Praise for **The Isabel Dalhousie Series**

"Mr. McCall Smith, a fine writer, paints his hometown of Edinburgh as indelibly as he captures the sunniness of Africa. We can almost feel the mists as we tread the cobblestones."
—*The Dallas Morning News*

"Charmingly told. . . . Its graceful prose shines, and Isabel's interior monologues—meditations on a variety of moral questions—are bemused, intelligent and entertaining."
—*The Seattle Times*

"Completely absorbing. . . . Will captivate and enthrall."
—*Detroit Free Press*

"McCall Smith's assessments of fellow humans are piercing and profound. . . . His depictions of Edinburgh are vivid and seamless. . . . His fans . . . are sure to embrace these moral peregrinations among the plaid." —*San Francisco Chronicle*

"Delectable. . . . Beguiling. . . . Alexander McCall Smith has done it again."
—*Newsweek*

"Utterly charming. . . . Alexander McCall Smith often celebrates the best of humanity—its compassion, its intuition, its empathy." —*The Capital Times* (Madison, Wisconsin)

"Endearing and often funny. . . . Scotland is a village . . . just as exotic and compelling, in its way, as Botswana. When authors as clever as McCall Smith pursue such parallel tracks, readers are doubly well served." —*The Wall Street Journal*

Alexander McCall Smith

THE RIGHT ATTITUDE TO RAIN

Alexander McCall Smith is the author of the international phenomenon The No. 1 Ladies' Detective Agency series, The Isabel Dalhousie Series, the Portuguese Irregular Verbs series, and the 44 Scotland Street series. He is Professor Emeritus of medical law at the University of Edinburgh in Scotland and has served on many national and international bodies concerned with bioethics.

www.alexandermccallsmith.com

BOOKS BY ALEXANDER McCALL SMITH

IN THE NO. 1 LADIES' DETECTIVE AGENCY SERIES
The No. 1 Ladies' Detective Agency
Tears of the Giraffe
Morality for Beautiful Girls
The Kalahari Typing School for Men
The Full Cupboard of Life
In the Company of Cheerful Ladies
Blue Shoes and Happiness
The Good Husband of Zebra Drive

IN THE ISABEL DALHOUSIE SERIES
The Sunday Philosophy Club
Friends, Lovers, Chocolate
The Right Attitude to Rain
The Careful Use of Compliments

IN THE PORTUGUESE IRREGULAR VERBS SERIES
Portuguese Irregular Verbs
The Finer Points of Sausage Dogs
At the Villa of Reduced Circumstances

IN THE 44 SCOTLAND STREET SERIES
44 Scotland Street
Espresso Tales
Love Over Scotland

The Girl Who Married a Lion and Other Tales from Africa

THE RIGHT ATTITUDE TO RAIN

THE RIGHT ATTITUDE TO RAIN

Alexander McCall Smith

Anchor Books
A Division of Random House, Inc.
New York

FIRST ANCHOR BOOKS EDITION, JULY 2007

The Library of Congress has cataloged the Pantheon edition as follows:
McCall Smith, Alexander.
The right attitude to rain / Alexander McCall Smith.
p. cm.
1. Edinburgh (Scotland)—Fiction. 2. Women editors—Fiction. 3. Housekeepers—Fiction. 4. Americans—Scotland—Edinburgh—Fiction. I. Title.
PR6063.C326R54 2006
823'.914—dc22
2006043214

Anchor ISBN: 978-1-4000-7711-3

www.anchorbooks.com

Printed in the United States of America
10 9 8 7 6 5 4 3 2 1

This book is for Edward Mendelson

THE RIGHT ATTITUDE TO RAIN

To take an interest in the affairs of others is entirely natural; so natural, in fact, that even a cat, lying cat-napping on top of a wall, will watch with half an eye the people walking by below. But between such curiosity, which is permissible, and nosiness, which is not, there lies a dividing line that some people simply miss—even if it is a line that is painted red and marked by the very clearest of warning signs.

Isabel adjusted the position of her chair. She was sitting in the window of the Glass and Thompson café at the top of Dundas Street—where it descended sharply down the hill to Canonmills. From that point in the street, one could see in the distance the hills of Fife beyond: dark-green hills in that light, but at times an attenuated blue, softened by the sea—always changing. Isabel liked this café, where the display windows of the shop it had once been had now been made into sitting areas for customers. Edinburgh was normally too chilly to allow people to sit out while drinking their coffee, except for a few short weeks in the high summer when café life spilled out onto the pavement, tentatively, as if expecting a rebuff from the elements. This was a compromise—to sit in the window, protected by glass, and yet feel part of what was going on outside.

She edged her chair forwards in order to see a little more of what was happening on the other side of the road, at a slight angle. Dundas Street was a street of galleries. Some were well established, such as the Scottish Gallery and the Open Eye, others were struggling to make a living on the work of young artists who still believed that great things lay ahead. Most of them would be disappointed, of course, as they discovered that the world did not share their conviction, but they tried nonetheless, and continued to try. One of these smaller galleries was hosting an opening and Isabel could see the crowd milling about within. At the front door stood a small knot of smokers, drawing on cigarettes, bound together in their exclusion. She strained to make out the features of one of them, a tall man wearing a blue jacket, who was talking animatedly to a woman beside him, gesturing to emphasise some private point. He looked vaguely familiar, she decided, but it was difficult to tell from that distance and angle. Suddenly the man in the blue jacket stopped gesturing, reached forward and rested a hand on the woman's shoulder. She moved sideways, as if to shrug him off, but he held on tight. Her hand went up in what seemed to be an attempt to prise off his fingers, but all the time she was smiling—Isabel could see that. Strange, she thought; an argument conducted in the language of smiles.

But more intriguing still: an expensive car, one of those discreet cars of uncertain make but with unambiguous presence, had drawn up on the café side of the street, just below the level of Isabel's window. It had stopped and a man and a woman had emerged. They were in a no-parking zone, and Isabel watched as the man pressed the device on his key ring that would lock the doors automatically. You are allowed to drop things off, thought Isabel, but not park. Don't you know that? And then she thought: People who drive cars like that consider themselves above the regulations, the rules that prevent those with humbler cars, and shallower pockets, from parking. And these people, of course, can afford the parking fines; small change for them. She found herself feeling irritated, and her irritation became, after a few moments, animosity. She found herself disliking them, this man and woman standing beside their expensive car, because of their arrogance.

She looked down into her coffee cup, and then up again. No, she thought. This is wrong. You should not dislike people you do not know. And she knew nothing about them, other than that they appeared to imagine that their wealth entitled them to ignore the regulations by which the rest of us had to abide. But then they might not know that one could not park there because they were from somewhere else; from a place where a double yellow line might be an invitation to park, for all she knew. And even as she thought this, she realised that of course they were not from Edinburgh. Their clothes were different, and their complexions too. These people had been in the sun somewhere, and their clothes had that cut, that freshly dry-cleaned look that Scottish clothes never seem to have. Scottish clothes are soft, a bit crumpled, lived-in, like Scottish people themselves really.

She craned her neck. The two of them, the man considerably older than the woman, were walking down the road, away from the car. They paused as the man pointed at a door, and the woman said something to him. Isabel saw her adjust the printed silk scarf around her neck and glance at the watch on her wrist, a small circle of gold that caught the sun as she moved her arm. The man nodded and they climbed the steps that led into the

Scottish Gallery. Isabel sat back in her seat. It was not remarkable in any way; a wealthy couple from somewhere else, driving
into town, leaving their car where they should not—but out of
ignorance rather than arrogance—and then going into one of
the galleries. There was nothing particularly interesting about
all that, except for one thing. Isabel had seen the man's face,
which was drawn up on one side from Bell's palsy, producing the
condition's characteristic grimace. And the woman's face had
been, by contrast, a beautiful one—if one's standards of beauty
are the regular features of the Renaissance Madonna: soft, composed, feminine.

They are none of my business, she thought. And yet she had
nothing to do until twelve o'clock—it was then ten-thirty in the
morning—and she had been half thinking of going into the
Scottish Gallery anyway. She knew the staff there, and they usually showed her something interesting by the Scottish artists she
liked, a Peploe sketch, a Philipson nude, something by William
Crosbie if she was in luck. If she went in now, she would see the
couple at closer quarters and reach a more considered view. She
had been wrong to dislike them, and she owed it to them now
to find out a little bit more about them. So it was not pure
curiosity, even if it looked like it; this was really an exercise in
rectifying a mistaken judgement.

THE ENTRANCE TO the Scottish Gallery was a glass door,
behind which a short set of open stairs led to the upper gallery,
while a slightly longer set led down into a warren of basement
exhibition spaces. These lower spaces were not dark, as base-
ments could be, but brightly lit by strategically placed display
lights, and brightened, too, by the splashes of colour on the

walls. Isabel went up and passed the desk of her friend Robin McClure to her right. He sat there with his list of prices and his catalogues, ready to answer questions. What impressed her about Robin was that although he could tell who bought paintings and who did not, he was civil to both. So those who wandered into the gallery because it was wet outside, or because they just wanted to look at art, would receive from him as courteous a welcome as those who wandered in with the intention of buying a painting or, in the case of those who were weaker, a readiness to be tempted to buy. That, thought Isabel, was what distinguished Dundas Street galleries from many of the expensive galleries in London and Paris, where bells had to be rung before the door was opened. And even then, once the door had been unlocked, the welcome, if it was a welcome, was grudging and suspicious.

Robin was not at his desk. She glanced around her. It was a general exhibition, one where a hotchpotch of works were displayed. The effect, thought Isabel, was pleasing, and her eye was drawn immediately to a large picture dominating one of the walls. Two figures were before a window, a man and a woman. The man was staring out at a rural landscape, the woman looked in towards the room. Her face was composed, but there was a wistful sadness about it. She would like to be elsewhere, thought Isabel; as so many people would. How many of us are happy to be exactly where we are at any moment? Auden said something about that, she remembered, in his mountains poem. He had said that the child unhappy on one side of the Alps might wish himself on the other. Well, he was right; only the completely happy think that they are in the correct place.

She glanced about her. There were several people on the main floor of the gallery: a man in a blue overcoat, a scarf around his neck, peering at a small painting near the window; a couple of middle-aged women wearing those green padded jackets that marked them immediately as leading, or at least aspiring to, the country life. They were sisters, Isabel decided, because they had the same prominent brow; sisters living together, thoroughly accustomed to each other, acting—almost thinking—in unison. But where were the man and the woman she had seen? She took a few steps forwards, away from the top of the stairs, and saw that they were standing in the small inner gallery that led off from the main floor. He was standing in front of a painting, consulting a catalogue; she was by the window staring out. It was the reverse of the large painting that she had spotted when she came in. She was looking out; he was looking in. But then it occurred to Isabel that in other respects the scene before her echoed the painting. This woman wanted to be elsewhere.

"Isabel?"

She turned round sharply. Robin McClure stood behind her, looking at her enquiringly. He reached out and put a hand lightly on her arm in a gesture of greeting.

"Don't tell me," he said. "You're standing in awe before our offering. Overwhelmed by the beauty of it all."

Isabel laughed. "Overcome."

Robin, his hand still on her arm, guided her towards a small picture at the edge of the room. Isabel glanced over her shoulder into the smaller room; they were still there, although the man had now joined the woman at the window, where they seemed absorbed in conversation.

"Here's something that will appeal to you," said Robin. "Look at that."

Isabel knew immediately. "Alberto Morrocco?" she asked.

Robin nodded. "You can see the influence, can't you?"

It was not apparent to Isabel. She leaned forward to look more closely at the painting. A girl sat in a chair, one arm resting on a table, the other holding a book. The girl looked straight ahead; not at the viewer, but through him, beyond him. She was wearing a tunic of the sort worn by schoolgirls in the past, a grey garment, with thick folds in the cloth. Behind her, a curtain was blown by the wind from an open window.

"Remember *Falling Leaves*?" Robin prompted. "That painting by James Cowie?"

Isabel looked again at the painting. Yes. Schoolgirls. Cowie had painted schoolgirls, over and over, innocently, but the paintings had contained a hint of the anxious transition to adolescence.

"Morrocco studied under Cowie in Aberdeen," Robin continued. "He later discovered his own palette and the bright colours came in. And the liveliness. But every so often he remembered who taught him."

"Morrocco was a friend of your father's, wasn't he?" Isabel said. Scotland was like that; there were bonds and connections everywhere, sinews of association, and they were remembered. Isabel had a painting by Robin's father, David McClure; it was one of her favourites.

"Yes," said Robin. "They were great friends. And I have known Morrocco ever since I can remember."

Isabel reached out, as if to touch the surface of the painting. "That awful cloth," she said. "The stuff that schoolgirls had to wear."

"Most uncomfortable," said Robin. "Or so I imagine."

Isabel pointed to the painting beside it, a small still life of a white-and-blue Glasgow jug. There was something familiar about the style, but she could not decide what it was. Perhaps it was the jug itself; there were so many paintings of Glasgow jugs—to paint one, it seemed, had been a rite of passage, like going to Paris. Artists, she thought, were enthusiastic imitators, a thought that immediately struck her as unfair, she conceded to herself, because *everyone* was an enthusiastic imitator.

"Yes," said Robin. "Well, there you are . . ." He turned his head. The man whom Isabel had seen had left the inner gallery and was standing a few steps away from Robin, wanting to speak, but reluctant to interrupt.

"Sir . . . ," began Robin, then faltered. Isabel saw his expression, the slight air of being taken aback and the quick recovery. And she thought: This is what this man must experience every time he meets somebody; the shock as the distorted face is registered and then follows the attempt to cover the reaction. She remembered how she had once had lunch with a young man, the nephew of a friend of hers, who had come to seek her advice about studying philosophy at university. She had met him for the first time in a restaurant. He had come in, a self-possessed, good-looking young man, and when they had moved to the table she had seen the scar which ran down the side of his cheek. He had said immediately: "I was bitten by a dog when I was a boy. I was thirteen." He had said that because he had known what she was thinking—how did it happen? Presumably everybody thought that and he supplied the answer right at the beginning, just to get it out of the way.

The man fingered his tie nervously. "I didn't want to interrupt," he said. Then, turning to Isabel, he repeated, "I'm sorry. I didn't wish to interrupt."

"We were just blethering," said Robin, using the Scots word. "Don't worry."

THE RIGHT ATTITUDE TO RAIN

He's American, thought Isabel, from somewhere in the South. But it was difficult to tell these days because people moved about so much and accents had changed. And she thought of her late mother, suddenly, inconsequentially, her *sainted American mother* as she called her, who had spoken in the accent of the American South, and whose voice had faded in her memory, though it was still there, just.

She looked at the man and then quickly turned away. She was curious about him, of course, but if she held him in her gaze he would think that she was staring at his face. She moved away slightly, to indicate that he should talk to Robin.

"Isabel," said Robin. "Would you mind?"

"Of course not," said Isabel. "Of course not."

She left Robin talking to the man while she went off to examine more paintings. She noticed that the woman had also come out of the smaller gallery and was now standing in front of an Elizabeth Blackadder oil of the Customs Building in Venice.

"Elizabeth Blackadder. She's a very popular artist," said Isabel casually. "Or at least on this side of the Atlantic. I'm not sure whether people know about her on your side."

The woman was surprised. She turned to face Isabel. "Oh?" she said. "Black what?"

"Blackadder," said Isabel. "She lives here in Edinburgh."

The woman looked back at the painting. "I like it," she said. "You know where you are with a painting like that."

"Venice," said Isabel. "That's where you are."

The woman was silent for a moment. She had been bending to look more closely at the painting; now she straightened up. "How did you know that I was American?" she asked. Her tone was even, but it seemed to Isabel that there was an edge to her voice.

"I was over there when your . . . your husband spoke," she said quickly. "I assumed."

"And assumed correctly," said the woman. There was no warmth in her voice.

"You see," continued Isabel, "I'm half-American myself. Half-American, half-Scottish, although I've hardly ever spent any time in the States. My mother was from—"

"Will you excuse me?" said the woman suddenly. "My friend was asking about a painting. I'm interested to hear the answer."

Isabel watched her as she walked across the gallery. Not married, she thought. Friend. It had been abrupt, but it had been said with a smile. Although Isabel felt rebuffed, she told herself that one does not have to continue a conversation with a stranger. A minimum level of politeness is required, a response to a casual remark, but beyond that one can disengage. She was interested in this couple, as to who they were and what they were doing in Edinburgh, but she thought: I mean nothing to them. And why should I?

She went to look at another painting—three boys in a boat on a loch somewhere, absorbed in the mastery of the oars, the youngest looking up at the sky at something he had seen there. The artist had caught the expression of wonderment on the young boy's face and the look of concentration on the faces of his companions; that was how artists responded to the world— they gaze and then re-create it in paint. Artists were allowed to do that—to look, to gaze at others and try to find out what it was that they were feeling—but we, who were not artists, were not. If one looked too hard that would be considered voyeurism, or nosiness, which is what Cat, her niece, had accused her of more than once. Jamie—the boyfriend rejected by Cat but kept on by

Isabel as a friend—had done the same, although more tactfully. He had said that she needed to draw a line in the world with *me* written on one side and *you* on the other. *Me* would be her business; *you* would be the business of others, and an invitation would be required to cross the line.

She had said to Jamie: "Not a good idea, Jamie. What if people on the other side of the line are in trouble?"

"That's different," he said. "You help them."

"By stretching a hand across this line of yours?"

"Of course. Helping people is different."

She had said: "But then we have to know what they need, don't we? We have to be aware of others. If we went about concerned with only our own little world, how would we know when there was trouble brewing on the other side of the line?"

Jamie had shrugged. He had only just thought of the line and he did not think that he would be able to defend it against Isabel in Socratic mood. So he said, "What do you think of Arvo Pärt, Isabel? Have I ever asked you that?"

AFTER SHE HAD FINISHED her business in town, Isabel decided to walk back to the house. It was by then afternoon, and the sunshine of early June, now with a bit of warmth in it, had brought people out onto the streets in their shirtsleeves and blouses, optimistic, but resigned to being driven back in by rain, or mist, or other features of the Scottish summer. Her walk back, like any walk through this city, was to her an exercise in association. One would have to have one's eyes closed in Edinburgh not to be assailed by reminders of the past, she thought—the public or personal past. She paused at the corner of the

High Street where the statue of Edinburgh's most famous philosopher, David Hume, had been placed. What a disaster, she thought. Isabel admired Hume and agreed with Adam Smith's view that he approached *as nearly to the idea of a perfectly wise and virtuous man as perhaps the nature of human frailty will permit*. But the good David was a natty dresser, interested in fine clothes (there was Allan Ramsey's portrait to prove that), and here he was, seated in a chair, wearing a toga, of all things. And there were some who had voiced further objections. Hume was a reader, they said, and yet here he was merely holding a book, not reading it. But what, she wondered, would the statue have looked like if he had been portrayed in elegant clothes with his nose stuck in a volume of Locke? There would have been objections to that too, no doubt. This was the public past, about which we often disagree.

She walked back across the Meadows, a wide expanse of common ground on which people strolled and played. To the south, along the edge of the park, rose the high Victorian tenements of Marchmont, stone buildings of six floors or so, topped with spiky adornments—thistles, fleurs-de-lis and the like. There were attics up there, rooms looking out of the sharply rising slate roofs, out towards the Forth and the hills beyond, rooms let out to students and later, during the summer, to the musicians and actors who flocked to Edinburgh for the Festival. As she walked up towards Bruntsfield she could make out the door that led to the narrow hall and, up five long flights of stone stairs, to the flat where more than twenty years ago her schoolfriend Kirsty had at sixteen conducted an affair with a student from Inverness, her first boyfriend and lover. Isabel had listened to her friend's accounts of this and had felt an emptiness in the pit of her stomach, which was longing, and fear too. Kirsty had spoken *sotto voce* of what had happened, and whispered, "They try to stop us, Isabel. They try to stop us because they don't want us to know. And then we find out . . ."

"And?" Isabel had said. But Kirsty had become silent and looked out of the window. This was the private past; intimate, unquestioned, precious to each of us.

Reaching Bruntsfield, she found herself outside Cat's delicatessen. She could not walk past without going in, although she tried not to distract Cat when she was busy. That time in the afternoon was a slack period, and there was only one customer in the shop, who was in the process of paying for a baguette and a tub of large pitted olives. There were several tables where people could sit and be served coffee and a small selection of food, and Isabel took a seat at one of these, picking up an out-of-date copy of *Corriere della Sera* from the table of newspapers and magazines beside the cheese counter. She glanced at the political news from Italy, which appeared to be a series of reports of battles between acronyms, or so it seemed. Behind the acronyms there were people, and passions, and ancient feuds, but without any idea of what stood for which, it was much like the battle between the Blues and Greens in Byzantium—meaningless, unless one understood the difference between the orthodox and the Monophysites who stood behind these factions.

She abandoned the paper. Eddie, Cat's shy assistant, to whom something traumatic had happened that Isabel had never fathomed, took the money for the baguette and the olives and opened the door for the customer. There was no sign of Cat.

"Where is she?" asked Isabel, once they had the shop to themselves.

Eddie came over to the table, rubbing his hands on his apron. His nervousness in Isabel's presence had abated, but he was still not completely at ease.

"She went out for lunch," he said. "And she hasn't come back yet."

Isabel looked at her watch. "A long lunch," she remarked.

Eddie hesitated for a moment, as if weighing up whether to say anything. "With her new boyfriend," he said, adding, after further hesitation, "Again."

Isabel reached for the folded *Corriere della Sera* and aligned it with the edge of the table, a distracted gesture, but one which gave her time to absorb this information. She had resolved not to become involved in the question of her niece's boyfriends, but it was difficult to remain detached. Cat's short-lived engagement to Toby had led to a row between Isabel and her niece—a row which had been quickly patched up, but which had made Isabel reflect on the need to keep her distance on the issue. So when Cat had gone to Italy to attend a wedding and had been followed back by an elegant Italian considerably older than she was, Isabel had refrained from saying very much. Cat decided not to encourage her Italian visitor, and he had responded by flirting with Isabel. She had been flattered in spite of herself, and tempted too, but he had not really meant it; flirtation, it seemed, was mere politeness, a way of passing the time.

The only boyfriend of Cat's of whom she approved was Jamie, the bassoonist, whom Cat had disposed of fairly quickly, but who had continued to hanker after her in the face of every discouragement. Isabel had been astonished by his constancy to a cause that was clearly hopeless. Cat had told him bluntly that there was no future for them as a couple, and while he respected her and kept his distance, he secretly—and sometimes not so secretly—hoped that she would change her mind. Isabel could not understand why Cat should have abandoned Jamie. In her view, he was everything, and more, that a woman could want. He was striking in appearance, with his high cheekbones, his dark hair that he tended to wear short, and his Mediterranean, almost olive complexion; unusual colouring for a Scotsman, perhaps, but one which in her eyes was fatally attractive. And he was gentle too, which added to his appeal. Yet Cat spelled it out to Isabel in unambiguous terms: I do not love him, Isabel. I do not love him. It's as simple as that.

If Cat was not prepared to love Jamie, then Isabel was. There was a gap of fourteen years between them, and Isabel realised that at Jamie's age this was significant. Would a young man in his twenties want to become involved with a woman who was in her early forties? Some women of that age had younger lovers—and there was nothing shameful about it, but she suspected that it was the women who started such affairs, rather than the young men. Of course, there might be some young men who would be looking for the equivalent of a sugar daddy, and who would seek out an older woman who could pay the bills and provide some diversion, but most young men were not like that, unless, as sometimes happened, they were looking for their mother.

Isabel could never have Jamie; she could never possess him, precisely because she loved him and she wanted what was best for him. And what was best for him was undoubtedly that he should meet somebody his own age, or thereabouts, and make his life with her. Of course that was best for him, she told herself. He would be a good father, he would be a good husband; he did not need to anchor himself to somebody older than him. He did not. But she still loved Jamie, and at times she loved him

achingly; but she controlled that, and only occasionally, in private, did the tears come for what just could not be. At least she
had his friendship, and that was something for which she felt
grateful. She did not have his love, she thought. He is fond of
me, but he does not return what I feel for him. *Let the more loving one be me,* wrote Auden, and Isabel thought, Yes, that is
what I feel: let the more loving one be me. And it is.

She would not interfere, but who was this new boyfriend?
She looked up at Eddie. Could he be jealous? she asked herself.
The tone of his voice had sounded resentful, and she supposed
that it was quite possible that he saw the arrival of a new man as
being in some way a threat to his relationship with Cat. She was
kind to him; she encouraged him; she was the ideal employer.
Eddie could not expect to amount to much in Cat's eyes, but at
least he was there, in her life, somehow, and he would not want
that to come to an end.

"Well, Eddie," said Isabel. "That's interesting news. I hadn't
heard. Who is this new man?"

"He's called Patrick," said Eddie. He put his hand a good six
inches above his head. "He's about so high. Maybe a bit less.
Fair hair."

Isabel nodded. Cat inevitably went for tall, good-looking
men. It was all very predictable. "This Patrick," she asked, "do
you like him?"

She studied Eddie's reaction. But he was watching her too,
and he grinned. "You want me to say that I don't," he said.
"That's what you want, isn't it? Because you won't like him."

We all underestimate Eddie, thought Isabel. "I'll try to like
him, Eddie," she said. "I'll really try."

Eddie looked sideways at her. "He's not bad, actually. I

quite like him, you know. He's not like the others. Not much, anyway."

This interested Isabel. Perhaps Cat was breaking the pattern. "Why?" she asked.

The door opened and a woman with a shopping bag came in. Eddie glanced over his shoulder at the customer and gave his hands a last wipe on his apron. "I'm going to have to go," he said. "I'll make you a coffee, if you like. After I've served this person."

Isabel glanced at her watch. "I'm going to have to go too," she said. "But I've got time for a quick cup. And then you can tell me about him. You can tell me why you like him."

AS ISABEL WALKED BACK along Merchiston Crescent, back to her house in one of those quiet roads that led off to the right, she thought about what Eddie had told her. In their brief conversation he had opened up more than he had ever done with her before. He had told her why he had disliked Toby, who condescended to him, who made him feel . . . "Well," he said, "he made me feel not quite a man, if you know what I mean." Isabel did; she knew precisely what Toby would have thought of Eddie and how he would have conveyed his feelings. And then Eddie had said, "Patrick is more like me, I think. I don't know why, but that's what I feel. I just feel it."

That intrigued Isabel. It told her something—that Patrick was an improvement on Toby—that was information of some significance, but she still could not visualise him. Eddie had thought that Patrick was more like him, but she found it difficult to imagine that Cat would deign to look at somebody really like Eddie. No, what it did convey was that there was more of the feminine in Patrick than there had been in Toby, or any of the others. Another possibility, of course, was that Patrick was simply more sympathetic than the others, and Eddie had seized on this. One can be masculine and sympathetic, and that, perhaps, was what Patrick was.

She turned the corner and started to walk down her road. Walking towards her, having just parked his car in the street, was one of the students who attended lectures in Colinton Road nearby. Isabel caught his eye as they passed. He was masculine and sympathetic. But then she thought: I have no evidence for that conclusion—none at all; apart, perhaps, from the fact that he smiled at me, just a hint of a smile—and the smile was one of those little signals we flash to one another: *I understand. Yes, I understand.*

CHAPTER TWO

ISABEL CALLED GRACE a housekeeper. She used that term
because it was frankly kinder than the other words on offer: to
call somebody a cleaner suggested that the job was a menial
one—a matter of dusting and polishing and mopping up. And
the words *daily* and *domestic* were adjectives used as nouns, and
whether or not it was this that gave them a dismissive ring, she
thought that they sounded that way. *Housekeeper*, by contrast,
implied a job of responsibility and importance—which it was.
One kept a house, just as one might keep a zoo, or indeed a
collection of paintings. To be the keeper of anything, thought
Isabel, was an honourable calling; she had no time for the tendency to look down on jobs involving physical labour. Lawyers
and accountants had a good conceit of themselves, she felt, but
why should they consider themselves superior to bus drivers
and the people who kept the streets clean? She could see no
reason. So Grace, who came to Isabel's house every day to clean
and tidy and put things back in their place, was called a housekeeper by Isabel, and generously paid. Isabel's father, for whom
Grace had worked during his final illness, had asked Isabel to
ensure that Grace was looked after, and Isabel had given her

word that she would be, even to the extent, now, of setting out to buy a flat for her. Grace rented, which Isabel thought was a waste of money, and subject to the vagaries of landlords. But when she had raised the matter with Grace, and offered to buy a flat, she discovered a curious inertia on Grace's part. Yes, it would be very nice one day to have a flat, and yes, she would look, but nothing was ever done. So Isabel had decided she would do it. She would look for something suitable and set Grace up in it.

She could easily afford to do this. Isabel was discreet about her financial position, but the Louisiana and Gulf Land Company, a large part of which she had inherited through her mother, had done and continued to do well. There was no shortage of funds, as the quarterly statement of assets from the Northern Trust revealed. These statements came from an alien land—from the land of money, a world of figures, of profit-earnings ratios, of bonds, of projections that meant little to Isabel. But she understood very well this world's siren call, and she resisted it. Money could claim one's allegiances very quickly; this happened all the time. It was like a drug: the hit faded and more was needed for the same high. So she did not think about it, and she quietly gave away much of her income, unnoticed, uncomplimented; she was often the *anonymous* at the end of lists of donors; that was her.

Grace was older than Isabel, but not by much—forty-six to Isabel's forty-two. These four years, though, were important, as they reinforced her tendency to question Isabel's judgement from time to time. Four years' seniority in adult life was nothing, whatever it may count for in childhood; yet these four years gave Grace the advantage of Isabel—in Grace's view. She thought her employer's view of the world was unduly theoretical and that one day it would be moderated by experience. But that experience, she felt, was slow to come.

The next morning Isabel was eager to tell Grace about Cat's new boyfriend, but the conversation started off in a totally different direction. Guests were expected the following week and arrangements had to be made. Grace did not like visitors to be sprung upon her; she wanted to know exactly who was arriving, why they were coming, and when they would leave. After this had been sorted out, then the details could be addressed: which room they would stay in, what meals would be required, and so on.

"You mentioned guests," said Grace as she slipped out of her blue macintosh and hung it on the peg behind the kitchen door. "Next week, isn't it?"

Isabel, rising from the kitchen table where she had been attempting the first few clues of the *Scotsman* crossword, put down her pencil. "Yes," she said. "Mimi and Joe. And they're coming for just under a month. They'll be going on to Oxford for a while and then back to Dallas."

Grace moved over to the sink and reached for her blue washing-up gloves. "Mimi and Joe? The ones who were here three or four years ago?"

Isabel nodded. Mimi McKnight was her cousin, her mother's first cousin, to be precise, and she and her husband, Joe, had visited her some years ago. Grace had met them then and, as far as Isabel remembered, got on well with them. There was no point in having guests with whom Grace disagreed: that could be disastrous.

Grace picked up a plate from the drying rack and examined it. Isabel had washed it, and it might have to be washed again. But the specks she saw turned out to be part of the design and it was set aside for shelving. She picked up another plate. This one was definitely still dirty, and the discovery pleased Grace. Isabel thought that she could wash up, but she was really no good at it, according to Grace. She had no idea how to load the dishwasher correctly and was always putting things away half-washed. She looked at the plate again, ostentatiously, so that Isabel might see her scrutiny. "A month?" she said as she began to fill the sink with water. "That's a long stay."

"She's my cousin," said Isabel. "Cousins can stay indefinitely, and sometimes do. They're different."

"I wouldn't care to be away from my own bed for a month," said Grace. "And I wouldn't put up with a cousin who stayed indefinitely."

"Mimi and Joe are different," said Isabel. "I like having them to stay. And . . ." She was about to say, "And they're my guests, after all," but stopped herself. It was no business of Grace's how long her guests should stay (and that plate is *not* dirty, she thought), but that was not the way the house, or Isabel's life, was ordered. Isabel *was* Grace's business, at least in Grace's mind, and that was the view which prevailed.

Grace dipped the plate into the water and began to scrub at the recalcitrant fragments of food. "What will they do?" she asked. "Not that I'm being nosy." She cast a glance at Isabel. "But why do they want to be away from home for that long?"

Isabel folded up her copy of the newspaper. "Dallas in summer is not very pleasant," she said. "It gets very warm. Baking, in fact. Think of Spain in summer, and then think hotter. Anybody who's in a position to escape the heat does so."

She rose from the table. She would usually spend the first half-hour of the morning after Grace's arrival immersed in the crossword, but today she felt disinclined to follow that routine.

She felt uneasy about something, and she thought that she might have been unsettled by the news of Cat's new boyfriend. Nieces found new boyfriends every day—there was nothing unusual in that; nor was there anything uncommon in the dismissal of one boyfriend in favour of another. From what Eddie had said, Patrick might be an improvement on Cat's previous boyfriends, and yet, she thought, there is something that makes me feel uneasy; I am not mistaken about this.

She left Grace in the kitchen and went out into the hall. From behind her she heard Grace switch on the radio, as she often did when engaged in housework. It was a studio discussion, a regular programme in which four or five people were invited to debate issues of the time. They were well-known voices—people who could be counted on to give a view on most things—and Isabel found it irritating. Grace did too, on this occasion, and Isabel heard the radio switched off quickly. She smiled. This was Grace's reaction to a well-known politician whose voice, she confessed, she could not bear. "I know he can't help it," she had said once. "I know it's not his fault, but I just can't tolerate the sound of him. And I disagree with everything he says. Everything."

Isabel moved through to her study, closing the door behind her. The morning's mail had brought the usual selection of unsolicited manuscripts for the *Review of Applied Ethics,* which Isabel edited, but it had also brought the proofs of the next issue. The *Review* had taken to devoting every other issue to a single theme, and the topic for this issue was character and its implications for moral involvement in the world. She extracted the proofs from the padded envelope in which the printer had consigned them. This was always an important moment for her, when she saw the results of her work in printed form. And the editorial, which she often wrote at the last moment, would be there, in cold print, her own words invested with all the authority that printer's ink on the page can impart.

She looked at the editorial. It was a curious thing, but she sometimes found it difficult to believe that she had written these editorials, with their carefully balanced appraisal of the arguments that her authors marshalled in their papers. Was this really her, this deliberative, even-handed person who signed the editorial at the bottom *Isabel Dalhousie, Editor*? She wondered for a moment whether others felt this. Did artists sometimes look at their work and wonder how they did it?

Character, she had written, *is a term that almost requires explanation today. It means little to the psychologist, who talks about personality, but to the philosopher it is more than that. You may not be able to create a personality, but you can create a character for yourself.*

Had she said that? She had written it almost three months ago and the prose had a somewhat distant feel to it, rather like an old letter filed away. It worried her that she had been too enthusiastic about the possibility of creating character. If character and personality were the same thing, then somebody was wrong: either the psychologists for saying that personality was immutable, or the philosophers for saying that it was malleable. She was not sure, though, that psychologists said that personality was immutable: some did, perhaps, but others said that personality was just a collection of traits, some of which would be consistent across time and some of which would not.

Isabel had discussed this once before with her friend Richard Latcham, who was a psychiatrist. She had met Richard when she was in Cambridge and they had stayed in touch. A few months ago she had gone to a reunion in Cambridge and he had invited her out to Papworth St. Agnes, where he lived. He had shown her his cars in what he called his motor house, a pagoda-style garage in the grounds of the sixteenth-century manor house. While looking at an old Bristol hard-top that he was restoring, the conversation had got on to effort and to how one might become good at the restoration of cars.

"Even you, Isabel," Richard had said. "Even you could do this."

She laughed. "I couldn't. I wouldn't know where to start."

He said, "You'd learn. I'm not suggesting that you wouldn't need to learn. But you could make yourself into a mechanic if you wanted to. What are you now? You're a philosopher, aren't you? But we can all become something different, can't we?"

She had looked at the car. On the wall, pinned up, was a photograph of the car before he had started his restoration work. The transformation seemed to bear out what he had said. But we can't, she thought. We can't all become something different. We may try to reinvent ourselves, but we are the same people underneath, incorrigibly so. She had turned to Richard and said as much, and he had reached out as she was speaking and removed a small mark from the bodywork of the fine old car.

"Bats," he said. "No, that's not what I think of your view. It's just the occasional bat gets in here and makes a mess of the cars."

Isabel thought for a moment. And then she said, "We don't know what it's like to be a bat."

Richard looked at her in surprise, and she laughed. "Sorry," she said. "It's just that somebody once wrote a paper called 'What Is It Like to Be a Bat?' A professor of philosophy called Thomas Nagel."

"And did Professor Nagel reach any conclusion?"

"That we don't know. We can imagine. But we don't know."

And then Richard had said, "Of course, when I said that you could change, I should have said that there are some things you can't change entirely. Your personality, for example, is something that is always there. Certainly after about the age of thirty."

This had interested Isabel, because she thought that she had changed. The woman who had married John Liamor all those years ago, the young woman in Cambridge, her head turned by the cynical Irish historian with his unkempt good looks and his witty disparagements of what he called "the creaky gerontocracy" (by which he meant the University of Cambridge) and the "queerocracy" (by which he meant the Fellows of his College). That would be called homophobia now, but not then, when straight Irishmen could present themselves as victims, too, whose prejudices were beyond censure.

She had changed, because now she would see through John Liamor; and she had changed in other respects too. She had become more forgiving, more understanding of human weaknesses than she had been in her twenties. And love, too, had become more important to her; not love in the erotic sense, which obeyed its own tides throughout life and could be as intense, as unreasonable in its demands, whatever age one was, but love in the sense of *agape,* the brotherly love of others, which was a subtle presence that became stronger as the years passed; that, at least, was what had happened with her.

"So there's not much that we can do about that central bit of ourselves—the core?" she had asked. "Would you call it that— the core?"

"A good enough name for it," said Richard. "No, I don't think there's much we can do about that. The very deep bits of us, the real preferences, are there whether we like it or not. But if these deep bits are not very pleasant we can keep them under control. We can adapt to them." He laid a hand on the polished bonnet of the old car, gently, with fondness, as on a precious object. "And I suppose we can develop positive attitudes which mean that in our dealings with others, in our day-to-day lives, we behave a bit better."

"And we would deserve credit for all the effort involved?"

Richard gave Isabel the answer she herself would have given. "Yes. A lot of credit." He paused. "I had a patient once who had a problem." He smiled. "Well, all my patients have a problem, I suppose, but this one had a particularly difficult problem. He was a liar. He just felt compelled to tell lies— about all sorts of things. And he knew that it was wrong, and he had to fight with it every day. Life for him was one constant effort, but he managed to stop lying. And, do you know, I really admired that man. I really did."

He was right, she thought. It was easy to be moral when that was the way you felt anyway. The hard bit about morality was making yourself feel the opposite of what you really felt. That was where credit was deserved.

Richard gestured that they should leave the motor house. He wanted to show Isabel the dovecote, with its small, carefully wrought bricks, an eighteenth-century addition.

"That man, the liar, really liked monopole Burgundy," he said as they walked out into the open air. "I remember that, for some reason. Monopole Burgundy from a single vineyard." He looked at Isabel and smiled. "Or that's what he told me."

"Maybe he didn't," she said. And immediately she regretted saying this, because it made light of that man's effort. So she quickly said that she was sure that he liked it.

Richard was uncertain. "He might have liked it," he said.

SHE WORKED ON THE PROOFS, her study door closed behind her. Grace seemed to be busy upstairs, as Isabel heard her footfall through the ceiling. Something was dropped at one point, and fell with a thud, which was followed by a silence. Isabel looked up at the ceiling, and waited until the footsteps continued so she knew that Grace was not lying unconscious under some piece of furniture. Grace shifted things, which were never in quite the right place for her. Wardrobes would inch across a room; chests of drawers cross the carpet; occasional tables disappear into corners. Isabel thought that it might be something to do with the principles of feng shui. Grace had an interest in these things, although she was reluctant to talk about them, fearing Isabel's scepticism. "There are some things we can't prove," she had once said to Isabel. "But we know that they work. We just know it." And this had been followed by a challenging look, which left Isabel feeling unable to defend the position of empiricism.

By lunchtime she had read and corrected almost half of the issue. Several of the authors' footnotes had been mangled in the setting, with page numbers disappearing or inflating impossibly and requiring to be deflated. Page 1027 could not exist; page 127 could, or page 102 or 107. This involved bibliographic checking, which took time, and sometimes required getting back in touch with the author. That meant e-mails to people who might not answer them quickly, or at all. And that gave rise to the thought that an article on the ethics of e-mail would perhaps be a good idea. Do you have to answer every e-mail that you get? Is ignoring an electronic message as rude as looking straight through somebody who addresses a remark to you? And what, she wondered, was a reasonable delay between getting a message and responding to it? One of her authors had sent her an enquiry only two hours after sending an initial e-mail. *Did you get my message? Can you give me a response?* That, thought Isabel, could be the beginning of a new tyranny. Advances in technology were greeted with great enthusiasm and applause; then the tyranny emerged. Look at cars. They destroyed cities and communities. They laid waste to the land. Our worship at their altar choked us of our very air, constrained us to narrow paths beside their great avenues, cut us down. And yet . . . she thought of her green Swedish car, which she loved to drive on the open roads, which could take her from Edinburgh to the west coast, to Mull, to the Isle of Skye even, in four or five hours, just an afternoon. The same trip had taken the choleric Dr. Johnson weeks, and had been the cause of great discomfort and complaint. It was an exciting tyranny, then, one which we liked.

She went through to the kitchen to fetch herself a sandwich and a bowl of soup for lunch. Grace had made the soup, as she often did, and it was simmering on the stove, a broth of leek and potato, salted rather too heavily for Isabel's taste, but good nonetheless. It was while Isabel was helping herself to this that Cat telephoned. There was often no particular reason for a telephone call from Cat, who liked to chat at idle moments, and this was such a call. Had Isabel seen that new Australian film at Film House? She should go, because it was excellent, better than anything else that Cat had seen that year. The Australians made such good films, didn't they? So perceptive. And witty too. Had Isabel seen . . .

Isabel sat down at the kitchen table, her soup before her, and continued to listen while Cat expounded on the merits of

Australian cinema. Then, as Cat drew a breath, she asked, "Did you go that film with Patrick?"

"Yes," said Cat. "I did. He was working late and so we met at the—" She stopped. "You haven't met Patrick, have you? Did I tell you about him?"

Isabel thought quickly. She did not want to tell Cat that she had heard about Patrick from Eddie, because it might embarrass Eddie if Cat were to know that he discussed her affairs. She might not mind, of course, but one never knew with Cat.

"I can't remember," she said, which was not true. And she thought: Why should I feel inclined to lie in a matter as petty as this? So she said, "Actually, I was speaking to Eddie and I asked where you were. He mentioned Patrick."

Cat was silent.

"It would be nice to meet him," Isabel went on. She tried to sound unconcerned, as if meeting Patrick was not all that important. "You could bring him round, perhaps."

"All right," said Cat. "Whenever you like."

After that the conversation trailed off. No date was chosen for Cat to bring Patrick to meet Isabel, but Isabel made a mental note to herself to call Cat the following day and suggest an evening. She did not want to press her, as she was meant not to be too interested in something which was none of her business.

She thought of Richard Latcham's lying patient and his struggle to tell the truth. This was not a great moral battle that she faced, the battle not to get involved in matters that did not concern her; it was really quite a small one. But it was nonetheless her battle; unless, of course, one took the view that it was entirely natural to be interested in her niece's boyfriends.

Grace came into the room. "Was that Cat?" she asked.

Isabel took out a bowl and began to help Grace to soup. "It was," she answered.

Grace opened a cupboard to put away a duster she had been carrying. "I met her new boyfriend," she said casually. "I was passing by the deli and I popped in. He was there."

Isabel looked down at her soup. "And?"

"He's called Patrick," she said. "And he seemed all right."

"Oh," said Isabel. "Well, that's something."

"Apparently Jamie knows him too," Grace volunteered. "They were at school together. Same age. Twenty-eight."

This was unexpected information, so Isabel again said, "Oh," and continued with her soup. That gave her something to think about, and she did so, while Grace continued to talk about something that had happened at her spiritualist meeting the previous evening. The medium—somebody new, said Grace, somebody from Inverness (and they're all a bit fey up there, she added)—had contacted the cousin of a young man who had been coming to the meetings for weeks but who had never said a word until then.

"At the end of the meeting he had changed completely," said Grace. "He said that he had blamed himself in some way for his cousin's death and now the cousin had reassured him that it was all right."

Isabel half listened. To be forgiven from beyond the grave could be important if that was the only quarter from which forgiveness could come, which, for many of us, she reflected, might well be the case.

CHAPTER THREE

"THERE'S SOMETHING I don't quite understand," said Jamie. "I hope you don't mind my talking about it. But I just don't see why you should be doing this."

They were sitting in a small pâtisserie round the corner from St. Stephen Street. The early afternoon light filtered through a corner of the window, illuminating floating particles of dust in the air; there was a smell of freshly made coffee in the air, and vanilla from the pastries. On the table behind them the day's newspapers were untidily folded, outraged headlines half obscured by creases in the paper: WARNS . . . RESIGNATION . . . ERUPTS IN SOMALIA . . .

Isabel leaned back in her chair. "It's because it's Grace," she said. "I don't want to sound like the on-duty philosopher, but, frankly, I have a moral obligation to her." And Somalia? she thought. What about Somalia? There was a book somewhere in the house, a book that had belonged to her father, which bore the title *A Tear for Somalia*. Did we owe it our tears?

Jamie continued, "But buying a flat . . ." He trailed off. It was an expensive gift, it seemed to him, and although he knew that Isabel was generous, this seemed to be generosity taken too far. "How much is it going to cost you? Two hundred thousand?"

Isabel looked away. She did not like talking about money, and in particular she did not like talking about actual figures. It could be more than two hundred thousand, but the funds were there and she thought that what she did with them was her own affair.

"It could cost that," she said quietly.

"And that's an awful lot of money," said Jamie. "A quarter of a million pounds. Just about."

Isabel shrugged. "That's what flats cost in this city," she said.

"Why can't Grace get a mortgage? Like everybody else?"

It was a perfectly reasonable question, and one which Isabel had asked herself. But the answer was that Grace was reluctant to take on debt and Isabel had given her word to her father that she would do what was necessary to look after her. In Isabel's view, that meant that she needed to provide her with a roof over her head. And even if she had not made that promise, she would probably have done it anyway.

"Grace is not the sort of person who would like a mortgage," said Isabel.

Jamie frowned. "Well, all right. But why you? Why do you have to do it?"

Isabel looked quizzically at Jamie. "Are you trying to protect me?" she asked.

Jamie said nothing for a while, but then a smile broke out on his face. "I suppose I am," he muttered. "You do some . . . some odd things." Then he added, "Sometimes."

"Well, that's very reassuring," said Isabel. "I'm busy trying to do something for Grace. You're busy trying to do something for me. And Grace, in her own inimitable way, spends a lot of time trying to look after me and you too—to an extent. A nice illustration of what moral community is all about."

The flat she was to look at that day was halfway along St. Stephen Street, a street of second-hand shops and bars; a street which prided itself on its slightly bohemian character yet was too expensive for students who might fancy living in such a quarter. People who lived there had to tolerate a certain amount of noise from the bars and the restaurants, but enjoyed, in return, the convenience of the coffee shops and bakeries round the corner, and the sheer beauty of the architecture, which was classical Georgian. Isabel was not sure about it as an address for Grace, who might be hoping for something more conventional, but thought that she would take a look at it, in case it proved to be suitable. The price was about right, and she had been told that she might even be able to lower it if she found cause to shake her head and complain about something.

She had asked Jamie to look at the flat with her because she thought that his local knowledge might help. Jamie lived in Saxe-Coburg Street, which was only a couple of blocks away to the north, and he often walked along St. Stephen Street on his way into town. He had known some people who lived there, he said, and they had talked to him about the locality, although he was having difficulty remembering what they had said. "I think they liked it," he said. "Or did they say they didn't? Sorry, I just can't remember."

That had not been very helpful, and it had reminded Isabel, inconsequentially, of Wittgenstein's account of his last meeting with Gottlob Frege. "The last time I saw Frege," he said, "as we were waiting at the station for my train, I said to him, 'Don't you ever find any difficulty in your theory that numbers are objects?'

He replied, 'Sometimes I seem to see a difficulty—but then again I don't see it.' " Isabel was not sure whether this was funny. She thought it might be, but stories told by philosophers which appeared to be funny were sometimes not funny at all, but very serious. And sometimes very serious remarks made by philosophers were, in fact, jokes, and intended to be taken as such.

Jamie had arrived at the café first that morning, and she found him already seated at the table near the window, paging through a musical score. He rose to greet her—Jamie always stood for women—and he reached out to shake her hand. They did not exchange a kiss of greeting; they had never done this, although it had become the social norm in some circles in Edinburgh. Friends, even friends of a single meeting's standing, kissed one another when they met; or at least men and women did. Isabel was unhappy about this rash of kissing. A kiss, she thought, was an intimate gesture, which was not enjoyable in any way when you did not know the person very well. Indeed it could be embarrassing: spectacles could get in the way and lipstick be left on male cheeks. There were other arguments against it: the recent consumption of garlic had a tendency to make an impression, and it was, she assumed, a good way of passing on a cold.

She would have enjoyed kissing Jamie, though—even through a miasma of garlic. He is so beautiful, she thought. He is at the moment of his greatest beauty, round about now. He will never be so beautiful again.

"You look thoughtful," said Jamie as they sat down together.

Isabel blushed. She could hardly say to him: I was thinking of what it would be like to kiss you. We often cannot tell people just what is going on in our minds, she thought, and so we hide things. And that was inevitable—to a degree—although there was a danger, surely, that if one concealed too much it would show. One would become furtive.

"I was thinking, I suppose," she said lightly. "I find I think too much. You yourself have accused me of that, haven't you?"

He had. He had told her on several occasions that she complicated matters and that the world was simpler than she imagined. But she had paid no attention, or, if she had heeded his advice, she had been unable to change her ways.

Jamie smiled. "Yes. I've told you plenty of times. Don't make things difficult for yourself. And do you do anything about it? You don't."

Isabel knew that he was right about her. But what he said raised the broader issue of whether anybody ever listened to advice. She suspected that few did.

"And do you listen to my advice?" she retorted.

Jamie looked puzzled. "What advice have you ever given me?"

Isabel was already asking herself this even as he posed the question. The only advice she had given him had to do with Cat. She had told him to give up any thought of getting Cat back because there was just no prospect of it ever happening.

She looked at Jamie, and he knew immediately what she was going to say. He looked down at the table in his embarrassment. "I know," he said. She waited for him to say something more, but he was silent.

She felt sorry for him. People made bad choices when it came to other people; and some people never recovered from the mistakes they made. Everybody knew just how sad it was to have a hopeless love, but still people, including herself, fell for the unattainable. There is no point in my loving this young man, she told herself, because it can never go anywhere. And yet did it matter if love was not reciprocated? Was it not possible to love somebody hopelessly, from a distance even, and for that love to be satisfying, even if never reciprocated, even if the object of one's affections never even knew? Jamie could love Cat even if he never, or only rarely, saw her. And she could love Jamie even if he never knew that she did. Both of us give love, she thought, and that must do something for us. Perhaps it was a bit like giving an anonymous gift. If one derived pleasure from the giving of something even if the recipient never knows who gave it—and it was a pleasure to give anonymously, as Isabel knew—then could not the giving of love be satisfying even if the person one loved never knew that he or she was loved? People did that all the time when they loved the inaccessible: the great romantic heroes, the film stars, the rock musicians, who were loved by legions of people who never saw them. Or the saints, and, if one came to think about it, God—although he, if one believed in him, loved one back, and so that was different; that was reciprocated love.

"Does it matter?" she asked Jamie. "Does it matter if one loves somebody who doesn't love one back? Do you think that it makes a difference?"

He looked up at her. "Of course it does. It's sad."

"Sad?" she mused.

"Yes," he said. "It's like . . ."

She raised an eyebrow. "Like what?"

"Like talking to somebody who isn't listening," Jamie said. "Yes, that's what it's like."

Isabel thought about that for a moment. "Is it because one can't share the feeling of love? Is it like having dinner all by oneself?"

It was then that Jamie had asked her about why she was

buying Grace the flat, and the conversation had drifted off unsatisfactorily into theories of moral obligation. After a few minutes of that, Jamie signalled to the waitress. "We're going to have to hurry," he said to Isabel, tapping his watch. "Isn't this person expecting you in the flat in ten minutes?"

Isabel replied that she was. So they placed their order for coffee and moved off the subject of morality, which was intractable, to house prices, which was a depressing subject. Both of them owned their houses; Jamie by virtue of the generosity of an elderly relative eager to avoid inheritance tax, and Isabel because her father had left it to her: old money, or at least money in late adolescence. Neither had earned the place in which they lived; many of those who earned what they had could hardly afford to live in Edinburgh now, with its high prices, just as people in London and New York found salaries inadequate for the cost of buying a roof to go over one's head. There was something wrong with this, Isabel thought, but it seemed to be an inescapable aspect of economic life: those who came in latest had the most uncomfortable chair, or no chair at all.

THERE WAS NO TIME for further conversation. They gulped their coffee down and then walked round the corner into St. Stephen Street.

"Here we are," said Isabel, pointing to a door at the top of a short flight of external stone steps. "That's the number."

Outside the door, mounted on a shabby brass plaque, were the names of the residents. Isabel found the name she was looking for, Macreadie, and rang the bell.

"Just walk right up," issued a woman's voice from a small intercom. "Top floor."

The mutual stairway was shabby and smelled of cat. And there, on the second-floor landing, was the possible culprit, a large tom in ginger, with ears tattered by conflict and a wall eye.

"A pugilist," said Isabel, pointing to the cat.

"Somebody loves him," said Jamie. "But let's not go into that again."

They reached the top landing and found that the door had already been opened for them. Standing in the doorway was a woman of about sixty, her hair swept back in the way used by Grace, wearing an intricately knitted Shetland sweater. Isabel noticed the pattern immediately. Somebody had sat for hours over that, working in all the natural colours, putting the sky and sea of those beautiful bare islands into the design.

Isabel introduced herself. "I'm Isabel Dalhousie. We spoke on the phone."

The woman smiled at her and then she looked at Jamie.

"My friend, Jamie," Isabel said. She saw the woman's eyes move to Jamie and then come back to her quickly. Something had crossed the woman's mind—and it occurred to Isabel that she was wondering what the relationship was. She had experienced this before—in restaurants, in cafés—when people had let their curiosity become apparent, or masked it too slowly.

They entered the flat, following the woman into the hall. Being on the top floor, the flat had an old-fashioned skylight, a small cupola, set into the roof, and this gave the hall an airy feeling.

"Falling light," said Isabel. "Very nice, Mrs. . . . ."

"Macreadie," said the woman. "Or Florence, if you like."

They left the hall and went into the kitchen. It was old-fashioned and a bit cramped, but there were useful cupboards built up against one wall and a well-used stone surface round the deep-set sink. Jamie went to the window and peered out, down into the drying green below, a small square of communally owned grass.

"I used to sit out there in the summer," said Florence. "In the days when we had a summer. A long time ago."

"Global cooling," said Isabel. "Everybody else gets warmer while Scotland gets colder."

"That's not true," Jamie corrected her.

They left the kitchen and went into the living room. This was also not particularly large, and Isabel thought that there was too much clutter. She tried to imagine the room without the glass-fronted display cabinet with all its trinkets, without the table covered with framed family photographs, without the ungainly Canterbury stuffed with magazines.

"This looks out onto St. Stephen Street," said Florence.

"There's a pub opposite, isn't there?" asked Jamie.

Florence nodded. "It can be a touch noisy on Friday and Saturday," she said. "But the bedroom is round the back. That looks out over the green. That's as quiet as the grave."

"Of course it will be," said Isabel. She liked the feel of the flat and she liked the owner. She had decided that Florence was a retired schoolteacher; she had that look about her and the bookshelves, she had noted, were those of an intelligent reader. But what had decided it was the presence on a shelf of *A History of Scottish Education.*

As they walked back through the hall to inspect the bedroom, Isabel asked Florence whether she was leaving Edinburgh altogether. When buying a house it was useful to know what the sellers were doing: a sudden departure or a sideways move was a danger signal.

"I was left a house in Trinity," Florence explained. "I have been very fortunate. It was my aunt's place."

That, thought Isabel, settles that; at least it ruled out the sudden arrival of an impossible neighbour. But what about the cat? Could somebody else's incontinent cat prompt a move?

"We saw a cat," she said. "On the stairs . . ."

"That's Basil," said Florence. "He belongs downstairs. I'm very fond of him. He comes in here for a visit from time to time."

"And the neighbours?" asked Isabel.

Florence reached out and touched Isabel on the arm. "I'd tell you," she said. "I really would tell you if they were a problem. They're angels, actually. All of them."

Isabel felt embarrassed that her questions had been so transparent. Yet the way in which she had been gently reproached made Florence appeal all the more to her. She felt that there was a current of fellow feeling emanating from this woman to her. It was reassuring—and touching, though she wondered what lay behind it. There were occasions—and they were quite common—when two people met and instantly got along together; something happened, possibly at a subconscious level, some sensing of sympathetic chemicals, which led to a rapport. Grace, who believed in telepathy, would say it was that. "I can tell what people are thinking," she said. "I really can."

And Isabel had said, "Oh yes, well, tell me what I'm thinking then."

"You're thinking that I can't tell what you're thinking," said Grace. And in that she was right.

Jamie did not follow them into the bedroom, but returned to the kitchen, to peer again out the window. Florence pointed

out the cupboards, the old fireplace in which stood an arrangement of dried flowers and which, she said, could be opened up
again if one wanted an open fire. "So many flats had their fireplaces taken out," she said. "Beautiful old Victorian fireplaces.
Georgian too. Such a loss."

Isabel looked at the dried flowers, dusty and pale, washed of
colour. "Such a tucked-away bedroom," she said. "So snug."

Florence gave her a conspiratorial look. "Yes. I can see you in
this place, you know. You and your friend." She looked through
the open door in the direction of the kitchen.

For a moment Isabel said nothing. She felt embarrassed by
the misunderstanding, but she also felt flattered that Florence
should imagine that she and Jamie were together in that sense.
Yes, she thought, it would be good to be living here with him,
living together as lovers. But she could not let Florence continue to believe something that was false, and so she started to
explain. "Jamie and I—" she began. But she did not continue, as
Jamie had appeared in the doorway.

"The bedroom," said Isabel, letting him look past her. "Isn't
it nice?"

Jamie nodded his approval. Again he went to the window
and looked out, poking at the wooden frame as he did so. He
had told Isabel about rotten window sills in New Town flats and
the importance of knowing just what repairs one was letting
oneself in for. This wood appeared to be solid, though, and he
turned to face into the room. Florence was staring at him, a
smile about her lips.

Isabel could not say anything about Jamie now, could not
give the explanation that was needed, and so she looked at her
watch and then at Jamie. "We should be getting along," she said.
"We have to . . ." She left that unfinished. They did not have to

do anything, but she felt that she had seen enough of the flat and she wanted to be out in the street. She would offer for it, she thought. She would talk to Simon Mackintosh, her lawyer, and make an offer.

They said goodbye to Florence, who saw them off in the hall. Then, on the stairway, on the way down, Jamie turned to her and said, "As nice as it gets around here."

"Really?"

"Yes. Top floor, which will make a difference to the noise. Bedroom at the back. Well maintained. And the wiring's new. I had a quick look."

Isabel smiled at him. "I knew that it was a good idea to bring you."

They went out onto the street, closing the heavy, blue-painted communal door behind them. A young couple walked past them, going in the direction of Royal Circus, the woman's midriff was exposed, the mottled white flesh shaking as she moved, and the man's jeans were fashionably torn, affording a view from the rear of dark-blue undershorts. Display of the body, thought Isabel; changing conceptions of the private. It was no longer socially impermissible for men to show their undershorts, and perhaps that was not unreasonable. Was there anything inherently more private about one garment rather than another?

Jamie was going to Castle Street, and Isabel, who was returning home, had planned to go in that direction, so they walked together up Gloucester Lane towards the end of Heriot Row. Gloucester Lane was a narrow cobbled alleyway on both sides of which were mews houses. Jamie pointed out how much more expensive these were, although sometimes they were smaller than the flat they had just looked over.

"It's strange how much people will pay for an address," he said. "Don't you think that rather odd?"

"Not at all," said Isabel. "Jockeying for social position is what people do. Instinctively. We're competitive creatures."

He looked up at a window in which a black-and-white cat was seated, eyeing them disdainfully. "You're a bit of a snob, Isabel."

He had not intended to say it; it had just come out. And now it was uttered, and he regretted it, as he sensed Isabel bristle beside him.

She stopped and turned to him. "I most certainly am not," she said. "That's most unfair. It really is."

He reached out and took her arm. "I'm sorry, I didn't mean that seriously. You're not a snob. You're not."

Isabel brushed his hand away. "All I said was that people do tend to go for what they think of as socially prestigious. And they do. Everywhere, in every society you care to mention. That's just a factual observation. A snob would say that it mattered where you came from, what your address was, and so on. I don't say that for a moment. Not one moment."

Jamie knew that she was right, and that his comment had been wrong and hurtful. Poor Isabel. She tried so hard to do the right thing—she agonised over these things all the time—and he had gone and accused her of something really nasty, which she did not deserve.

She had started to walk off without him, and he ran to catch up with her. "That was a stupid remark I made," he said. "Really stupid. Will you forgive me?"

Her voice was cold. "Think nothing of it."

"I meant—*really* forgive me," he said.

She was silent, and so Jamie persisted. "You know, you often go on about forgiveness. Yes, I've heard you. And yet do you practise it yourself?"

She looked at him. "So now you're accusing me of hypocrisy as well as snobbery? Is that it?"

"Oh, Isabel, for God's sake . . ."

She closed her eyes. He was right in what he said about forgiveness; it was just that she was vulnerable to insensitive words from him—not that his words had been particularly insensitive—and this vulnerability was all the greater because she could not talk to him about it. To him she was just another friend, nothing more, and one could talk like that to a mere friend. And that, she thought, is my personal tragedy. As long as I am afraid to tell him of my love, to confess it to him, then I shall have to pretend that we are just friends on this level. But I cannot tell him. That would end even the friendship. He would be appalled. He would run away.

"We're arguing over nothing," she said. "Of course I know you didn't mean it. Sorry."

They resumed their walk up the hill. At the top of Gloucester Lane, the mews houses gave way to broader, more elegant streets, to Heriot Row and Darnaway Street. Heriot Row, which faced south, was a long sweep of Georgian terrace, with formal gardens on the other side. It was a street and an attitude rolled into one; most of those who lived here played the part expected of them and furnished their houses and flats with Georgian furniture. The high windows of the drawing-room floors were draped with long-drop curtains, bunched at the sides, secured with formal tassels; the windows at street level afforded a glimpse of dining rooms with rise-and-fall lights above large mahogany tables, of grand pianos, of book-lined studies. It was a world which Isabel understood, and in which she could move, and yet it was not the world in which she chose to live. There was a deadness of the soul in such places, she thought; it was like being in a museum, living a life devoid of colour and spontaneity.

"Heriot Row has always given me the creeps," she said.

Jamie looked up at the windows. "I don't know," he said. "I went to a party here once. I didn't get the creeps. In fact, it was rather fun."

"It's too perfect," she said. "I suppose most cities have places which are just too perfect. There's Mayfair in London. All very clean and well looked after. But sterile too. And there are those streets in the smart parts of New York. The ones with those unwelcoming doormen. Too rarefied for me."

She was about to say something about Paris, too, when something caught her eye. She and Jamie were about to cross the road when a car swung down from Wemyss Place and turned right into Heriot Row.

"That's a beauty of a car," Jamie said. "Look at it."

Isabel was uninterested in cars, but interested in those within. And in this case she recognised them, the man and the woman from the gallery. He was at the wheel, occupied with driving, but the woman turned and looked at Isabel and Jamie as the car went past. She looked at Isabel for only a moment, a look which gave no sign of recognition; then her eyes moved to Jamie, and for a brief second she stared at him before the car moved beyond them and made its way down Heriot Row.

"That woman looked at you," said Isabel. "Did you see?"

"What a stunner," said Jamie.

"Not close up," said Isabel. "I met her in the Scottish Gallery."

"I was talking about her car," said Jamie.

A few minutes later they parted company. Jamie had to visit

an insurance office in Castle Street and so they said goodbye at the corner of Hill Street. Then Isabel continued her walk home, thinking, as she did, of the coincidence of seeing the American visitors twice in so short a time. What were they doing? Who were they? She was barely any further along the road to knowing anything about that than she had been when she first saw them from the window of Glass and Thompson. But why that should be of the slightest importance, she had no idea. She meant nothing to them, and they should mean nothing to her. And yet they did.

CHAPTER FOUR

MY DEAR," said Mimi McKnight, "just look at us! Bedraggled! In need of . . . well, in need of everything, I suspect. Hydration, certainly."

Isabel had offered to fetch Joe and Mimi from the airport, but had been firmly turned down. They would find a taxi, they said, and arrive under their own steam, which they did, laden with several months' worth of luggage and gifts for Isabel and the various others with whom they would be staying on their trip. Isabel received two large bottles of Tabasco sauce, a copy of Robert Lowell's *Collected Poems* and a nineteenth-century Mexican miniature silver candelabra.

Mimi was first cousin to Isabel's mother, Hibby. Mimi was from Dallas, but Hibby had been born and raised in Mobile, on the Alabama coast, a city of elegant oaks and long stories of the blood. Mobile was a proud place, and did not care for the ignorant condescension of outsiders. "We invented Mardi Gras," Isabel had been told by her mother. "New Orleans thinks it did, but it's wrong. We did. That's your heritage, Isabel." But there was another side to the heritage of well-to-do Mobile, of course: the dark side of the South—and this was not talked about, or used not to be. It was there, though, and could be seen in the musty family photograph albums, where the servants stood in the background, under a tree, beside the cars, carrying things. That's what can lie behind money, thought Isabel; not always, but often: expropriated lives; the lives of people in the background, nameless, forgotten, who never really owned very much.

As a teenager Isabel's mother had been sent to Dallas in the summer, away from the humidity of the Gulf Coast and into dry heat of the Texas plains, thought to be better for you and more tolerable. There she stayed with her cousin, Mimi, and did the things which teenagers of the time and place did: shopping at Neiman Marcus on Commerce Street, swimming at the club, waiting for something to happen, which it never did.

Then their paths had diverged. Hibby had gone to New York, to the Katherine Gibbs Secretarial School, and had then worked for two years with a firm of Wall Street lawyers. Several of these lawyers would have been quite happy to marry her; she was good-looking and had that Southern charm that young men found irresistible. But she, in turn, found the attractions of a Scottish graduate student at Columbia Law School equally irresistible, and married Isabel's father instead. Back in Mobile, they put a brave face on this, and those relatives who had met her intended husband reported positively. It was not the end of the world. Mimi, in particular, who had met Isabel's father at the engagement party that Hibby held in New York, could not understand their misgivings. "Everything about him is perfect," she said. "Even his imperfections."

Mimi's marriage to Joe McKnight was a second marriage for both of them. Joe, a professor of law at Southern Methodist University in Dallas, was an authority on Texas legal history and the law of the Spanish colonies, of which Texas had been one.

Had been, Joe stressed. "We stole it from the Mexicans fair and square," he pointed out, half seriously.

His interests were antiquarian, and these were shared by Mimi, who dealt in rare books. Joe restored and rebound these books in the small bindery that he had set up in an upstairs room in their Dallas house, a room stacked with pots of glue, bolts of soft binding leather, all the tools of that trade. He knew all about these leathers and endpapers and bookworms. And Mimi knew all about choral music and old cookery books and cats.

They arrived in the early evening. Isabel had shown them to their room, the guest room at the back of the house, which, although it got little direct sunlight, had a view over the garden.

"The room we were in last time," said Mimi. "And there's that painting." She crossed the room to look at the large oil hung on the wall above the chest of drawers. A man and his wife, their arms around two young children, huddled together on the deck of a sailing ship. Behind them the waves were swelling, whipped to white at the crests, almost obscuring the shores of a distant island. "That's Skye, isn't it?" she asked.

Isabel nodded. "McTaggart," she said. "And yes, I think that it is Skye. He painted quite a few pictures like that. People leaving Scotland, setting off for their new lives in Nova Scotia or Boston, or wherever it was."

Mimi stood before the large picture, which she gazed at through her large oval glasses. "And off they went," she said. "Look at the children's expressions. Look at them."

Isabel joined Mimi in front of the painting. She was not particularly fond of McTaggart, and this explained the painting's presence in the guest bedroom, where she rarely saw it. It had been a favourite of her father's, though; he liked nineteenth-century Romantic painters and had bought this cheaply at an auction, one of the first paintings he acquired, and had given it to Isabel's mother. Isabel suspected that her mother had not liked it either, but had never said as much.

The children in the painting seemed impervious to their fate. The parents saw before them only a hazardous sea voyage, weeks of seasickness and privation, and, at the end of it all, a landing in a hard and unknown country. For the children, though, setting sail was a great adventure. The boy, his face bright with excitement, was pointing at a seagull that was riding the boat's slipstream; the girl was saying something to a doll she was clutching—some maternal words of encouragement, a lullaby perhaps.

"It makes me think of 'Lochaber No More,'" said Isabel. "Do you know that song, Mimi? It's about leaving Scotland. About never again seeing the place you've loved."

Mimi, lost in the painting, said nothing.

Isabel recited:

> *"Farewell to Lochaber, farewell to my Jean,*
> *Where heartsome wi' her I ha'e mony day been,*
> *For Lochaber no more, Lochaber no more,*
> *We'll maybe return to Lochaber no more."*

Mimi turned to Isabel. "But that's very beautiful," she said. "Sad. Sad and beautiful. To be *heartsome* with somebody. What a lovely word."

Isabel smiled. "That's what this country's like, you know. It has a way of surprising you. It's hard to be indifferent to it." She turned away from the McTaggart. "But I have things to do. We're having company for dinner."

She was aware as she spoke that she had unconsciously

slipped into an American idiom. People in Edinburgh did not have company in the way in which they did in America. They had guests.

"Guests?" asked Mimi.

"Yes," said Isabel. "Cat."

"Good," said Mimi. "I have a gift for her. And Joe has always had a soft spot for Cat, haven't you, Joe?"

"Yes," said Joe. "Nice girl."

"And she has a new boyfriend, Patrick," said Isabel. "He's coming with her."

Mimi and Isabel exchanged glances. Mimi had heard of Toby, and of the others; or at least she had heard Isabel's version.

"I've not met him yet," Isabel admitted. "But preliminary reports . . ." She hesitated. There had been only one report so far, and that had come from Eddie. Was Eddie a good judge of these matters?

"Are favourable?" asked Mimi.

"Yes," said Isabel. "But we shall shortly see. I hope you don't mind, by the way, having something on your first evening. It occurred to me after I had arranged it that you might want a quiet evening."

Mimi assured Isabel that she and Joe would be very happy to be entertained that night. "And I want to meet Patrick," she said. "Poor young man. Do you think he'll mind being on display?"

"Nobody enjoys being on display," said Isabel. But then she thought: Some do, and so she added, "Except actors. And narcissists." Patrick could be both of these, she thought. She wondered whether a narcissistic actor would be an improvement on an unfaithful wine merchant, which is what Toby had been. Motor insurance companies rated people according to occupation when they assessed risk; poets and journalists paid a higher premium than lawyers and librarians. It had not occurred to her before, but now she saw it: the risk a man posed to a woman probably ran in parallel to the insurance risk he represented. Dangerous drivers made dangerous lovers. Safe, reliable personalities made safe reliable boyfriends and husbands. But how dull!

"You're smiling at something," said Mimi.

PATRICK, a glass of wine in his hand, was sitting on the sofa, talking to Mimi. Joe, standing near the fireplace, was engrossed in conversation with Cat. Isabel, who had left her guests for a few minutes to attend to something in the kitchen, took in the scene from the doorway. There had been no awkwardness when Cat and Patrick arrived; just the smallest of warning glances, perhaps, between Cat and Isabel. Cat knew that Isabel was making an effort not to involve herself in her affairs, and appreciated this, but old habits, she knew, died hard.

They had spoken to each other briefly in the kitchen, when Cat had come through to help. "He seems very nice," Isabel had said. It was a trite word—*nice*—but it would have to do in the circumstances. And what else could she have said? She had yet to talk to Patrick and get to know him; nice was about as far as she could go at present.

"We get on very well," said Cat quietly. "I thought that you'd like him."

"He's very good-looking," said Isabel, smiling.

Cat, carefully placing canapés on a plate, looked at Isabel sharply.

"Well, he is," said Isabel defensively. "I'm not accusing you

of going for looks. But if the looks are there, then all the better."
She was not sure if she believed what she said. Of course Cat
went for looks. It had been apparent to Isabel ever since Cat
had been sixteen and had produced her first boyfriend that she
was attracted to tall young men with regular features and blond
hair. It was a cliché of male beauty, really, and Cat subscribed to
it enthusiastically. Of course there was a biological message in
it, as there was in all messages of beauty. In choosing me, it said,
you choose somebody who is strong and reliable and who will
give you strong children. Ultimately everything that the poets
said about love was a romanticization of the fundamental biological imperative: find somebody with whom to produce children and who will help you raise them.

She did not have the chance to speak at length to Patrick
until they were seated at the table. Exercising her prerogative as
hostess, she had placed Patrick on her right, which would
enable her to find out what she needed to find out. He proved
forthcoming. He was a lawyer, he revealed. He worked for a firm
that specialised in takeovers, which he called acquisitions. "We
acquire companies," he said simply. "I draw up lists of things
that have to be checked. We call it compliance."

Isabel raised an eyebrow. There was something soft about
him, she thought. In spite of the masculine good looks, the
chiselled features, there was something yielding and feminine
about him. And yet here he was talking about pouncing. For a
moment, a ridiculous moment, she imagined Patrick pouncing
on Cat, his long limbs poised like springs, his thin, elegant fingers extended like claws.

"Redness in tooth and claw," she muttered.

"Money doesn't stay in a hole," said Patrick casually, dipping
his spoon into his soup. "It needs to be active."

Isabel felt herself becoming irritated. Money was an inanimate force. It was people who were active, who made money do things. "But these takeovers involve people losing their jobs," she said. "Isn't that true? From what I've heard, the first thing that the new owners do is try to get rid of as many people as they can."

Patrick put down his spoon. "Sometimes," he said. "But companies aren't charities. People can't expect a job for life. Not these days."

Isabel told herself that she should try to like Patrick. She had promised herself that she would give him a chance, and that she would not make any assumptions. But what she now felt was not an assumption. This was a conclusion: Patrick was self-satisfied. He was as shallow as Toby had been; more intelligent, perhaps, but just as shallow.

"Are you going to be a lawyer for the rest of your career?" she asked quietly.

Patrick looked surprised. He took a piece of bread roll from his plate and broke it. "Yes," he said. "That's what I want to do." He spoke in a slightly pedantic way, the words carefully chosen and articulated, as if everything that he said was the result of careful deliberation.

"In that case," said Isabel, "you yourself expect a job for life. Interesting." She waited a moment for her remark to sink in. Patrick was not slow, and he gave a wry smile when he saw the trap he had stepped into.

"Being a lawyer is a career," he said. "I don't expect to be with the same firm all my life. The people I'm with at the moment could get rid of me tomorrow if they wanted."

"But they won't, will they?" said Isabel.

"Probably not. But they could, you know."

"If they were taken over?"

"Law firms tend not to get taken over," said Patrick. And again he recognised the trap. The rules of the jungle did not apply to those who wrote the rules of the jungle.

"WELL," said Isabel to Mimi. "That's Patrick."

The two women were standing in the kitchen after dinner. Cat and Patrick had left, and Joe, tired from the journey, had gone upstairs to bed. They had brought the plates and dishes through, and these were now stacked above the dishwasher, ready to be loaded.

"Yes, Patrick," said Mimi neutrally.

Isabel knew that Mimi was charitable in her views. It was one of her great qualities: Mimi did not like to belittle others. And, I must remind myself, Isabel thought, that I have had a single meeting with him. I am fourteen years older than he is. Nobody is asking me to sit in judgement on him.

"He's bright," said Isabel. "Toby wasn't."

"No, so I hear," said Mimi.

"And I can see what she sees in him physically," said Isabel. "He's . . ."

"Yes," said Mimi. "He certainly is."

There was silence for a moment. "He lives with his mother," said Mimi. "When I was speaking to him through there, he told me. He says that he's lived with his mother all along. Through law school, through his traineeship, and he's still there."

"That's unusual," said Isabel. "Or is it, these days? Children are going back home, I gather, but they usually go away first." She paused. She remembered Eddie's remark: *Patrick is more like me.* What exactly did that mean? Now that she had met Patrick she thought that she might understand it better.

"I found him a bit . . . ," she began.

"A bit?" asked Mimi.

Isabel was not sure. "A bit something. But I'm not sure what it is. It's a sort of fussiness, perhaps. Yes, fussiness might be the word. I can imagine that he likes to have everything neat and tidy. I imagine that he disapproves of a lot of things. That sort."

"Do you think that he disapproved of us?" asked Mimi, picking up a heavy crystal glass and holding it up to the light. "This was his glass, by the way."

Isabel looked at the glass. There was nothing unusual about it. A few tiny grains of dark sediment from the red wine it had contained stuck to the bottom, just above the stem.

"Do you notice anything?" asked Mimi, handing the glass to Isabel.

She looked at it. There was nothing; just the grains. Were they significant? She looked at them again. "Just a bit of sediment," she said, puzzled.

Mimi looked amused. "Look at the rim," she said.

Isabel looked but could see nothing. Then she saw. Nothing was what she saw.

"Quite clean," said Mimi. "He wiped it after he used it. I saw him do it. He wiped it with his table napkin."

"An obsessive," said Isabel.

"Maybe," said Mimi. "But you know what I think? I think he's a mama's boy." She paused and took the glass back from Isabel. "I just get that feeling about him. I hope that I'm not doing him an injustice, but he reminds me very strongly of somebody I knew in Dallas, somebody just like him. He lived with his mother near the country club in Highland Park. In one of those large places on Beverly. She more or less wouldn't let him out of her sight."

Isabel remembered Beverly, with its ostentatious houses, mansions really, and their manicured lawns. And she imagined the mama's boy on Beverly drinking iced tea under the revolving fan, watched by a Dallas matron, from her chair, vigilant. "And?" she said.

"The mother saw off the poor boy's girlfriends," Mimi said. "Saw them off. Every one of them." It had been a matter of remark; people had laughed about it, although it was not a laughing matter, said Mimi. The mother had died, and for a time the son had remained where he was, in the same house, in thrall to the memory of the mother who was not there, stuck in the cautious rituals that she had instilled in him. Then he held a party, an immense blowout, and he went off with the party planner, a blonde from Fort Worth, who would have been the embodiment of his mother's worst nightmare. "Not an intellectual," observed Mimi. "The lady, that is."

"So Cat . . ."

"May encounter a problem," supplied Mimi. "Although we could be quite wrong, you know. Does that thought occur to you, Isabel? Do you think I could be quite wrong?"

That thought had occurred frequently. Isabel's training as a philosopher would have been in vain had she not opened herself up to doubt. Doubt was a constant, a condition of her being. "Often," said Isabel thoughtfully. Then she added, "But not now."

They left it at that. Isabel felt uncomfortable talking about Patrick in this way. She reminded herself that she had resolved to make an effort to like him, and she would do that, for Cat's sake. It was really no business of hers if Cat should take up with a mama's boy—or an obsessive, for that matter. Cat's life was her own, and she, Isabel, would welcome whomsoever Cat chose to share her life with. Isabel would have wished that this had been Jamie, but it was not, and if it was going to be Patrick, then so be it. I shall make the most of him, thought Isabel. I really shall. Patrick and I will become friends.

In bed that night, in the darkness, with the illuminated dial of her alarm clock glowing from the bedside table, she asked herself whether one could force oneself to like somebody, or whether one could merely create the conditions for affection to come into existence and hope that it did, spontaneously. *Open then our hearts*—these words came into her mind, dredged from somewhere in her memory, from some unknown context. If one opened one's heart, then friendship, and love, too, might alight and make their presence known. It was the act of opening that came first; that was the important thing, the first thing. But who was it who said, *Open then our hearts*? Where did that come from?

CHAPTER FIVE

"**M**ARMITE?" asked Isabel over breakfast.

"The National Library of Scotland," said Joe, buttering a slice of toast. He applied only butter, scrupulously avoiding the open jar of Marmite which Isabel had placed in front of him.

She noticed the spurning of the Marmite. That, she said, was her test of acculturation. Only the most determined of anglophiles would eat Marmite, and not even all of those. For the rest, it was an inexplicable British taste, quite beyond sympathy. Drinking lukewarm beer and taking tea with lashings of milk were understandable, even to a Texan for whom iced tea was only natural; but to spread on one's toast a salty black yeast paste was beyond comprehension. And Joe, who had been a Rhodes Scholar, and who liked nothing more than to spend the summer in a rambling house which they rented in Oxford, was an anglophile by any standard; but not by the measure of Marmite.

"Yes," said Joe. "I intend to spend the day in the National Library of Scotland. And no thank you, I don't like Marmite."

"Working on your history of adoption?"

"Precisely. They have some very interesting material there."

Mimi reached for the coffee pot. "And I shall be trudging round the bookstores," she said. "I don't know how you can eat that stuff. I really don't."

Isabel applied Marmite to her toast. "Looking for?" Mimi was a serial book collector, moving from author to author. Her collection of Andrew Lang was virtually complete, as was that of Graham Greene firsts. Isabel continued, "It's an acquired taste, I suppose. Like the hundred-year eggs that the Chinese eat. You know, the eggs they bury for a hundred days and then dig up and eat. They go wild over them."

"Arthur Waley," said Mimi in answer to Isabel's question. "He translated Chinese poetry. It was wonderful stuff. And he wrote biographies of some of his poets. It's quite a thought, isn't it—there they were in the eighth century or whenever it was and somebody should write their biography twelve hundred years later. An Englishman. So far away. Picking over the lives of these poets."

That, Isabel agreed, was strange. But so was any act of homage to the classical world. Would Catullus have imagined that he would be read after millennia had passed? That people would show an interest in the small details of his life? No, said Mimi, Catullus probably would not. But Horace would. He described, she recollected, his poems as a monument *more enduring than bronze;* that had struck her as a sign of excessive ego. "But I don't think that these Chinese poets would have imagined that degree of immortality," she said. "They led rather remote lives. They were often exiled for some tiny faux pas committed at court. They were sent off to be magistrates in the remote provinces somewhere. And that made their poetry rather wistful, full of regrets."

Isabel thought for a moment. She was trying to remember

something by Li Po. She had Waley's translation of his works in her library, but could only remember a poem about drinking wine by oneself. That was all.

"Li Po drank wine by himself," she began.

"Indeed he did," said Mimi. "But so did many of the others. Chinese poets were always drinking wine and then writing about it. Or waiting for boats to arrive from downriver. Or wondering what absent friends were up to. Brooding about what they were doing."

"That," said Isabel, "is the most painful feature of lost love. You wonder what the other person is doing. Right at this moment. What is he doing?"

There was silence for a moment. Joe put down his slice of toast and looked at his plate. Mimi, from behind the rim of her coffee cup, watched Isabel and thought: *Is that what she is thinking now?*

WITH MIMI AND JOE off on their respective outings, Isabel had the house to herself. It was Grace's day off, and she had gone to Glasgow to visit a cousin. The house, without Grace, seemed unnaturally quiet, but it gave Isabel the opportunity to work without interruption on her editing. Her desk was piled with manuscripts, the consequence of her dogged adherence to a policy of requiring the submission of articles in printed, rather than electronic, form. She could not read on screen, or at least not for long; the sentences and paragraphs became strangely disjointed, as if they were cut off from that which went before and that which came afterwards. That, of course, was an illusion; such paragraphs were just round the corner, just a scroll away—but where was that. Was electronic memory a *place*?

Before they appeared on the screen weren't they just endless lines of noughts and ones, or odd decimals? That, she thought, was the ultimate triumph of reductionism: Shakespeare's sonnets could be reduced to rows of noughts; or even the works of Proust; although how much electricity would be consumed to render Proust's long-winded prose digital? Patient wind turbines would turn and turn for days in that process. And what about ourselves, and our own reduction? We could each be rendered, could we not, down to a little puddle of water and a tiny heap of minerals. And that was all we were. *Imperial Caesar, dead, and turned to clay, Might stop a hole to keep the wind away.* Or, as binary code might so prosaically put it: 0100100101101 10101110000 . . .

She worked quickly, and by the time that her lawyer telephoned her she had managed to make an impression on the pile of manuscripts; she had read three, and had embarked on the fourth. None of them, she thought, was likely to get past the peer reviewers, which was sad, as each represented months of effort: thought, planning, hopes. But the problem was that they all had the feel of being written to order, by people who had to write these articles—any articles—because they were academics and it was expected of them. This was their output, the basis on which they would be judged; not on whether they were inspirational teachers who could hold a class of students spellbound, could inspire them to think, but on the production of this sheer *wordage,* which few would read. Most of these articles would not change the world, would not make one iota of difference to anything. She sighed, and looked at the title page of the next article on the pile. "Dust to Dust: Should We Rebury Old Bones?" Her interest was aroused, and she picked up the manuscript. "Bones of five hundred years of age have been the subject

of controversy. Should archaeologists rebury them, or can muse-
ums . . ." She sighed again, and imagined for a moment archaeologists digging up old bones, so carefully, with their trowels and
brushes, and then, more or less immediately, burying them once
more, with reverence.

She rose to her feet to answer the lawyer's call, taking the
telephone with her to the window of her study.

Simon Mackintosh's voice was precise. "That place that you
looked at," he began. "The one in St. Stephen Street—I registered your interest in it with the seller's lawyers, as you asked
me to do."

"Good," said Isabel. "And I've decided that I'd like to make
an offer. I liked it very much. I was going to call you today to talk
about what offer we should put in." Isabel did not like the Scottish system of selling houses. A property went on the market
with an invitation for offers, giving a general guide to where
offers should start. But then what started was a blind auction:
anybody interested in buying it could put in their best offer in a
sealed envelope and, at a preordained time, these would be
opened and the highest bidder—normally—would win the auction. This was all very well for sellers, but for purchasers it cre-
ated an agony of uncertainty, driving people to offer the very
most they could afford, just in case somebody else came up with
a bigger offer.

Simon laughed. "Well, I'm saving you that call—and with
good news. The woman who's selling it . . ."

"Florence Macreadie."

"Yes," Simon continued. "Her lawyer telephoned me and
said that she would be very happy to sell it to you—and at a
price which is actually lower than the current starting price. Ten
thousand below, in fact. So it's yours if you want it."

Isabel said nothing as she absorbed this news. She had never been obliged to bid for a house before, but everything that she had heard from friends who had done so had made her dread the process. It seemed that everyone had their stories of missed properties, of offers that had seemed to be high and yet turned out to be far too low, of houses lost to an offer only five pounds higher; and yet here she was being offered a flat in a popular area of town at a sum below the starting price.

"Isabel?"

"Yes, I'm here. Sorry, I was thinking. I was trying to take in what you said to me. Ten thousand . . ."

Simon sounded bemused. "Below. Yes. Ten thousand below."

So, thought Isabel, she's desperate to sell. This means that there is some snag. The neighbours? Basil, the cat they met on the stairway? Ground subsidence affecting the foundations of the building? Fulminating wet rot in the roof space?

Simon interrupted her thoughts. "My first reaction, of course, was to assume that there was some problem with the property. It sounded rather as if she wanted to offload it on you. That's what I thought at first."

Precisely, thought Isabel.

"But then," Simon went on, "her lawyer told me the reason. She does have a reason, you know."

"And that would be?"

Simon hesitated. He sounded embarrassed. "Apparently she was very taken with the idea of your living there. She said that she liked the idea of you living there with your young man. That's the term she used. *Young man*. She said that it appealed to her sense of the romantic."

Isabel stared out of the window at the spruce tree in the

front garden. A squirrel was sitting nervously on one of the lower branches, its tail twitching in that curious, jerky way, as if tugged by a string.

Simon continued. "I don't like to pry, of course. It's no concern of mine. I thought, though, that you were interested in the flat for Grace—"

"Of course I am," Isabel said quickly. "Young man . . . Look, Simon, this really is rather funny. I asked Jamie, who is indeed a young man, to help me look over the place. He lives round the corner down there. I thought that she got the wrong end of the stick but couldn't set her right." She laughed. "So now she wants to help set me up in a love nest."

Simon cleared his throat. "Well, I must admit that I was rather surprised. Mind you, why not, Isabel? There's no reason why you shouldn't do something like that. You're a very attractive woman. Take a look in a mirror some day. I'm not speaking as your lawyer now, but as a friend . . ."

"It would be interesting," Isabel said. And she imagined herself—allowed herself to imagine—walking up the steps to the flat to find Jamie already home, inside, welcoming her, and her cooking a meal for the two of them in the kitchen with the late evening light of summer on the rooftops and a glass of wine in her hand and . . .

"But back to the matter at hand," Simon said. "What do you want to do? Do you want me to accept her offer to sell it to you?"

Isabel was about to say yes, and then she was struck by doubt. Florence Macreadie's offer was made on the basis of a false assumption. It was true that Isabel had done nothing to encourage the other woman's false belief, but could she let her act on it? If she did she would be taking advantage of another's mistake, which surely was wrong. It would be like . . . What

would it be like? Like buying a valuable antique from a vulnerable old person who had no idea of what the thing was worth.
People did that, did they not? Unscrupulous dealers would spot
a valuable item in the possession of somebody who had no clue
as to its value and they would buy it for a paltry sum. It would
be a valid sale from a strictly legal point of view, but morally it
was something quite different. If she took the flat from Florence
on these terms, then it would be taking something from her
which she would not have offered had she known the truth.

"Can you let me think about this?" asked Isabel.

"Of course."

"And is there any legal reason to turn it down?" she asked.

Simon paused before giving his answer. "No legal reason, as
far as I can see. But . . . morally, I think that you wouldn't
want somebody to be disadvantaged by a false impression she
laboured under." Simon paused for a moment. "I hope that you
don't mind my saying that. You're the one who knows all about
ethics . . ."

Isabel's response was immediate. "You're quite right. Of
course I can't let her act on that strange idea. Of course not."

Simon's relief was evident in his voice. "I thought you'd
come to that conclusion. I'll let her lawyer know that his client
was—how shall we put it?—misinformed. Then we can come
up with a bid, same as anybody else."

Isabel agreed, and after the exchange of a few niceties the
conversation came to an end. She turned back to her desk, but
did not sit down immediately. She stood for a good few minutes,
staring at the books on her shelf, the serried ranks of titles.
Kant. Schopenhauer. Midgley. Kekes. All these people who had
spent so much time, given up on so many other diversions (one
assumed) in order to devote themselves to the elucidation of

what was right. And here she had been faced with a moment of financial temptation—the saving of ten thousand pounds—and she had hesitated in her response. She had almost said yes. She had almost told Simon that they should accept Florence's offer immediately. She had almost done that. And everything on those shelves, all the elaborate structures of right and wrong, had been for a few moments forgotten. Which is how most people acted when it came to temptation. They gave in. And we should never forget, thought Isabel, that every one of us is capable of doing the same thing if the gain that we see for ourselves is large enough. She had often thought that if she were ever to give in to a yearning for the material it would have to be a very large sum; her price would be a high one—a kingdom. But now she had seen that the opposite was, in fact, true. Her price was as low as anybody else's. And if she could give in over a mere matter of ten thousand pounds, could she not give in over the mere matter of a young man, a musician, whose company she so appreciated and whose profile, at the right angle, stopped her heart?

I have learned something about myself, thought Isabel.

CHAPTER SIX

JOE AND MIMI settled into their routine. He went off to the
National Library each morning and returned shortly after five in
the evening. He seemed pleased with what he found. It was
slow work, he said, and he was not sure what it would bring
forth—a book, perhaps, but not a big book; an article certainly,
that he would send to people who were interested in this sort of
thing. Joe knew them all and they would send him their articles
too. "The dean loves us to write these things," he said. "It gives
him a warm feeling."

Mimi looked for Arthur Waley and one or two other authors.
She found a first edition of the life of Li Po, in good condition,
with the dust jacket, which pleased her, and some Auden, which
pleased Isabel, but which would not have pleased Auden, as it
was a pamphlet, elegantly set and printed, of "Spain 1937," a
poem which he disowned.

"I feel disloyal when I read the poems he disliked," said
Isabel. "Even that marvellous 'September 1, 1939.' Remember
the poem? It had those lines at the end which people in New
York copied and sent to one another in consolation in that other

terrible September. But Auden said it was all wrong. He didn't mean it any more."

Mimi took off her spectacles and polished them on a square of soft silk. "But people take different things from works of art. The poem, the painting, changes."

Isabel suddenly laughed, and Mimi looked at her cousin in puzzlement. "Amused?"

Isabel shook her head. "Sorry, not anything you said. I've just remembered what happened to my friend Gill Salvesen. She's an amateur printmaker. One of her prints was taken by a gallery and they inadvertently hung it sideways. She heard about it and was going to tell them about their mistake, but before she could do so, a friend of hers bought it and hung it in her house—sideways. Gill didn't know what to do."

Mimi smiled. "Well, that makes the same point, doesn't it? People see different meanings."

"But there may be a real meaning. And if somebody doesn't know that, shouldn't we tell her?"

Mimi pointed upstairs. "What about that McTaggart in our room? What if I thought that it represented people *arriving* in Scotland rather than emigrating?"

"In art, immigrants don't look sad," countered Isabel. "They look apprehensive. Or even quite excited."

"But would you tell me that? Would you tell me that if what gave the painting meaning for me was the thought that it was all about arrival?"

"I might let you carry on thinking that," conceded Isabel.

"Well, there you are," said Mimi.

Then Mimi said something which was to make a difference. It had nothing to do with their discussion of art, but was a social arrangement which she and Joe wanted to propose.

"We wondered if you were free the weekend after next," Mimi said. "There are some people we know who are here in Scotland for the summer. They've taken a large house outside town—Joe knows exactly where it is. One of these Scottish fortified houses. Somewhere near Peebles, I think. Anyway, they—or rather he, we don't really know her—asked us whether we would come out for the weekend. They're happy to make it a house party. They know we're staying with you, so you're invited."

Isabel was free that weekend, and the idea of a house party appealed.

"Good," said Mimi. "We'll get in touch with them. Or Joe will, rather."

Isabel was curious. "Who are they?"

"Dallas people," said Mimi. "He's called Tom Bruce. She's called Angie. She's his fiancée. Second time round, of course. For him. I don't know about her."

There was something in Mimi's tone that made it clear to Isabel that Angie was not in favour. That was not unusual, of course; an old friend remarried and, try as one might, the new wife was not quite the same. Countless friendships had foundered on that rock.

"You're not too keen on her?" Isabel asked gently.

"I don't like to be uncharitable," said Mimi.

"Which is what people say before being uncharitable."

"Well," drawled Mimi. "Well . . . Let's give her the benefit of the doubt. But put it this way: she's a good bit younger than he is. And he's . . ."

"Very well-off?"

"Exactly. Even by the standards of Preston Hollow, where he lives, he's not hard up. Do you remember Preston Hollow from your Dallas visits?"

Isabel did not. But Mimi's point was clear.

"He was one of those property people who acquired large tracts of land out near the airport. All that nothing acreage that nobody was interested in. Well, that changed, and Tom did very nicely. Not that anybody resented it. He's a really nice man. He supports the symphony and the new museum. And he always said that he would support the law school too, but hasn't exactly gotten round to it just yet.

"Yes," Mimi continued. "Everybody has time for Tom. We don't see a great deal of him, but now and then we do. He's quite a shy man, really. His confidence was pretty dented by his condition. Do you know about Bell's palsy?"

They were sitting together in the drawing room at the time. Isabel had given Mimi a glass of New Zealand white wine, and she was holding her own glass, half full. She put it down on the table beside her. In her mind she saw the man in the gallery. She saw the face wrenched up at one side in that disfiguring grimace. That was Tom. That was who he was.

"I knew I was going to see him again," she muttered. "I knew it."

"Knew what?" asked Mimi, taking a sip of her wine.

"I think I've met them," said Isabel. "Just pure coincidence. I saw them in a gallery. They were buying a painting, I think."

"That's them," said Mimi. "She's on a spending spree, I gather. Paintings. Rugs. Even a racehorse, somebody said."

"But I had the impression that he was the one who was—"

"He'll do anything to please her," said Mimi. "Poor Tom."

ISABEL MET CAT for lunch that day, at two o'clock—a late lunch, but that was when the busy time in the delicatessen came to an end and Cat could leave Eddie at the counter while she took a break with Isabel at one of the tables. She had made Isabel a special Greek salad, which is what she knew she liked: salty cheese crumbled over olives and sliced boiled egg. Cat herself liked tomatoes and mozzarella.

"I haven't thanked you for the other night," said Cat. "We both enjoyed it. I love seeing Mimi and Joe, although they always make me feel a bit stick-in-the-mud. All the travelling they do."

"I don't know," said Isabel. "You went to Italy not all that long ago. And you had those six months in Australia."

Cat looked wistful. She had spent six months in Australia after university, working in a series of casual jobs, travelling and seeing the country. It had been the most perfect time of her life, and she could not think of it without a feeling of nostalgia. "Yes. There was that. But that was then. Now is different. Now is here. And tomorrow will be here."

Isabel speared an olive with her fork. "Not necessarily," she said. "All sorts of things can happen. You might . . ."

Cat looked at her. "Yes? I might what?"

Isabel had been thinking of marriage. That was the obvious thing that could change Cat's life and get her out of her rut, if that's what she thought she was in. Marriage had changed Isabel's own life—for the worse, but not every marriage did that. One would have to be massively cynical to see marriage in that light. Were most marriages happy? Somewhere she had read that with increased participation by women in economic life— as more women began to have their own careers—so the levels of happiness in marriage went down. Women in Sweden and countries like that, where women were free and independent, were apparently less happy in their marriages than women in those countries where they had less power and participated less in the working world. Well, if that were the case, she thought, then that meant that there was something wrong with conventional marriage, rather than something wrong with freedom.

She could not tell Cat that she had been thinking of marriage, because she was not at all sure whether Cat wanted to get married. So many people no longer bothered, but just lived together, or left it for years and years before doing anything about formalities. But was that what Cat really wanted? Or did she want somebody to come along and make a public commitment to her, as people used to do with marriage, as she had done with John Liamor?

"I might what?" repeated Cat.

"You might meet somebody," said Isabel.

Cat looked down at her plate, and Isabel knew that they were in awkward territory. She had learned her lesson, and was determined not to repeat the mistake she had made over Cat's involvement with Toby. But there was no reason for Cat to take offence over a very ordinary reference to the possibility of meeting somebody, and so Isabel said, "You could find yourself in a relationship with somebody who worked somewhere else, for example. That happens, you know. What if you met an Australian you liked and you thought you might go off together to Melbourne or Perth or somewhere? That happens, a lot. And the other way round too. Somebody from Australia meets somebody from London and goes to live there."

It did. There were love stories happening all the time in circumstances just like that; stories unsung, but as heroic and moving in their way as those that had been sung; we could not all be Tristan and Isolde, even if we were separated from one another by oceans and circumstance, but the whole point about the great myths was that they were about exactly the things that we all experienced and recognised.

"You could meet somebody too," said Cat. "An Australian philosopher. How about that? And then you'd be living in Melbourne."

"I'd like that," said Isabel.

"Melbourne? Or meeting somebody?"

She thought for a moment. "Well, I did go to Melbourne once, you know. And I found it fascinating. I'd be very happy there, I think. I love the Australian landscape. I like Australians."

But that was not what Cat had wanted to find out. She had hardly ever discussed John Liamor with Isabel—there had been an unspoken understanding about that—and she knew that there was concealed pain there. But Isabel was a vivacious, attractive woman, and men liked her. There was no reason why she should not have a lover; or none that Cat could see.

"But what about meeting somebody?" asked Cat. "Australian or otherwise. There are plenty of men in Scotland, you know. Have you thought . . ."

Isabel had another olive to attend to. She thought: She doesn't know, Cat doesn't know that I have met somebody and that it's Jamie. Yes, she had met him, but that was not what Cat meant. Cat's question was about the meeting of somebody who would actually be suitable for her, who would be about her age, in his early forties, maybe a bit older. That's what her question meant.

And for a few moments, Isabel was confused. She was confused because she knew that this was something that she had not confronted. She had been so scarred by what had happened with John Liamor that she had decided that she would be best off by herself. And then what had happened was that she had

found that of course she needed a man, and she had found herself falling for Jamie because he was there and he was so attractive and sympathetic and nobody could help but fall for him.
The point about love, the essential point, was that we loved
what we loved. We did not choose. We just loved. WHA again
had seen that when he had written about his love, as a boy, for a
pumping engine. *I . . . thought it every bit as beautiful as you.* Of
course it was. Love required an object, he said. That was all.

"I'd like to meet somebody," she said. "Yes. I would. Yes."

She looked up from her Greek salad, from the small, bliss-
ful world of olives and sliced boiled egg, and met Cat's gaze.
Now Cat did not know what to say. What she thought was:
Good, she's over that awful Irishman. Good. But she did not
know what to say because she had said that there were plenty of
men in Scotland, but the fact of the matter was that there were
not. There was a shortage of eligible men because of . . . what?
Demographic reasons: the death of men; all those men who
died from working too hard and living at the wrong pace, whose
final seconds must be filled with such regrets for all they had
given to their work? The social acceptance of the gay alternative? She could not think of anybody suitable for Isabel, not one
man, not one. He would have to be intelligent and urbane; he
would have to have a sense of humour. She knew nobody over
thirty-five who fitted those requirements who was not already
married or with somebody or gay.

Isabel smiled at her. She felt better for having said, and
thought, what she had just said. She felt that she had revealed
something to Cat, and with revealing something about oneself
there always comes a sense of lightening of the load that we all
carry: the load of being ourselves. "But of course," she said, "I
shouldn't talk about meeting other men. There's Patrick."

There was a slight cooling of the atmosphere. "I haven't known him that long," said Cat defensively. "He's not necessarily the one."

"Of course not," said Isabel hurriedly. "I enjoyed meeting him, by the way."

Cat looked away. "He enjoyed meeting you too." Isabel was not sure if this was true or if it was just politeness on Cat's part—or on Patrick's part, for that matter. She doubted whether he would really have enjoyed meeting her; there had been no warmth in their encounter—although she told herself that she really had tried; they were just too dissimilar.

There was a silence. Over at the counter, Eddie finished serving a customer and stretched his arms above his head, yawning. He looked towards Isabel and lowered his arms sheepishly, as if caught doing something furtive. "Tired?" Isabel mouthed to him across the room, and he nodded.

"Patrick is fun," said Cat suddenly, as if she had just thought of a reason why she should like him. "He makes me laugh. He's witty."

Isabel tried to conceal her surprise. She could not recall much of Patrick's conversation, but it did not seem to her it had been witty. "That's important in a man," she said. "I can imagine nothing worse than being with a man who has no sense of humour. Just imagine it. It would like being in the desert." She paused. "Have you met his mother yet? He lives at home, doesn't he?"

"I've met her once or twice," Cat replied. "She's a local politician. She used to be in charge of—"

Isabel raised a hand. "Of course! I thought that Patrick's name was familiar. Cynthia Vaughan. That's his mother. I've met her too. Several times. We were on a committee together."

"That's her," said Cat. "They live in Murrayfield. Near St. George's School."

Isabel placed her knife and fork on her empty plate. This was not particularly good news. Cynthia Vaughan was the last woman she would wish on Cat. She was a powerful, rather hectoring woman, almost a parody of the pushy local politician. Any son of hers would have a battle escaping from a mother like that. That was why he still lived at home, thought Isabel. She won't let him leave.

"She's not a woman I would care to disagree with," Isabel said cautiously.

The note of defensiveness came back into Cat's voice. "She was perfectly nice to me."

"I'm sure she was," reassured Isabel. But she thought, with some relief perhaps, Patrick is not going to last. The choice is going to be between Cat and his mother. And the mother will win, because she was the sort who had never allowed herself to lose a political battle, and the fight between mothers wanting to hold on to their sons and the women who wanted to take their sons away was a battle royal, more dogged than the Battle of Bannockburn, more poignant than the clash at Culloden Moor.

CHAPTER SEVEN

SHE CLIMBED THE STAIRS to Jamie's flat in Saxe-Coburg Street. She occasionally called in unannounced, which he did not seem to mind, and he did the same to her; neither was offended if the other was busy and made that apparent. Jamie had to practise, and she had to edit. Both knew that these activities took precedence over social activities.

He had an old-fashioned bell pull, which he had restored to working order and of which he was inordinately proud. A small brass arm, complete with clenched hand and cuffs, that hung at the side of his door could be pulled downwards, causing a bell inside to sound briefly. A couple of tugs would produce a longer, more insistent peal. Isabel pulled the bell handle, glancing at the fanlight above the door. The glass in the fanlight, Jamie had said, was the original pane put in when the tenement was built in 1850. "You can tell old glass," he said. "It is thicker at the bottom than at the top. It's liquid, you see. It very slowly sags downwards." Like people, thought Isabel.

Jamie answered the door and from his expression she knew immediately that he was not busy; this was not the I'm-in-the-middle-of-something face. He smiled at her and gestured for her to come in. "I was about to phone you," he said.

Isabel took off the light raincoat she had been wearing—it was one of those days which could not decide between wet and dry—and hung it over the chair in the hallway. Jamie's flat was not large: a small hallway gave onto a living room off which was a bedroom; these rooms, together with a generous-sized kitchen and a cramped bathroom, completed the accommodation. Jamie taught bassoon in the living room, where there was an upright piano in one corner. Most of his teaching was done in schools, but the occasional private pupil came to the flat, especially boys from the Academy, which was more or less next door. If the wind was in the right direction, as it was now, one might hear the school's pipe band practising, the wailing of the pipes drifting across the rooftops. It could be worse, Jamie had said. Imagine living in Ramsey Garden and having the Military Tattoo taking place in one's backyard every night for a month. And Isabel had listened for a moment and said: "I have nothing against 'Lochaber No More.' That's what they're playing."

"Something like that," said Jamie. "I don't notice it, really. It's just part of the background. Like the traffic."

Isabel listened. There was no traffic sound, as far as she could tell, just the pipes. She glanced at Jamie. How strange it must be to be entirely beautiful—did one think about it? Did one see the heads turn? He did not, she thought; he seemed blissfully unaware of what he looked like, and seemed not to care. He was just easy with it, which was part of his charm. There was nothing more unattractive than narcissism, she thought; nothing could transform beauty into a cloying, unattractive quality than that self-conscious appreciation of self. There was none of that in Jamie.

"Mimi and I were talking about it. 'Lochaber No More,'" said Isabel. "That McTaggart upstairs in my house made me think about it. And now . . ." She moved to the living-room window and looked out over the roofs towards the Academy. The pipes died away; the last notes had been reached. The air now seemed very still; what had been light rain was now mist, and there were signs of the sun trying to break through. "That's the trouble with our weather," she continued. "It doesn't know what it's doing."

"I like it," said Jamie. "It keeps us on our toes. I'm not sure that I would like the predictability of living in Sicily or somewhere like that. I'd miss our skies."

"I suppose so," said Isabel. "But then, every so often I have this yearning to go away altogether. To get away from Scotland and its weather. I could very easily live in the south of France, you know. In fact, I may go one of these days."

Jamie, who had been standing near the piano, fiddling with a bassoon reed, looked up sharply. "You're not seriously thinking of going, are you?" There was an edge of anxiety in his voice, which Isabel had noticed and which had given her a sudden, wild moment of hope. He did not want her to go.

She smiled at him. "A fantasy," she said. "From time to time I see myself doing something completely different, something exotic, but I never do anything about it. And it's not just the south of France. It's Thailand, Cambodia, India. Can't you see yourself in a small village on one of those Thai islands, leading the life of a Gauguin . . . that was the South Seas of course. Not exactly next door."

"Or Robert Louis Stevenson," interjected Jamie.

"Yes," said Isabel. "Or RLS. Yes. But not quite."

"Maybe we could go away together," mused Jamie. "You could be Robinson Crusoe and I could be your Man Friday."

Isabel laughed. "Have you ever looked at Defoe's illustra-
tions?" she asked. "Have you noticed that all that Robinson Crusoe sees on the beach is a single footprint? Not two footprints,
just one. Have you ever thought of how odd that is?"

"Because he had two feet?"

"Precisely. When we see him later in the book, he definitely
has two legs and two feet. We see him."

"He must have been hopping at the time." Jamie suggested.
"Very odd."

"Yes. Authorial inattention. I see it all the time when I'm
editing the *Review*. Even my philosophers can be very sloppy."

Then she thought: He said, *Maybe we could go away together*. He had said that, and she, stupidly, had started on about
Defoe and Man Friday having only one foot, when what she
should have said was, *Yes, let's. Let's go away*. She should have
said that straight away because it was the time to say it, and now
she could hardly go back to the lost moment. Patrick Kavanagh,
she thought. He wrote a poem which she always remembered,
about two young people in a boat and one does not say what he
wants to say to the other and has a lifetime to regret his mistake.
A lifetime. And Robert Graves wrote a poem about the bird of
love and said that when he is in your grasp you must clutch him
tightly; and there was Herrick, too, busy gathering his rosebuds,
as everybody could recite, or at least everybody who had sat at
the feet of the dry-as-dust Miss Macleod at George Watson's
Ladies College in George Square; all these poets who warned
us, warned us not to lose the opportunity, and yet we did, as
Miss Macleod herself had obviously done.

"Yes," said Jamie, suddenly. "Yes. We could go off somewhere. I've always wanted to go to Kerala. I've always wanted to
see—what's the name of that place? Cochin?"

"It's Kochi now," said Isabel. "But it's the same place." She paused. The sun had won the struggle with the mist and there was a broad ray of light slanting in from the window onto Jamie's red Turkish rug. Tiny flecks of dust floated in the light, like miniature planes swirling in space. She looked up at Jamie. "I'd like that," she said. "I went to Cochin once. I could show you."

Jamie had taken a step forward and was standing in front of her. The ray of sun now fell on his forearm. Isabel saw how it penetrated the thin cotton of his shirt, revealing the arm beneath. When she was a child she had held her hand up to the light and imagined that she could see the bones of her fingers through the flesh. And one of the boys from further down the street, the one who became a doctor and who died in Mozambique, had possessed a pair of X-ray specs which he had donned and claimed to be able to see through clothing. She thought of him from time to time, and of his sad, avoidable death at the hands of a youthful carjacker, and saw not the grown man, who had tried to do something about human suffering, but the small boy with his X-ray specs and his tricks.

"Look at this reed," Jamie said, handing Isabel the shaved double reed that fitted to the end of the bassoon's elegant crook. "Look how badly it's twisted. I've used it four, maybe five times, and now this."

She took the reed from him and examined it. It was an intricately made, rather fiddly object: two thin strips of reed, curved, laid side to side, and then bound at the base in a neat turban of red thread. Jamie sometimes made his own reeds, but he also bought them from a man who lived on a farm somewhere in England. He had spoken of this man before, who was called Ben, and she had imagined a bucolic scene with Ben sitting under a tree in his farmyard, shaving and tying reeds, while geese strutted around him. It would not be like that, of course; the farm would have stopped producing anything except bassoon and oboe reeds, and Ben would be a displaced urbanite.

"They're such odd-looking things," said Isabel. "And they make that ridiculous squawk when you blow them. Not that I can do it."

Jamie took the reed from her hand. "You don't know how to do it properly. I'll show you." He turned the reed round so that the tip was towards Isabel. "Open your lips. Just a little bit. Like this. See. Like this."

She did so, and he positioned the reed, but then withdrew it suddenly, and the back of his hand was against her lips, pressed gently against them. It was as if he had given his hand to be kissed in some courtly gesture. He moved it away. He was looking at her. Now he leaned forward and the hand kiss became a real kiss. Just briefly. Then he drew back and stared down at the carpet, at the now-enlarged square of sunlight.

"I'm sorry," he mumbled without looking at her. "I shouldn't have done that. I'm sorry."

She was about to reassure him, to reach out and take his hand, but he had turned away. "I was going to make you coffee," he said. "Come through to the kitchen. Or stay in here, if you prefer. I can bring it through."

Isabel said that she would go with him, and she followed him into the kitchen. She looked at the nape of his neck. She looked at his shirt, tucked carelessly into his jeans; for some reason, she glanced at her watch and noticed the time, as if to commit to memory the moment, the precise moment, of her transformation.

He busied himself with the making of coffee. He could have turned round, but his back was to her and the thought crossed her mind that this was to hide his embarrassment. He made a remark about a concert in which he was to play the following week. He said something about one of the pieces of music, about how he had met the composer and of how disappointing it had been. "He had nothing to say about his work, you know; nothing."

Isabel said, "People don't always like to talk about what they've done." And she thought immediately: Yes, he had kissed her and now would not talk about it. She had not meant it in that sense, but Jamie picked up on it. "Sometimes we do things on impulse," he said. "And the best thing may be to pretend that it never happened. But that hardly applies to a composition, surely?"

It was a ridiculous idea, and they both laughed, which went some way to defusing the tension. But when he brought over her cup of coffee, she noticed that his hand was shaking very slightly. The sight touched her. So he had been affected by what had happened in the same way as she had. It had been something important for him, not just a peck on the cheek between friends.

She put her coffee down on the square pine table that dominated the kitchen and sat on one of the chairs beside it. "Jamie—" she began, but he cut her off.

"Let's not," he said. "Let's not go there."

For a moment she felt wounded. It seemed to her that he was viewing their moment of intimacy with distaste, as one would remember but decline to dissect a social solecism. And what exactly did *Let's not go there* mean? Did it mean that the incident itself was not to be remembered, or that he did not wish to get emotionally involved with her? Was *there* a state of entanglement that he wanted to avoid? There were many reasons why he should think that way about it, and Isabel had thought about them all. And dominating everything was the sheer brute fact that fourteen years lay between them. Fourteen years. Jamie would want a contemporary; indeed she knew which contemporary he really wanted. Cat. And Cat was her niece. Did that not make matters problematic?

And yet, and yet . . . Would anybody raise an eyebrow if a man of thirty-eight took up with a woman of twenty-four? That was a gap of fourteen years, and there were plenty of such liaisons, which people seemed to accept readily enough. How old were Levin and Kitty? That sort of thing was quite different from the real cradle-snatch, from Humbert Humbert and his Lolita. She and Jamie were two adults, one a bit older than the other, but with the same interests and the same sense of humour. Why should I not love him? she asked herself. How absurd that we should deny ourselves something when our moment of life is so brief, our very world so transitory.

And now, sitting with her coffee, in silence, she thought of Auden's line: *how rich life had been and how silly.* She knew what that meant, she understood it; but the difficulty lay in trying to explain to somebody that it didn't matter, it simply didn't matter. Jamie did not want to take a risk. She now did. They were simply not in the same place. She was here, and he was there. That was the topography of unrequited love; there were many hills, unscalable peaks, continents separated by wide oceans of misunderstanding, of indifference.

She drained the last of her coffee, glanced at her watch and rose from her seat. She took a step forward and placed a kiss on the side of his cheek, a chaste kiss of the sort that friends give one another. She noticed that he was tense as she approached him—the body conveys so much without movement of any sort—and then the tension dissolved after her kiss. "I have to go."

He nodded. "And I have a pupil coming in"—he looked at his watch—"fifteen minutes."

She said goodbye and made her way down the stairs. Out in Saxe-Coburg Street she stood still for a moment and looked at the gardens. He kissed me, she thought. He made the move; I didn't. The thought was an overwhelming one and invested the everyday world about her, the world of the square, of trees, of people walking by, with a curious glow, a chiaroscuro which made everything precious. It was the feeling, she imagined, that one had when vouchsafed a vision. Everything is changed, becomes more blessed, making the humblest of surroundings a holy place.

CHAPTER EIGHT

IT WAS MIMI who suggested over breakfast that Isabel should meet their hosts before they went to spend the weekend with them. "They come into Edinburgh a lot," she said. "And Joe and I would like to entertain them. It would be a way of returning their hospitality before the occasion, so to speak."

Isabel agreed; it would give her an opportunity to meet Tom and Angie before she went to stay with them, which would be helpful. The meeting in the gallery, such as it was, had not been a positive one, and a relaxed meeting in a social setting could help. They could come to her house, she suggested, but Mimi objected that this would not involve Joe and her reciprocating hospitality. Isabel still thought it better. Angie had snubbed her once already, in the gallery; she could hardly do that in Isabel's own home. "Mimi, you cook," Isabel said. "It can be your show. I'll hand over the kitchen. And you're a better cook than I am. Far better."

There was another reason why dinner at her house would be a good idea. She had not seen Jamie since that afternoon encounter in his flat, and she was waiting for an occasion when they could see one another in the company of other people; this would make it easier. She would put it to him that she needed to make up numbers—which she did—and he would not think that she was pursuing him. Which she was not—she was definitely not pursuing him—but did she want to see him again, and soon? Yes, she did.

When she called him with the invitation, she was relieved to discover that everything seemed normal. He would be very happy to come to dinner, he said. He was having a trying week of rehearsals with a conductor who for some reason didn't like him. Isabel privately thought that unlikely; nobody could dislike Jamie, except Cat perhaps, and that was odd, and Cat's fault, her blind spot, her perversity.

But Jamie was sure. "He has it in for me," he told Isabel. "He always picks on me. Always. He says that I don't have the dynamics quite right. He says my playing sounds feverish. What does he mean by that?"

"Con fuoco," said Isabel. "That's the closest I can get to it."

"But why do you think he picks on me?" Jamie asked peevishly.

Isabel could guess. Envy. That, in her mind, was one of the commonest causes of petty behaviour like that. "He envies you," she said.

Jamie laughed. "Why should he envy me? He's a successful conductor. Much in demand—for some inexplicable reason. He has no reason to envy anybody."

At the other end of the telephone, Isabel smiled. "Do I know him?" she asked. "Describe him to me."

Jamie gave her the name, which she did not recognise. Then he went on, "He's on the short side. Rather pudgy. Gets red in the face when the tempo increases. Waves his arms about."

Envy, she thought. Jamie was tall. He was good-looking. He never went red in the face. What she was tempted to say was: *He wants to be you,* or, perhaps, more poignantly, *He wants you and cannot have you,* but she could not say that. Jamie would not imagine that he could be the object of desire; it was not in his nature to think that. So she simply said, "Envy," and left it at that.

Isabel accompanied Mimi to buy the provisions for the dinner. They walked into Bruntsfield; they could get some of the things from Cat, the others from the collection of small stores that lined Bruntsfield Place on both sides. They walked along Merchiston Crescent slowly, as if out for a stroll; Isabel was a quick walker, but not now, as Mimi stopped several times to remark on a glimpse of garden or to address remarks to cats she saw sunning themselves on low garden walls. "Paying my respects," she said to Isabel. "This is their territory, you know." And Isabel saw that the cats appeared to understand this, and sidled up to Mimi, recognising their ally.

And then, on the way back, laden down with shopping bags, when they had stopped briefly at the top of East Castle Road, Mimi turned to Isabel and asked her how much she remembered of her mother. Nothing had provoked the question—it just occurred. "You were still so young when she died," she said. "Eleven is young. Memories of the years before that can become hazy. Unreliable even."

"Some memories are clear enough," said Isabel. "Walking along this street, for example. I remember that very well. I remember holding her hand and walking along here. Just as we've been doing."

Mimi nodded. "I can see the two of you. I can see it." She touched Isabel on the arm, briefly, the gesture of an older cousin. "Whatever time it happens in your life—whenever it is that your parents die—you miss them, don't you? It's the end of such a chapter. Two of the most important actors in the play are written out."

"I miss her a lot," said Isabel. "I can't say that I think of her every day, but I think of her often. She comes into my mind, as if she's still here. A presence."

"As it should be," said Mimi.

"We idealise them, don't we?" Isabel went on, swapping her bags from hand to hand to redistribute the load. "I've sometimes tried to imagine what it would be like to have a parent who did something really awful—what it would be like if one discovered that. I knew somebody who did, you know. The effect on her life was devastating. Everything changed for her. She was happy one moment and then the next . . ."

"What happened?"

"It was a girl I knew at university, at Cambridge. She was in my college; a rather sporty girl who played tennis, I think, and something else. She found out that her father had been seeing a prostitute. He was the chairman of a bank and this woman was blackmailing him."

"That's hardly unusual," said Mimi. "And the fact that he was being blackmailed almost turns him into a victim, doesn't it?"

They resumed their walk. "He would have been the victim of the story," Isabel continued, "except, as they say, for one little thing. He tried to hire somebody to kill her. And he was discovered. The man he approached developed cold feet and went to the police. They wired him with a tape recorder and this gave them the evidence they needed. His trial was all over the papers, and this poor girl had to sit it out. Nobody spoke to her about it. In fact, somebody thoughtfully removed the newspapers from the common room on the day his conviction was reported. We all pretended it just hadn't happened, whereas we should have talked to her about it. We should have given her some support."

"Of course," said Mimi. "But at that age one doesn't want to face up to things like that. One thinks that cheerful denial is better. But I suppose it never is."

Isabel wondered about that. She knew people who did very well on cheerful denial; rather better, she suspected, than if they faced up to the problem. Cheerful denial was certainly one way of dealing with an illness, and those who denied often fared better because optimism, and laughter, had a strong psycho-somatic effect. But this conversation was about parents. "I don't know how I would have handled it if my parents had had affairs," said Isabel. "Or tried to kill somebody. I think that it must be one of the most difficult things for children to handle—having affairs, that is. I know that people can't help themselves—well, I count myself fortunate that I didn't have that to deal with."

Mimi was silent for a few moments. Then she said, quietly, "No. It can't be easy. It can't be easy for anybody."

They came to the top of Isabel's street. In a garden on the corner, a large secluded square of land behind a high stone wall, the branches of a cluster of elms moved slowly in the breeze. Behind them, the sky was clear, intersected by the vapour trail of an aircraft, heading west. Isabel pointed to the line of white, and Mimi looked up, through her large oval glasses. Isabel saw the sky reflected in the lenses, a shimmer of blue.

"One of the things I regret," she said to Mimi as they looked up, "one of the things I regret most is never having known my *sainted American mother* as an adult. I suppose I would have known more about her if I had. As it is, I don't really know that much."

Mimi let her gaze move earthwards. "Of course, that's what you call her, isn't it? Your *sainted American mother*. That's very nice."

"Would you be able to tell me about her?" Isabel asked suddenly. She looked at Mimi, her eyes filled with eagerness. "Would you mind? Just tell me everything you know about her. What sort of person she was—from the adult point of view. Was she happy? What moved her? Give me an idea of who she was."

Mimi did not reply, and Isabel asked her again.

"Do you want the unvarnished truth?" Mimi asked.

Isabel's expression was serious. The truth was a serious matter. "Of course I do," she said. "You wouldn't tell me anything but the truth, would you?"

"People sometimes don't want to hear everything about their parents," said Mimi. "Not everything."

Isabel was vehement in her denial of this. She wanted to hear it all, she said. After all, it's not as if there were any serious skeletons in the cupboard.

Mimi stopped and stared at Isabel. "But what if there were?"

Isabel's answer came quickly. "I'd want to hear about them," she said. "Definitely."

Mimi seemed unconvinced. "Are you sure?"

"Very sure. And the fact that you've mentioned this means that there is something." She paused. "Tell me, Mimi. You have to tell me now."

"I hadn't planned to," said Mimi, doubtfully. "It's not . . ."

Isabel spoke gravely now. "Please. You've made me doubt— not that I'm blaming you for that—but you have. You can't stop now." If Mimi left anything unsaid now, then it would prey on her mind. She might even wonder if her mother had tried to have somebody killed—ridiculous thought. The grocer, perhaps. Or one of her bridge four—for irresponsible bidding.

Mimi spoke evenly, in a matter-of-fact way, as a lawyer might do in addressing a court. "Your mother had an affair," said Mimi. "She had an affair and never had the chance to confess to your father, or to make her peace with him. It was while she was having the affair that she discovered she was ill—that she was diagnosed with cancer. And by then she couldn't bring herself to tell him. So he never found out. Or that's what she told me. Which was better, don't you think?" She had not understood why Hibby had had that affair. Sex? Is that all that affairs were about, or was it boredom, the sense of being trapped, the need for a form of companionship that a spouse cannot provide? Their marriage had been a good one, Mimi had thought, and there had been no signs of an itch. But that, perhaps, was what itches were by nature: invisible.

They were halfway down the street. Isabel did not stop, but looked firmly at the pavement below her feet. The concrete was broken—the result of years of civic neglect, because this was a prosperous area and the authorities had other priorities. The well-off are never popular; they are tolerated, envied too, but not actually liked. She saw one or two places where weeds had taken hold in the cracks and had forced the surface upwards with the power of their roots. She listened to Mimi.

"And the man with whom she had this affair," Mimi went on, "this man, who's still around by the way—I saw him the other day, here in town—he dropped her; he dropped your mother when he heard that she was ill. That wasn't his plan, you see. Your mother was very attractive, and it was fine to have an

affair with a beautiful, engaging woman, even if she was somebody else's wife—that made it more exciting for him, I suppose.
But it was quite another thing to have an affair with a woman
who was dying of breast cancer. The sick are not romantic, not
really, in spite of Rodolfo and my namesake in their garret. It's a
different sort of love that puts up with illness. Old love."

They were at Isabel's gate now. Mimi looked anxiously at
her. She wondered whether she should have told her. She had
never intended to, but Isabel had insisted, and she had thought
that it was the right thing to do. But now, looking at Isabel, she
wondered whether it would have been better to lie.

"Should I have told you all that?" she asked, taking hold of
Isabel's arm. "Or should I have kept it from you?"

Isabel was a philosopher. She was perfectly aware that in
moral philosophy it was widely agreed that paternalism was
unjustifiable except in a very limited number of cases. We should
not lie to people, and we should not keep from them the truth
that they want to hear. Of course Mimi should have told her,
because truth had to be told. And yet, could she ever use the
expression my *sainted American mother* again?

She had had an affair. Well. She was human. Red-blooded.
Women had affairs all the time; only a false sense of propriety
made us pretend that this did not happen; the Madame Bovary
within us, she thought, within every married woman. But what
about this man, the man who had treated her so shabbily? What
had been the allure that had driven her mother—her *sainted
American mother*—yes!—out of the arms of her husband and
into his? At the door to the house, as she slipped the key into the
lock, she turned to Mimi and asked her, "What was he like?
This other man. What was he like?"

"He was much younger than she was," said Mimi.

CHAPTER NINE

Later that day, Isabel stood in Rutland Square, that quiet, perfect Georgian square tucked away behind the busy end of Princes Street, under the shadow, almost, of the castle and its towering Calvinist rock. Like so many places in the city, it had its associations for her. There was the Scottish Arts Club on the other side, where she had gone to parties that had gone on into the small hours, where utterly memorable conversations had taken place, and been forgotten in spite of their brilliance; there was the corner where, during her student days, home from Cambridge, she had embraced that boy she had met in the bar at the Caledonian Hotel, that student from Aberdeen, who had met up with her a few evenings later and with whom she had enjoyed a brief flirtation; and then he had gone back to Aberdeen and she had realised that they meant nothing to each other. That was before John Liamor, about whom now, curiously, she seemed to be thinking less.

Was she? Since she had met John, just over twenty years ago, she had thought about him, one way or another, every day. In the beginning, when she had been in his thrall, she had thought about him all day; he was just there, constantly, and her thoughts of him were pleasant, almost numbing, like the feeling, she imagined, that an opiate would give. Then, when she had discovered that he was having an affair with one of his students, she had thought about him with anxiety and alarm, as one thinks of somebody whom one is afraid to lose. And that had been replaced by resentment and anger and aching feelings of love: emotions that were all inextricably mixed up and which fought with one another in a hopeless lack of resolution. The precise memory of him became less vivid, as a drawing in pencil on paper may blur, become less clearly delineated with handling and folding. But he was still there, and every so often—more often than she would have liked to admit—there came a pang of longing. At such times all she wanted was for him to come back into her life as if nothing had happened, for her to be lying in his arms listening to the song that he liked to play at such moments, the gravelly voiced singer with his mid-Atlantic drawl singing about love and heartache; music that she could not listen to now, because of its associations and the sense of loss that it triggered. We act out our lives to a soundtrack, thought Isabel, the music that becomes, for a spell, our favourite, and is listened to again and again until it stands for the time itself. But that was about all the scripting that we achieved; the rest, for most of us, was extemporising.

Yesterday, and the day before, she had not thought of John Liamor—not once. And she had not thought about him today, either, until that moment when in front of the lawyer's office in Rutland Square she had thought about his absence from her thoughts. And it was different, she decided. When she thought about him now, he was just another person, not John Liamor, the man who had dominated her life. *He was my North, my South*—those desolate words of WHA about lost love. And he went on to say: *I thought that love would last for ever: I was wrong*. Well, of course.

I am free of him now, she said to herself. I am a free woman. I thought that he would last for ever: I was wrong. She went up to the door and pushed it open, thinking: I am free. But then she thought: Why am I free? And she knew intuitively that it was because of what had happened with Jamie. Something had been changed by that moment of contact. Jamie would be her lover. It was John who had been stopping her—not some notion of appropriateness—those were intellectual doubts and it was really far more simple than that. She had been tied to an incubus, the memory of a love that had been rejected and had had nowhere to go; she had been locked into a dead relationship and now the last dried skin of it had fallen away, like the scab on a wound, and she was free.

She faced the receptionist, who looked up at her with an enquiring smile. Isabel thought: What if I told this woman, if I said to her, "I have just decided, out there on your doorstep, that I am going to have an affair with a younger man?" And then, presto, had taken a photograph out of her bag and said, "There. Look at him."

We do not do these things, and she did not. She had once, in casual conversation about the mind, discussed such impulses with her psychiatrist friend, Richard Latcham, who had said: "Of course we all have those thoughts. We have them when we stand on the edge of waterfalls. We all think: What if I jumped now? Or we think of saying something outrageous, or taking all our clothes off. It's entirely natural, but we never do it. It's the mind exploring possibilities, which is what our subconscious minds do all the time. Most of the possibilities are very straightforward likelihoods, but there are others, which are set aside and disregarded. Don't worry, Isabel."

"But surely it happens," Isabel had said. "Surely sometimes people give in to these urges. After all, some people actually do jump over waterfalls, and maybe not all of them had thought it all out beforehand."

Richard thought for a moment. "I think it's pretty rare," he said. "But I do know of one case. Somebody I know, in fact. He told me all about it. He's a classicist here in Cambridge, a tremendously erudite man. He writes about late Latin poetry. Apparently he's *the* man for late Latin poetry. They had a dinner in his college and they were all in the senior common room afterwards—you know, one of those old panelled rooms with portraits of the founder and Isaac Newton and so forth on the walls, and he was sitting with a friend drinking a glass of port when a visiting professor of archaeology from Canada walked past with his wife. They had just helped themselves to coffee and had the cups in their hands. Apparently she was a rather substantial woman who was particularly broad in the beam. And this classicist suddenly said very loudly, in the hearing of everybody, 'My God! What a massive rump!' "

"Apparently this poor professor of archaeology dropped his coffee cup and the coffee spilled down the front of his trousers. And his wife stood frozen to the spot. That was it. The classicist apologised and said that he did not know what had come over him. He really felt terrible about it. He later wrote them a letter and offered to make a substantial donation to a charity or cause of their choice. They accepted his apology, which is exactly what you would expect of decent people like the Canadians, and then they suggested some association for Anglo-Canadian understanding, which I suppose was appropriate, in a way. But I think that was one case where the inner urge to do something impermissible overcame the inhibitory mechanisms." Richard paused. "Mind you, it could have been worse."

"Hardly," said Isabel.

"He could have been standing at the edge of a waterfall," said Richard thoughtfully. "Or he could have been standing behind her at a waterfall."

"And pushed her over?"

"I'm afraid so," said Richard.

"What a—" She was about to say terrible disaster, but Richard said: "Splash."

THE RECEPTIONIST INVITED ISABEL to take a seat. The lawyer, she said, would be down to see her in a few minutes and would see her in the small conference room off the reception area. Isabel sank into a large black leather sofa and paged through a social magazine. It was about cocktail parties and receptions and openings at galleries. The same faces appeared in several of the photographs, faces which looked confidently into the camera as if to say, "Yes, me again." She turned the pages quickly, and then stopped. A dance had been held at Prestonfield House: somebody's birthday, the daughter of a man in a kilt with an elaborate ruff at his throat, the full Highland rig, an East Lothian grandee. And there were the bright young people, smiling, laughing, glasses of champagne in their hands. And there was Jamie standing in a group of three young men, all of them in their kilts and formal jackets, their arms around one another. She stared at the photograph, stared at the faces of the other two young men, and at Jamie, and her heart gave a lurch.

She was not part of that world. But there was something else about the photograph that intrigued her, something almost homoerotic in the easy intimacy of the three young men, their friendship, their closeness. She looked closer. Their arms were on one another's shoulders; the face of one of them was turned to another, facing him. Jamie had pulled back from the kiss that afternoon; could it be that, for all his obsession with Cat, who was, after all, boyish in her appearance, his inclinations, or some of them, were otherwise? That was quite common, and one should not be surprised that a man might be attracted to one or two women but still be attracted to his own sex. There were many such relationships. And a young man like that might find the company of an older woman appealing, because it was easy and interesting and sexually undemanding. She looked at the photograph again, and, in a quick movement, furtively tore it out, folded it and tucked it into her bag. There was a rustling of paper from the desk near the window, and she gave a glance in the direction of the receptionist, who had clearly seen her. She smiled and shrugged, a gesture which came naturally to her but which was ambiguous in its meaning.

"I'm sorry," Isabel said across the room. "I simply had to keep that. It's someone I know. And it's pretty out of date . . ."

"Of course," said the receptionist politely. "It's just that we tend to keep the magazines for a while. People like to read them."

"Good," said Isabel, meaninglessly, looking up at the ceiling, like a child caught in an act of flagrant disobedience who simply pretends that it has not happened.

The lawyer, an attractive woman in the dark skirt and high-boned looks of her profession, came through the door and shook hands. She gestured to a door and led Isabel into a small, windowless conference room furnished with a beechwood table and chairs. There was coffee in a vacuum jug and a small plate of biscuits.

As she helped Isabel to coffee, the lawyer explained that although she was happy to talk about the purchase of the flat, any formal offer would have to come through Isabel's own lawyer in the proper legal form.

"I understand," said Isabel. "But there was something I wanted to discuss with you personally."

"I haven't seen the flat myself," warned the lawyer. "I have some particulars about it, but I don't have details. If there is something about it that needs further looking at, then you need to speak to your surveyor. I take it that—"

Isabel interrupted. "It's nothing to do with that," she said. "We had a survey done. Everything was fine. No settlement in the building."

"Which is very much a plus in the New Town, isn't it?" said the lawyer. "There are some parts where the floors are at quite an angle. I suppose it's the penalty you pay for living in an old building. Lots of character, but sometimes lots of cracks. No, I gather it's a very nice little flat." She looked at Isabel enquiringly.

"Simon Mackintosh said that the owner—"

"Florence Macreadie."

"Yes, I met her. He said that Florence Macreadie was prepared to let me have the flat for substantially under the starting price."

The lawyer nodded. "It's unusual. Very unusual. But yes, I can confirm that. Ten thousand below."

Isabel sipped at her coffee. She looked at the lawyer's hands, which were resting on a pad of paper, an expensive, lacquered fountain pen held loosely between the fingers. But her hands did not move. They were perfectly still.

"It's very generous of her," said Isabel. "But I fear that she has the wrong impression." She looked at the lawyer, whose eyes moved away from hers. It was embarrassing for her, she decided. This was not a matter of conditions and clauses. "Yes," she went on. "She formed the impression that the young man who was with me was there because we were going to move in together. She was . . ."

"Touched," supplied the lawyer, and smiled at Isabel, as one woman to another. She looked down at her hands and placed the pen very deliberately on the pad of paper. It rolled slightly and then came to rest. Isabel watched it.

"Well, we're not," said Isabel. "I asked him to come simply because he knows the area."

The lawyer was silent for a moment. Then she laughed. "Ah! So you're not . . . Well, I suppose one must say that you're not . . . together. I'm sorry. The way she described it to me made it sound rather romantic. I'm sorry, Miss Dalhousie."

Isabel looked again at the lawyer's hands. The wedding ring. And her mind was made up. She would not be an object of pity. She would not. "We are actually," she said.

The lawyer did not understand. "You're . . ."

"We are in a relationship," said Isabel.

The lawyer blushed. "Oh . . . I didn't mean to . . ."

"It's all right. It's at an early stage. But we're not going to live there. That flat will be for someone else altogether. I have a . . . a lady who helps me. I'm buying it for her." To say that it was at an early stage was not enough. She should have said that they were close friends, and that was all. But suddenly she was tired of being by herself, tired of being seen by others as being in some way disadvantaged because she was single, or as incapable of getting herself a man. She was not. She was not. But she knew at the same time she should not make what amounted to a childish boast of a relationship with a younger man. She had no reason to wish to make this other woman feel envious, and yet it had slipped out and now it was difficult to retract it without looking foolish. Leave it, she thought. It's not important. Leave it.

The lawyer seemed flustered, but after a moment or two she regained her composure. "But don't you think that Miss Macreadie's offer might still stand? I'll have to ask her, of course, but it seems to me that she might still wish to help you by selling you the flat, even if it's for your . . . your lady. The way she put it to me was that she wanted to do something for you because she liked the idea of your being with that young man—and she did describe him as a bit younger than you. Not of course that . . . But the point is, I think she wants you to have it."

Isabel sat back in her chair. She had not expected this. She had stretched the truth. Jamie was not her lover—yet—and now it seemed as if she might be offered the flat nonetheless. And that would mean that a potential advantage secured on the basis of a misunderstanding would become a potential advantage secured on the basis of a clear lie. So she had made the situation worse.

The lawyer stood up. "Let me speak to her," she said. "Then I'll get back to Simon Mackintosh to confirm things. That's what I'll do."

Isabel could not bring herself to object. She knew that she should, but she thought that she might do so later, when she had the time to think of a reasonable way out of a ridiculous misunderstanding. So she said nothing, and was shown out cordially by the lawyer. As she left through the front door she saw the receptionist glancing at her. There was disapproval in the glance but it was well concealed; disapproval of one who tore pictures from the magazines of others, which would have been compounded, surely, had she known that this magazine-mutilator was one of those people who boasted of romantic exploits that they simply had not had. Those are the worst sort of people in every way. Inadequate lovers. Inadequate people.

CHAPTER TEN

JAMIE ARRIVED EARLY for dinner, as he often did, since he enjoyed talking to Isabel while she prepared the meal. He would sit at the kitchen table, glass in hand, listening to her; he liked to listen to her. But this was not possible this evening, as it was Mimi's dinner and she had forbidden Isabel to enter the kitchen. "Unless I can't find anything," she said. "Then you can come in and get it for me. Otherwise, this is my show. You're off duty."

As Joe was busy with correspondence in the study, Isabel took Jamie through to the music room and they sat in front of the high Victorian fireplace. During the summer Grace filled the fire basket with dried hibiscus from the garden, and the faded blue-grey petals of the flower heads were covered with little fragments of masonry that had fallen down the flue.

"Somebody told me that my chimneys were crumbling inside," Isabel said. "And every so often a good chunk of masonry falls down to make the point. But I can't be bothered to do anything about it. I really can't. They can reline them, but it's another expense."

"But you're not short of money," said Jamie. "You can have

lined chimneys if you want. You can have anything you want. Anything."

Isabel looked at him. She did not like discussing her finances with anybody, even with Jamie, but now she considered what he had said. *You can have anything you want.* And anyone too? she wondered. The idea was offensive, and she tried to put it out of her mind, but the question was insistent: Could money really get you people, if that was what you wanted? Was it a crude trans- action, or were there people who were simply drawn to those with money and therefore prepared to take up with them, even if they would never have done so otherwise? She thought of an aged magnate who had married one of the world's most glam- orous women. Would she have married him if he had no money? It was difficult to imagine, but then she thought: I know nothing about that woman, and what she wanted, or saw in him. How do I know that she didn't love him?

"It's not that simple," she said to Jamie. "In the first place, I don't have that much. And in the second place, I don't like to waste it." She did not intend to sound peevish, but she did.

Jamie looked apologetic. "I'm sorry," he said. "I didn't mean to be rude."

"I know," said Isabel, melting.

"The point is," said Jamie, "that you shouldn't let things go with a house. If something needs attending to, then you should do it before it gets worse. My dad's got a builder who keeps say- ing that to him."

"And it's true," said Isabel. But then she remembered a con- versation with a German friend, Michael von Poser, on one of his visits. He was a prominent German conservationist who be- lieved that old buildings should be left to age gracefully. "And if your ceiling should fall down," he had said to Isabel, a twinkle in his eye, "then you have lost a room, but gained a courtyard. Think of it that way."

Isabel told Jamie about this remark and they both laughed. Then Jamie looked up at the ceiling, as if to detect signs of imminent collapse. "What about that flat in St. Stephen Street?" he asked. "What's happening about that? Have you put in an offer?"

Isabel did not respond immediately. She looked into her glass of wine. New Zealand white. "Cloudy Bay," she muttered.

Jamie held his glass up to the light. "And so clear," he said, smiling. "But the flat—are you going to go for it?"

"Do you think I should?" she asked.

"Of course. If you really want to get a place for Grace, then that seems to me to be perfect. It's really nice. She'll love it. And it's not far for her to toddle up the hill to those spiritualist meetings of hers. Ideal."

Isabel plucked up her courage. "Something has happened," she said cautiously. "Since you ask. My lawyer was in touch. We had noted an interest with her lawyers, and they had contacted us. They said that Florence Macreadie wanted me to have the flat and that she would take an offer, from me, of the asking price . . ." She paused. Then, "Less ten thousand."

Jamie's eyes widened. "Ten thousand under? Is she desperate or something? If it goes to bids then somebody's bound to offer at least ten thousand *over*. Maybe that's what she said, and they got it wrong."

Isabel shook her head. "They didn't," she said. "Ten thousand under. There's a reason."

"Oh?"

"Yes," said Isabel. She had decided to tell him, but how was she to put it? Although everything had changed for her, he was behaving as if nothing had happened the other day in his flat. She felt slightly injured by this because it implied a certain indifference on his part, and she wanted to talk to him about it, to see what he had meant. But if she did so, then he might take fright, or he might be embarrassed, or he might . . . There were any number of ways in which he might respond.

She steeled herself. "Apparently Florence Macreadie thought that we were planning to buy the flat together."

She looked at Jamie. But all he did was shrug and take a sip of wine from his glass. "So?" he said. "I was helping you. I can see why she thought that. People take friends to look at places they're buying."

"No," said Isabel. "You've got it wrong. She thought that you and I were going to live in it. Together."

Isabel was surprised by Jamie's reaction. He smiled. "As flatmates? Would you do your share of the washing-up, Isabel?"

"As lovers," she said quietly.

Jamie was silent. Isabel glanced at him, but he did not look at her. "I see," he said.

"It's ridiculous," Isabel said. It was a ridiculous misunderstanding, that is; it was not ridiculous that she and Jamie should be lovers. Not now.

Jamie looked up, and for a moment she saw something in his eyes. She was certain of it. "Is it all that ridiculous?" he said quietly.

"Well, no . . ."

He seemed to be thinking of something for a moment, and she waited anxiously, but then he said, "Have you put in the offer?"

Isabel sighed. "I can't," she said. "I can't let her sell it to me on the basis that we're going to live there when we aren't. It would be wrong. It really would."

Jamie thought about this for a moment. "No. No you can't. I can see that—now that I think about it." He put down his wineglass. "I once bought a bassoon from a man who was drunk," he said. "He had put an advertisement in the paper saying that he was selling a load of old musical instruments. I went along to his place, and he showed me a room with about seven old instruments in it, all in fairly sick condition. He had bought them, he said, at a garage sale. Some instrument-repair man had died and his family had sold the contents of his workshop. They were his project, but he died before he got round to restoring them."

"And the man who advertised was drunk?" asked Isabel.

"Yes," said Jamie. "It was about seven in the evening, and he had been in the pub with his friends. He told me he had. But he must have been there for hours. He was pretty far gone."

Isabel became the philosopher. "A very nice problem," she said. "Is a drunken agreement a proper agreement? Very nice. I suppose that drunk people can still know what they want. In fact, sometimes the fact that they're drunk reveals to them even more clearly what they really want. *In vino veritas.*"

Jamie said that this was true, but in this case there was a complication. "There was a bassoon on the ground. I recognised the model immediately. Quite a nice one. It needed a bit of work, but it would make a very nice instrument. So I asked him what he wanted for it, and he said, 'That clarinet?' and he quoted a really low price."

Isabel laughed. "So you bought it as a clarinet?"

Jamie looked for a moment as if he was ashamed. "I'm afraid I did."

Isabel wanted to reassure him. Those who entered the market did so at their peril; it was *caveat venditor* as well as *caveat emptor*. But what was the difference between buying an antique from an elderly person who was unaware of its value—which she was sure was not right—and buying something from an ignorant drunk? There was really no difference except for the fact that we felt sympathy for the vulnerable and we did not for the drunk. But that was not enough to make a moral difference. That was the problem with morality; it required a consistency and evenhandedness that most of us simply did not possess. Or some schools of morality required that; and the more she thought about it, the more Isabel came to believe that such requirements were simply inhuman. That was not the way we worked as human beings. We were weak, inconsistent beings, and we needed to be judged as such.

Jamie looked at his watch. "They should be arriving soon," he said. "Tell me something about them. Tell me who these people are."

Isabel also looked at the time. The moment, she realised, had been lost. They had skated round the issue, but at least she had seen something in his eyes and he had implied that it was not ridiculous that they should be more than friends. So now she knew that, and that was something.

"TOM BRUCE."

Isabel took the hand that was extended to her. It was a firm handshake, of the sort that Americans give, a token of directness and no nonsense.

"And this," he said, "is Angie."

Isabel was in the hall, with Mimi and the guests. She turned to Angie, noting the low-cut cocktail dress and patent-leather shoes. "We've actually met," said Isabel. "I'm sure that you won't remember, but it was in a gallery in Dundas Street, a week or so ago. We spoke . . ."

"Of course!" Angie smiled. "Of course I remember." She turned to Tom. "We were buying that picture by . . . What's his name again, hon?"

Tom looked flustered. "Cal . . . Cal . . ." His words were distorted by the twisting of his mouth.

"Cadell?" suggested Isabel.

Tom looked at Isabel with gratitude. "Yes, that's him."

"One of our most distinguished painters," said Isabel. "My father had one of his paintings, but gave it away. That was before they became so expensive. I've often wondered whether I could ask for it back."

"Tom adores Scottish art," said Angie. "In fact, anything to do with your country. He's Scottish, of course. That name. Bruce. Descended from Robert the Bruce."

Tom's embarrassment was palpable. "I don't know about that," he said. "It's a possibility that we're looking into. I've got somebody doing the research and he says that there are interesting things coming up. He thinks that it might be the same family. But I'm sure it's only a remote possibility. We're east Texas really."

"But if it were true," said Isabel, "that's a royal connection. Think of that. Of course, the Scottish throne has gone south now, with the Hanoverians. Some people still resent that, you know." She led them into the drawing room, where Jamie was waiting, talking to Joe. Introductions were made while Isabel poured drinks for Tom and Angie.

"Talking of Scottish kingship," said Isabel as she handed Tom a glass of wine, "Jamie here has Jacobite sympathies."

Tom and Angie turned to look at Jamie. Isabel noticed that while Tom turned away, Angie continued to look at him, as one watching. Jamie raised a hand in protest. "Not really."

"Well, I suspect that he has," said Isabel. "He seems to know a bit about the Stuarts and he sings Jacobite songs."

"You don't always believe in what you sing," Jamie said, looking to Joe for support.

"No," said Joe.

"Sometimes lost causes have all the best songs," said Isabel. "And the best poetry too. Look at the Spanish Civil War. The Republicans had all the poetry. Lorca, for instance."

"Who are the Jacobites?" asked Angie, turning to face Tom.

"Followers of the Stuart kings," said Isabel. "Jacobus is James in Latin, and a lot of the Stuart kings were called James. Bonnie Prince Charlie was a Stuart."

Tom tapped Angie on the shoulder. "The house we're staying in, my dear. Remember, I told you that it was associated with the Jacobite cause. And there's that bedroom . . ."

Angie brightened. "Oh yes! The Prince's bedroom."

Tom took the explanation further. "Legend has it that Prince Charlie stayed in it at some point. Just one night, apparently, and then he had to move on." He looked at Joe. "We thought that we might put you and Mimi in it when you come out there."

"As long as you don't mind a ghost," said Angie, giggling. "I thought I saw him the other day. He was sort of white— insubstantial . . ." She trailed off, and then suddenly turned to Jamie. "Do you believe in ghosts, Jamie?"

Jamie laughed nervously. "I haven't thought about it very

much . . . But, no, probably not. I haven't seen any evidence. Or any ghosts, for that matter."

"Grace is the person," said Isabel, glancing at Jamie. "My housekeeper. She doesn't call them ghosts, of course. She's a spiritualist. She talks about 'the other side.' " She felt vaguely disloyal, talking about Grace in this way, and her voice dropped at the end. It was true, though, Grace did go to seances, which had always struck her as being so out of character, given Grace's good sense in everything else. We all have our weak points, she thought. Mine . . . This was no time for self-evaluation, though; she would change the subject of the conversation, she decided. But then she remembered Mobile, which was said to be the city of ghosts. That had always amused her. "Mobile is the place for ghosts, isn't it?" she volunteered.

Mimi looked up. "So we're told," she said. "Though why there should be more ghosts there than anywhere else, I don't know."

"Perhaps they move down from the North," Joe observed drily. "People move to Florida in their retirement. Ghosts move to Mobile."

It was typical of Joe's dry humour, and Isabel looked at him in appreciation. Angie, however, seemed puzzled. "Do ghosts move?" she asked.

"That's something we can't tell," answered Isabel. She turned to Tom. It was kind of him and Angie to issue the invitation for the house party, and she thanked him. On the contrary, he said: it was good of Isabel and her friends to fill the house for them. They were spending almost three months in Scotland and knew very few people. It would be pleasant to have some company.

You have each other, thought Isabel. But was that enough?

Even when one was in love, it was not really enough just to have the other person—not if one needed stimulation. The company of just one person could be reassuring, could stave off loneliness, but would it be enough for three months?

Angie had been talking to Joe and Jamie, and so she said to Tom, "We need to see people, don't we? I sometimes have to get out of the house just to do so—not necessarily to talk to anyone, just to see them. We have some shops nearby. I drive round there and have a coffee. See people."

"Yes," he said. "I guess that's why we come into Edinburgh a lot. I thought that we might just stay out in that house, buried in the country, but we need to get in."

Isabel nodded. She could imagine what it would be like to be stuck in the country with Angie. But then she had no interest in Angie, and he did. He must find her exciting. Sexually? Strange.

She stole a glance at Tom. What would his face have looked like before the Bell's palsy? He must have been good-looking, with those strong features, the regular nose, the fine eyes; only the mouth was wrong, twisted into its grimace by the condition. And his physique was impressive too. He must be in his fifties, but there was no spare flesh and he was well put together. If one looked beyond the grimace, one saw a fine man; as Angie must have done, unless she was looking at something else: at the house in Preston Hollow, at the staff who presumably looked after him—the Mexican maid, the groundsman, the driver.

Her thoughts were interrupted by Tom asking her what she did. Isabel explained about the *Review* and he listened attentively. He had done several courses in philosophy at Dartmouth, he said. They discussed that for a while and then Mimi caught

Isabel's eye and pointed in the direction of the kitchen. It was time for dinner.

Isabel had left the seating plan to Mimi, and she found herself next to Tom; Jamie, across the table, was on Angie's right. Isabel watched as the evening wore on. Each time she looked across, she noticed that Angie was deep in conversation with Jamie and she heard odd snatches of what she said. *Tom's been so kind to me . . . We toyed with the idea of Paris, but Tom's so interested in Scotland . . . You don't know Dallas? You should . . . some time . . . And then, would you believe it, she shot him. Everybody knew it wasn't an accident, I certainly knew . . .*

Why, Isabel wondered, had she shot him? And who was she? Women shot abusive husbands, in desperation, or husbands who went off with other women, in fury. It seemed unlikely, but she was talking about Texas, where guns, shamefully, were part of the culture. And that was an absurdity, she thought, and such a blot on American society, this little-boy fascination with guns and toughness. Something had gone so badly wrong.

The dinner finished reasonably early, as Tom and Angie had to drive back to the house outside Peebles where they were staying. In the hall outside, Angie said, "Now, Jamie. Everybody here is coming out to see us in a week's time. They can't leave you here in Edinburgh. Will you be our guest too?"

Tom looked up. He was slightly surprised, thought Isabel. "Yes, why not?" he said. "It would be very pleasant. There's plenty of room."

Jamie looked uncertain. He glanced at Isabel, who smiled at him. "It would make the party," she said.

"Thank you. I'd love that."

After they had left, Isabel insisted that she and Jamie would clear up as Mimi had prepared the meal. In the kitchen with Jamie, she closed the door behind her. "Well," she said.

Jamie's expression was passive.

"Well," said Isabel again. "That was Tom and Angie."

"Yes," said Jamie, putting a plate into the dishwasher. "That was."

Isabel reached past him to put a couple of glasses on the top rack of the machine. "You seemed to get on well enough with her." She picked up another glass and threw out the dregs. "I couldn't help but hear something she said. Something about some woman shooting a man. What was that about?"

Jamie shrugged. "Some Dallas story," he said. "Somebody who married somebody else. Some oil man. Then shot him. So she said."

"Shot for his oil," mused Isabel. "Tom had better be careful."

For a moment Jamie said nothing. He stacked a few more plates and then turned to face Isabel. "Isabel," he said, softly.

For a minute, Isabel thought that he was going to embrace her. It was the right moment; they were alone; he was standing close to her. Her heart raced in anticipation. But then she saw that he was shaking a finger at her in mock admonition.

"You have an overactive imagination," Jamie said.

She turned away. She was tired, and he was right. Her imagination was overactive—in every respect. She imagined that people might dispose of one another for gain. She imagined that this young man, who could presumably have any girl who took his fancy, would choose to get involved with her, a woman in her early forties. She should rein in her imagination and become realistic, like everybody else. And you don't need the complications that would follow any deeper involvement with Jamie; that is what she said to herself. Why spoil a friendship for the sake of the carnal? And the carnal inevitably spoiled friendships. It took friends to another land—away from their innocence, to a place from which they could not return to simple friendship.

And yet, remember, she thought, none of us is immune to shipwreck. Come, beckons the fatal shore: come and die on my white sands, it said. And we do.

CHAPTER ELEVEN

THE FOLLOWING MORNING she made the decision to visit Florence Macreadie. There was an F. Macreadie listed in the telephone directory for St. Stephen Street and a quick call from Isabel established that she would be at home after eleven that morning—"after doing the messages"—and would be happy to see her; Isabel approved of the old Scots expression and liked Florence Macreadie all the more for using it. One did not go shopping in Scots; one went for messages.

She made her way to Stockbridge slowly, walking across the Meadows and down Howe Street, stopping to look into shop windows, and to think. While looking at a display of Eastern rugs in Howe Street, marked down in price, now *irresistible* according to a placard in the window, *Turkish delight,* in fact, she reflected on the fact that when she had last walked past this shop, a week ago, and had briefly glanced at the rugs in the window, she had been a different person. She had been Isabel Dalhousie, of course, the editor of the *Review of Applied Ethics* and resident of Merchiston; those aspects of identity, the externals, had not changed, but others had. A week ago, she had believed in the saintliness—whatever that was—of her mother; now she was a person who knew that there were no saints and that her mother had been a woman with human failings, and a younger lover. And a week ago she had believed in her own ability to resist temptation; now she knew that she, like everybody else, was too weak to do that. Two sets of scales, she thought, had fallen from her eyes. It was rather like growing up; the same process of seeing things differently and feeling different inside.

Mimi's disclosure of her mother's affair had raised conflicting emotions in Isabel. She had even felt cross with Mimi, in a shoot-the-messenger sense, but these feelings had not lasted long. She knew that she had given Mimi no alternative but to disclose what she knew, and indeed if anybody deserved censure for that it was Isabel herself. Ordinary consideration for the autonomy of others dictates that we should not browbeat information out of those who don't want to give it. What we know, and what we think, is our own business until we decide to impart it to others. Secrecy about the self may seem ridiculous or unjustified, but it is something that we can choose if we so desire. And this is true even if the information is something of very little significance. Isabel had read of an author of naval histories who had considered questions from journalists as to his date of birth to be unpardonably intrusive. That had struck her as being absurd—unless he was unduly sensitive about his age, which might have been the case, as that particular author had invented an entirely fictional boyhood in Ireland for himself. In which case, one might learn to be wary of those who did not offer their age: had they invented a past?

It had been wrong, she felt, to press Mimi to tell her. The information she had elicited had not been all that unusual—there were plenty of adulterous mothers—but what had shocked Isabel was that it showed that her mother had been just like she was. That was the information that she had found difficult and had led to several nights of sleeplessness. Her mother had had an affair with a much younger man, which was precisely what Isabel wanted to do. *I am like my mother in that respect. It comes from somewhere, and that is where.* And somehow the thought that an ingrained biological drama was playing itself out in the next generation made her friendship with Jamie something less individual, less personal. This was not something which had arrived as a gift; it was simply tawdry behaviourism.

She moved away from the rug shop. A man inside, anxiously waiting for customers, had seen her and had been watching her. Isabel had looked through the glass, beyond the piles of rugs, and had met his gaze. She was sensitive to such encounters, because in her mind they were not entirely casual. By looking into the eyes of another, one established a form of connection that had moral implications. To look at another thus was to acknowledge one's shared humanity with him, and that meant one owed him something, no matter how small that thing might be. That was why the executioner was traditionally spared the duty of looking into the eyes of the condemned; he observed him by stealth, approached from behind, was allowed a mask, and so on. If he looked into the eyes, then the moral bond would be established, and that moral bond would prevent him from doing what the state required: the carrying out of its act of murder.

Of course that was a long way from looking through the plate-glass window of a rug shop, but salesmen knew full well that once you engaged your customer in that personal bond, then the chances of their feeling obliged to buy were all the greater. Rug salesmen in Istanbul in particular understood that; their little cups of coffee, half liquid, half sludge, offered on a brass tray, were intended not only as gestures of traditional hospitality, but also as the constituents of a bond between vendor and client. So, as Isabel retreated from the window and looked fixedly down the street, she felt the tentative bonds snapping like overstretched rubber bands. And then she was free, looking down the road towards St. Stephen Street, and only five minutes early for her meeting with Florence Macreadie.

Florence had returned only a short while before Isabel knocked at her door. Isabel noticed the coat that she was wearing, a dark-blue macintosh that was beginning to fray around the cuffs. Yet its cut was good and it had in its day been fashionable, or at least in good taste.

"I've just come back," she said. "I haven't had time to make coffee or anything."

"I gave you very little warning," said Isabel apologetically.

Florence gave a dismissive gesture. "Oh, I don't stand on ceremony," she said. "Anybody can come to see me any time. Not that they do, of course. But they could if they wanted."

She led Isabel through the hall and into the kitchen. The house was slightly untidier, Isabel thought, than it had been when she had been there last. But that had been during a viewing time, when everything was on show. One had to be tidy, the estate agents advised; and ideally there should be the smell of newly baked bread when prospective purchasers came in—it made them feel positive about the place.

Florence began to spoon coffee into a cafetière. If the smell of newly baked bread was lacking, at least there was the aroma of fresh coffee grounds, as rich and tantalising. She shifted a pile of papers from one side of the table to the other. "I need to sort everything out," she said. "But I keep putting it off. One accumulates so much stuff in a place and yet it's hard to throw it away. Or at least I find it hard. It's like throwing away one's past."

Isabel glanced at the papers. They did not look like personal letters, but were old bills, letters from tradesmen, circulars. "Sometimes it's good to do that," she said. "It can be quite cathartic to get rid of everything."

Florence sighed. "And yet, don't you think that these little scraps of this and that make up our lives? Everything has its associations, painful or otherwise." She paused, looking at Isabel with eyes that Isabel now saw were an unusual flecked grey. "You know, when I was teaching—I was an English teacher, by the way—I used to keep the essays of some of my pupils. I still have them. I found that I simply could not throw them away. I kept them as a reminder of the young people who had written them. It's so sad."

"Why? Why is it sad?"

"As a teacher, you know, you frequently become very emotionally attached to the young people you see every day. How could it be otherwise? You get to love them, you know, and you miss them terribly when they go off and start their own lives. Suddenly everything changes. You've been a major part of their lives for so long, and then suddenly they no longer need you. I always found that very sad."

She finished talking and looked at Isabel, as if judging her response. Isabel realised that Florence was assessing her, as some people do when they are not sure whether the person to whom they are talking either understands or is prepared for a conversation of depth.

"I can understand that," said Isabel. "Yes."

"I think it was the hardest thing about the job," Florence said. "Saying goodbye to those young people. Although I suppose there were harder things from time to time." She was silent, lost in memory. Then, "I had a very promising pupil," she went on. "He was a very nice boy. But he had one of those childhood cancers, and although they tried all sorts of treatments they knew that it was a losing battle. He just wanted to get on with life and do the same things as everybody else did. Go to parties. Play sports. And he did, by and large."

Isabel said nothing. In the background, the kettle hissed and switched itself off. Florence left it.

"He knew what the score was," said Florence. "But he didn't talk about it. And we respected that. I remember when he left school. I wished him good luck and I tried not to cry but, my goodness, when he walked out that door, I dissolved in tears. I remember him standing there and smiling, and I wished him the best of luck with his career. He had his plans for university, you see. I know we all tried, but I don't think any of us was particularly good at dealing with it. Except for the chaplain." She stopped and looked at Isabel before continuing. "I don't know why I'm burdening you with this."

"It's not a burden," said Isabel. "Really, it isn't."

"I came into a classroom one afternoon, to fetch something I'd left behind. I didn't think there was anybody there. But then I saw the chaplain sitting with this boy, and he had his arm around his shoulder, to comfort him, and he was talking to him. And I could see that the boy had been crying. I closed the door quietly. I don't think they saw me.

"I can't believe in God, Miss Dalhousie. I've tried from time to time and I just can't. And yet, when we need them, who are the people who are always there for us? Who are the people who comfort us? Whom would you like to have at your ending? What kind of person would you like to have at your deathbed? An atheist or somebody with faith?"

Isabel thought. Were there not atheists who were just as capable of giving love and support as others? And might not it be better to die in doubt, if that had been one's condition in life?

"I know some very sympathetic non-believers," she said. "I don't think we should discount them."

"Maybe," said Florence. "But there's nothing in the atheist's creed that says that he must love others, is there?"

Isabel could not let this pass. "But he may have every reason! Even if you do not believe in God you may still think it very important to act towards others with generosity and consideration. That's what morality is all about."

Florence's eyes lit up. "Yes," she said, "morality—the ordinary variety—says that you shouldn't do anything to hurt others. But I'm not so sure that it tells you to go further, to love them." She thought for a moment. "And surely most people are not going to make the effort to love others on the basis of some theory, are they? I know that I wouldn't. We have to learn these things. We have to have them drummed into us."

"The moral habits of the heart," mused Isabel.

"Yes," said Florence. "And religion is rather good at doing that, don't you think?" She turned round and began to pour the hot water into the cafetière. "Anyway, I don't know how we got into that! You didn't come here to discuss theology with me, did you?"

Isabel laughed. "Not exactly, although I'm always very happy to talk about such things. I came—"

"About the flat."

"Yes."

Florence began to pour Isabel a cup of coffee. "I assume that your lawyer has been in touch about my offer?"

Isabel nodded. "He has. It is . . . it is very generous of you."

Florence sat down at the table, opposite Isabel. She placed both hands around her mug of coffee, warming them. "I've had so many people looking round the flat since it went on the market. Thirty, I'd say."

Isabel said that she could imagine the disruption.

"Of course, some of them haven't the slightest intention of buying it," said Florence, smiling. "Do you know that there's a type of person who goes to look at houses for sale? They have a good poke round and it's all sheer nosiness. They look in cupboards. They remark on the decor. And so on. I was warned about these people, and I think that I spotted one or two of them. There was one woman from Clarence Street, round the corner, who didn't realise that I recognised her. She just wanted to see what the inside of my house was like."

Isabel tried to imagine what it would be like to have that little to do, and to have the brass neck to nose round other people's houses. But then she thought: What about that house at the end of the road? She had always wanted to see the inside of that. If it were to come on the market, could she resist?

"I assure you," she said lightly, "I assure you that I was seriously interested."

Florence laughed. "Of course you were. I didn't think otherwise. Not for a moment. I could tell."

Isabel cleared her throat. "I feel that I should tell you something," she began. "When I came the other day—"

Florence raised a hand. "Please," she said. "It was not for me to say what I said to my lawyer. I've felt a little bit embarrassed about that. And now she tells me that you and . . . and that young man are not intending to live here after all."

"No," said Isabel. "We aren't."

"But that doesn't really make any difference," said Florence. "My offer stands. You can still have it for the figure I suggested." She paused, taking a sip of coffee from her mug. Isabel saw that she was looking at her over the rim. The look was that of a schoolteacher observing a favourite pupil who has perhaps just a touch too much character: a mixture of approbation and envy.

"May I ask why you want me to have it?" Isabel asked. "I hope that I don't sound rude, but I really would like to know."

Florence put down her mug. "Because I like you, Miss Dalhousie," she said. "That's one reason. I just do."

Isabel shook her head. "But you hardly know me. I really don't see how you can come to any conclusions about me on the basis of . . . on the basis of not much more than one meeting. And, anyway, your idea of my circumstances is, I'm afraid, wrong. That young man—"

"Is just a friend. Oh, I imagined that might be the case. After the lawyer came back to me and said that you had been to see her. She said that . . . Well, I'm sorry to have to say this. She said that she didn't believe what you told her—that you were, in fact, having an affair with that young man."

It is not easy to hear the news that we have been spotted in our lies, and Isabel's reaction, a simple human reaction, was to blush. This was burning shame, made physical, and Florence, seeing it, immediately regretted having said what she had.

"I'm sorry," she said. "I shouldn't have told you that. I made it sound more serious than it was. And I'm sure that she mis-understood what you said. I'm sure that you didn't deliberately mislead her."

"I did," said Isabel plainly. "I told her that Jamie and I were in a relationship. Those were my exact words."

"Well . . ."

"I don't know exactly why I did it," said Isabel. "Pride, probably. Perhaps I was just fed up with being condescended to by married people. You know how it can be sometimes."

Florence reached across and placed her hand on Isabel's arm. "I'm single," she said. "I know what you're talking about."

Isabel looked down at the design of the waxed tablecloth on the table. It looked French: a series of little pictures of a cornu-copia disgorging its contents before a group of surprised pic-nickers: *Déjeuner sur l'herbe* transformed.

"It's so ridiculous," said Isabel. "A week ago my life was all very straightforward. Now it seems that I've talked myself into a whole web of misunderstandings and deceptions. All over nothing."

Florence laughed, and her laughter defused the tension. "Let's forget about all that," she said. "The point is this: I gather you're buying this place for somebody who works for you. That's reason enough for me to want to sell it to you."

Isabel protested, but Florence was insistent. "If you could have seen some of the people who have been through this place since it's been on the market, you'd understand how I feel. Some of them were nice enough, but an awful lot of them were ghastly, just ghastly. Materialistic. Ill-mannered. And quite a few of them actually condescended to me. They thought, woman in her sixties. Very uninteresting. Unimportant. Practically non-existent. And then there was you, and that young man. And I

suddenly thought, Why should I sell this to somebody I don't
like? I don't need the money. I'm comfortably off, with my teaching pension and the money and that house in Trinity left to me.
I don't need anything more."

She stopped to take a sip of her coffee. On the other side of
the table, Isabel stared out of the window and thought about
what Florence had said. She could see the logic of the decision
and she knew that she should accept; to be able to accept is as
important as to be able to give—she knew that.

"You're being very generous," she said. Then she hesitated,
but just for a few moments, before she continued. "I can afford
to pay more, you know. I'm not short of money."

She felt the soft power of Florence's gaze; those grey, understanding eyes. "I know that."

But how did she know? thought Isabel. Do I seem well-off?
There is a well-off look, Isabel thought, but she did not imagine
she had it. It was an assuredness that came with not being anxious; that and a well-tended air. But how did one distinguish
between that and arrogance?

"Let's leave it at that," Florence suggested. "You can sleep
on my offer and then, in, let's say, two days, your lawyer can let
us know whether you want to go ahead. Would you be happy
with that?"

Isabel made a gesture with her hands, palms outwards,
which indicated acceptance, and resignation too. Florence, smiling, reached for the cafetière to top up Isabel's mug. "That
young man," she said. "You're lucky to have such a friend."

"Very," said Isabel.

"You're obviously fond of him," said Florence, and then
added, "And he of you, of course."

Isabel again said, "Very."

Florence put down her mug, exactly over one of the cornucopias. The picnickers, frozen in time, were dwarfed. "Could it
not become a love affair?" she said quietly. She watched Isabel's
face as she spoke, and her words were hesitant, as if ready for
withdrawal in the face of a hostile reaction. But Isabel was not
offended by the question.

"It's almost that," she said. "I think we're at a crossroads
now. But I just don't know."

"But you should," said Florence. "Look at yourself. You're
still quite young. You're not my age. If he wants it too, then why
deny yourselves?"

It's not as simple as that, thought Isabel. There was the question of friendship and the hazardous conversion of friendship into
erotic love. That was not always simple. "I can't help myself,"
she said. "I keep thinking through the implications of things. I
know that it's a guaranteed way of never getting anything done,
but it's just the way I am. I don't act spontaneously."

"Then be prepared," said Florence abruptly. "Be prepared to
shed tears when you get to my age and you think back on lost
opportunities. Somebody asked me to live with . . ."—there was
the briefest hesitation, and then—"with her. I said no, because
people would talk. They wouldn't now, of course, but it was different then. They didn't care about people's happiness, did
they? And I think that we would have been very happy together.
Just as friends, you know. Just as friends. She had a flat in the
Dean Village, you know, under the bridge, looking out onto the
mill pond. It would have been like living on an opera set. We
would have been happy."

"We shouldn't care so much about disapproval," said Isabel.
"But we do, don't we?"

Florence was looking down at the floor. There was regret in

her expression. She looked up at Isabel. "Go on," she said. "Go ahead. Have an affair with him."

"And if it goes wrong?"

"That's the last thing one thinks of on starting these things," said Florence. "Really, it must be. Otherwise . . ."

"Maybe."

There was silence. Isabel had reached a decision, but she did not want to tell Florence what it was. The conversation had been an intimate one, with revelations on both sides, and she had a natural caution. She had not come here to talk about herself and her feelings and she had been slightly surprised by the way in which the other woman had encouraged her. Was it just because she had a romantic streak? There were people who were forever trying to bring others together; it appealed to them to have the world paired off, as if this brought resolution of some sort. But she did not imagine that Florence would think that way. In which case, was she obtaining some almost voyeuristic pleasure from encouraging the affair? Again, some people derived something of that nature from the contemplation of the affairs of others, which was not surprising, thought Isabel, because much of our lives are spent in thinking about what others are doing, watching them, emulating them.

"I really must go," she said, rising to her feet.

Florence did not get up. "I've offended you, haven't I?" she said. "This is none of my business."

Isabel shook her head in denial. "You haven't offended me at all. You've made me think. That's all."

As she made her way down the stone staircase to the front door, Isabel encountered the cat she had seen on her first visit to Florence's flat. He was sitting on a chair on a landing, his tail hanging down beneath the seat. He watched her warily as she walked past, looking up at her, holding her gaze for a moment, before he turned his head away to stare at the banisters with affected interest in something invisible to a human being. Then he closed his eyes, as if to dismiss her, and she walked quietly on. Many people in pursuit of the cool, thought Isabel, would give anything to appear as indifferent, as insouciant, as this indolent cat, but they would never make it. Wrong species: we are too engaged, too susceptible to emotion, too far from the consummate psychopathy of cats.

CHAPTER TWELVE

THE WEEKEND with Tom and Angie was still some days away. Isabel was looking forward to getting out of town—she had not been anywhere that summer, because June, and the better weather it brought, had crept up on her unannounced. She wanted to go to Italy for a couple of weeks, or to Istanbul, but had done nothing about organising a trip. Perhaps September or October would be better, when the heat had abated and there would be fewer people about, and perhaps . . . No, Jamie would not be able to come then, as it was term-time, and there would be his bassoon pupils to think about. So perhaps she should suggest just a short trip, a three-day weekend, to one of the Scottish islands, to Harris, perhaps, to that landscape of grass and granite outcrops and Atlantic skies. Jamie might fish on one of the lochs, and she would walk out along that strip of land where the sea broke in waves of cold green water and where one could just imagine those early Scottish saints, their skirts wet, coming in on their small boats from Ireland.

But there was no point in thinking about that now. She had to contend with the preparation of the next issue of the journal and with a number of objections raised to her editing by one of her contributors. He was a professor of moral philosophy from Germany who prided himself on his ability to write in English. This pride was well placed in some respects, but not in others. Isabel had tried to tell him that inversions in English had to be handled carefully—otherwise infelicities of style would we encounter. The verb at the end of the sentence could be put, but only rarely. *Very seriously must the issue of moral imagination be taken,* he had written, and when Isabel had interfered with this sentence in the proofs he had responded testily: *Wrong it* might *be,* he had written, *but wrong here it is not.* That very sentence was technically correct, but was not easy modern English, as she had pointed out in a subsequent note, to which he had replied: *Must philosophy be easy? For whom are we writing? For the philosopher or the street person?* She smiled at the additional confusion; the man in the street was *not* a street person, by definition.

Grace came in, bearing a cup of coffee. "You look harassed," she said, placing the cup and saucer before Isabel. "I thought that you might need this."

"I certainly do," said Isabel. "And, Grace, how about this? What do you understand by *street person?*"

Grace frowned. "Street person? Oh, we see them all right. Have you walked down by the bottom of the Playfair Steps recently? You see street persons down there, if that's what you want to call them."

"Beggars?"

Grace looked disapproving. "Some of them. But some do other things. Deal in drugs."

"And use them."

Grace nodded. "But it's the beggars that get me. Beggars used to be old and crabbit, remember? There was that man whom everybody called the Glasgow Road Tramp. He was a great character. He wore an old army helmet and used to say to everybody that he had just come in off the Glasgow Road and could one spare him the price of a cup of tea."

Isabel smiled as she remembered him. He was a much-loved character in the city and everybody gave him money. But he was, of course, a genuine tramp, with boots stuffed with newspapers and a determined walk. Surely it was of the essence of a tramp that he should actually tramp; just as Shakers shook and whirling dervishes whirled.

"But these new beggars," Grace went on. "They're nineteen, twenty, or thereabouts. And they just sit there and ask for money. I never give them anything. Never. They could work. There's no real unemployment in this city, after all. Everywhere you go you see signs offering work. Just about every café has one. Dishwashers and so on."

Isabel listened politely. What Grace said was true, but only to an extent. Some of these street people were genuinely homeless—young people in flight from their homes in Dunfermline or Airdrie or somewhere, running away from abuse or tyranny, or sheer disorder. And they ended up on the street because they had no skills and it was easy.

"I don't give them any money," said Isabel quietly. "But sometimes I feel bad about that."

Grace snorted. "And why should you feel bad? Why should you feel bad when you know what they're going to do with it?"

Isabel did not answer Grace's question. The street people at the bottom of the Playfair Steps were a difficult case to defend, even if they deserved defending. She was thinking, instead, of India and of a ride from a hotel to the airport, in that chaotic Indian traffic, which has a choreography and a hedging divinity of its own, where cows and people and smoke-belching vehicles engage in a ballet that against all the odds seems to work. And she remembered, in the midst of her terror of collision, a woman running up to the white Ambassador car, her baby, a tiny scrap of humanity, in a dirty sling of rags on her hip, and clawing at the car window with a hand that was some sort of human claw; leprosy, perhaps, had done its work. And she had looked at the woman in horror, because that was what she felt and in the suddenness of the moment could not conceal. And then she had averted her eyes, as the woman trotted beside the slowly moving car, still scraping at the glass in desperate pleading. It had seemed to her that all of suffering humanity was outside that car door, all of it, and that if the car stopped it would sink and she would be consumed by it. Later still, in her airplane seat, with all the resources of jet fuel and technology to lift her out of teeming Bombay, she had thought of that poor woman and of the fact that she would be hungry, right now, unable to feed that tiny baby, and had she opened the window just a little and thrown out a few rupees she would have made life bearable for that woman for at least a couple of days. But she had not.

Begging, she realised, was one of those moral issues which she called *intimate;* they did not arise in the halls of academia so much as in the daily lives of people. These were the questions that reminded us we had a moral faculty, a conscience: What do we owe our friends? Do I need to be kinder? Am I being selfish? Should I declare even *that* to the taxman? And to most of us, this was what moral philosophy was all about.

She looked at Grace, who was still expecting an answer to the question she had posed. "Well, all right," said Isabel. "Perhaps I don't need to feel bad about it. But you know how I tend to think about these things too much. I know it's a failing, but I can't seem to help myself."

Grace, who did not respond immediately, was studying Isabel carefully. She knew her employer well; rather better, in fact, than Isabel realised. And although she agreed with Isabel's self-assessment of her tendency to conduct internal debates when others would simply make a decision and act, she was not sure that this was always a failing. Isabel talked about the good life and how we should try to lead it, and again Grace agreed with this. Isabel's life was a good one; she was a kind woman, and she felt for people, which was more than one could say about a lot of people in her position, Grace thought. But there were certainly areas of Isabel's life where what was required was a little less thought and a bit more action. Should she say something? Well, they had always spoken frankly to one another . . .

"Yes," said Grace. "I know how you think about things. But there are some things that you shouldn't think too much about. You just need to say to yourself: Here goes, and get on with it."

"Work, for instance," said Isabel, pointing to the pile of papers on her table.

Grace made a dismissive gesture towards the papers: there was always the wastepaper bin for those. No, and here she pointed to her heart; no, it was not work she was thinking about. "That boy," she said.

Isabel was perfectly still, as one confronted in misdeed. Only her eyes moved. "Jamie?"

"Yes, Jamie. You're in love with one another, aren't you?"

Isabel was at a loss as to what to say. It was not just her surprise at the fact that Grace had raised the subject; nor was it so much that Grace had detected feelings which she had no idea had been so obvious; it was the fact that she had said *in love with one another*. Her voice was small. "Do you think that he's . . . that that's how he feels?" And she added, in confirmation, because now there could be no concealing this from Grace, "Too?"

Grace did not hesitate. "Of course he does. He worships the ground you walk upon. It's obvious."

Isabel, who had been tense with anxiety, now relaxed. She felt gratitude to Grace, a warm feeling of having been told something that she really wanted to hear but had not dared hope for. Yet what did Grace think about it? She had not actually said that she approved, but neither had her attitude been one of manifest disapproval. "Do you think I should . . . do something?"

"He'll never take the first step," said Grace quickly. "He's younger than you, remember."

How could she forget that? That, after all, was the entire problem. But then, as if anticipating Isabel, Grace went on, "Not that age matters. Not these days."

"You don't think it does?"

"No, it doesn't," said Grace. "There's somebody who comes to the meetings—at the Psychic Institute—who has a much younger husband. At first, I thought he was her son. In fact, somebody said that at one of the meetings, but she simply laughed. No, that's not the problem."

Isabel waited for Grace to go on. If the age difference was not the barrier, what was?

"Cat," said Grace, frowning. "That's the problem."

"But I think that he's getting over her," said Isabel. "I think he realises now that she's never going to come back to him. It's taken a long enough time, but I think that the penny has finally dropped. I'm sure it has."

That was not what Grace had had in mind. "Oh, it's not him that I'm worried about," she said. "It's her. If she finds out that you and Jamie are . . . are together, then she's going to be furious."

This struck Isabel as being, apart from anything else, unfair. "But she's rejected Jamie. She's made it very clear that she's not in love with him and never will be. I can't understand that, of course, but that's how she feels. Why should she have any interest in what he does now?"

Grace looked at Isabel and thought: You may be a philosopher, but you sometimes don't understand at all. "Because you're her aunt," said Grace, chiselling out each word. "Her aunt. And I rather suspect that most women would feel jealous if an aunt took an old boyfriend of theirs. They just would."

Grace waited for Isabel to say something, but Isabel had nothing to say. Elation had been replaced by despair. Here was another complication, weightier still than all the others. Cat was her niece, her closest relative. They had had their disagreements in the past, but had always patched them up. This might be different. This touched that dark, primeval area of the human psyche: sexual jealousy.

Grace now continued. "You see," she said, "the reason we know Cat would feel that way is that people are human. That's something you need to write about in that *Review* of yours." She nodded to the pile of manuscripts. "People are human. Think about that."

THE SUMMER SOLSTICE came two days later. Isabel had always thought that Scotland did badly with its solstices. Summer, it seemed, had hardly started by the third week of June; it was no time for the days to start getting shorter, even if the difference each day was barely noticeable. And as for the winter solstice, that also seemed a cruel trick played on Scotland, as the worst was still to come then, even if the days were meant to be drawing out.

"We've decided to do something about the summer solstice," said Peter Stevenson over the telephone.

"To put it back a month? What a good idea. But can you? I know that you're influential, but . . ."

Peter laughed. "No. To have a midsummer party," he said. "Spontaneously, as you can see from the timing of this invitation. Two days' notice."

"I'm never booked that far ahead," said Isabel. "But I do have houseguests. A cousin and her husband."

"They sound perfect," said Peter. "And of course they're welcome too."

It was just the sort of invitation that Isabel liked to receive.

She did not enjoy cocktail parties, unless she was in the very special mood that made them bearable or unless she was the hostess, in which case she could busy herself with duties and would never get stuck. Getting stuck was the problem, thought Isabel. You could not talk to the same people for the whole evening, but how did one get away? Saying "I must let you circulate" was the same as saying "Would *you* please move on," and saying "I must circulate" was the equivalent of saying "*I* must move on; you stay here." In an extreme situation, one might say, "I think I'm going to faint," which would immediately bring about suggestions that one sit down—elsewhere. That enabled movement, but the excuse had to be used sparingly. One could acquire a reputation for fainting too frequently.

"You get invited to cocktail parties in hell," a friend of Isabel's had once observed. "There's one every evening. But I gather there's nothing to drink. And you have to go." He frowned and looked regretful. "I'm not looking forward to it," he went on. "Not one little bit!"

Isabel had asked him about how he dealt with the problem of being trapped, and he had thought for a moment before he gave his reply.

"You can mention your infectious diseases," he said. "That sometimes gets people moving. The other possibility is to say: 'Let's talk about religion. Let's *really* talk about it.' That works too."

But this was not a cocktail party. West Grange House, a Georgian house behind walls, stood in the middle of a large garden that had been transformed for the occasion. Long trestle tables, covered with white linen cloths, had been set up beneath the two large oak trees that stood mid-lawn. Along these tables were wooden chairs, at least forty of them, and places were laid before each: white napkins, glasses, silver. Near the large, sunken rockery, a table had been set up for the bar; next to it was a large tin bath in which stood a big lump of ice, like an ice sculpture awaiting its sculptor, with bottles nestling round its base.

Isabel liked this house. She liked the air of quietness, the feeling of being away from the fray, which, she thought, is exactly what a house should provide. She liked the feeling, too, that things were planned here; that what happened in this house happened because it was meant to. And this party, she thought, which had been decided upon only two or three days before, looked as if it were the result of weeks of preparation.

Joe and Mimi were introduced to Peter and Susie and taken off to meet somebody. Isabel, a glass of wine in her hand, walked out onto the lawn, nodding to one or two friends in the clusters of guests. It was a clear, warm evening, in spite of Isabel's foreboding that the Scottish weather would misbehave; perhaps this was global warming, the creeping of Mediterranean conditions northwards, the migration of species into northern zones; hammerhead sharks in the Irish Sea—that was a thought—scorpions in the villages of England. But we had been warned, she reminded herself, that global warming would bring Scotland only more rain and less sun.

She looked heavenwards, and felt dizzied, as she always did when she looked up into an empty sky; the eye looked for something, some finite point to alight upon, and saw nothing. It might make one dizzy, she told herself, but it might make one humble too. Our human pretensions, our sense that we were what mattered: all of this was put in its proper place by simply looking up at the sky and realizing how very tiny and insignificant we were. Our biggest cities, our most elaborate symphonies, the *Encyclopaedia Britannica,* the smartest gadgets, were nothing really, just a momentary arrangement of the tiny number of atoms we had in our minuscule patch of space. Nothing.

"A monkey puzzle tree."

Isabel turned round. Mimi, a glass of what looked like champagne in her hand, had come up behind her.

"Yes," said Isabel, glancing at the tree at the far end of the garden. "They used to be very popular. The Victorians loved them and put them everywhere."

"You're so lucky with your soil," said Mimi. "You have this lovely rich soil. My garden in Dallas is clay. And it gets so dry."

It sounded to Isabel as if Mimi were reproaching herself. "You can't help your soil," Isabel said. "Nor your weather."

Mimi looked at a clump of rhododendrons in flower along one of the garden walls, the blossoms pink and red against the dark green of the leaves. "Our soil *is* our fault—to an extent. Remember the dust bowl. Dust storms and tumbleweed? That was human greed. And we repeat that sort of mistake, don't we? Look at Las Vegas, if you can bear to. That's in the desert, we should remind ourselves. We've built that dreadful disaster in the desert, of all places."

"I suppose somebody likes Las Vegas," said Isabel.

Mimi was silent. There was a bird somewhere in the undergrowth, hopping about, making the leaves rustle.

"I'm sorry about the other day," Mimi said suddenly. "I'm not sure if I should have told you what I told you. About your mother."

Isabel continued to stare at the point where the bird had been. "I'm glad that you did. And I asked you to. If you had refused I would have felt that you were hiding something from me. And we have to know these things . . ."

"Do we?" asked Mimi.

"Once we suspect them."

Mimi was unconvinced. "I'm not sure," she said. "I'm not sure that we want our parents to be human. We know that they are, of course, but it's a special sort of knowledge—or I think it is. Like the knowledge that we're not here on this earth for ever. We know that, but we don't think of it all the time, do we? We put it to the back of our minds."

Isabel took a sip of her wine. Champagne had been on offer, but she had missed it for some reason. "Well, if we don't want to know too much about our parents—or about their faults, rather—then maybe that's because we see ourselves in what they did. We recognise their failings because they are our own failings too. Unacknowledged, perhaps."

Mimi nodded. "That may be."

Isabel decided that she would go on. She could talk to Mimi because she was family, but a friend too, and she had always felt that Mimi understood. But how could she put it? And would Mimi be shocked? She had to remind herself that there was nothing shocking about it. Not objectively, but talking to another person about what one felt at that most intimate level *was* an incursion into the private, whatever people said, however frank the climate of the day.

She turned and looked at Mimi, and saw herself again, for a moment, in the lenses of those oval glasses, as in a mirror. "I was surprised to hear that my mother had had an affair, but . . . but that's not all that unusual and people do. However, it was the fact that it was with a younger man, a far younger man. That . . ."

Mimi smiled. "Shows good taste? A certain spirit?"

"That's exactly what I'm on the verge of doing." She had said it, and it sounded ridiculous. To be on the verge of having an affair! Either one had an affair or one did not.

Isabel looked for signs of surprise in Mimi, but there were none. Mimi just looked at her, as if expecting her to say something else. "But I knew that," she said. "Jamie. I assumed that."

Now the surprise was Isabel's. "I didn't realise . . ."

"Of course you wouldn't," said Mimi, reaching out for Isabel's forearm. "We never realise how transparent we are. But people know. It was obvious at that dinner party you gave."

"You gave."

"I gave," acknowledged Mimi. "You can tell when somebody is in love with another person. There's a conspiratorial look. No, that's not quite right. There's a connivance. No, that's not correct either. There's something. Put it that way. There's something."

"And you saw that there was something?"

Mimi patted her gently on the arm. "I did." She paused, looking directly at Isabel. Now, thought Isabel, now come the words of warning, of caution. *Do you think that it's . . . I don't want to interfere, but . . .* Instead, Mimi said, "Who wouldn't? Or rather, who couldn't?"

"I'm sorry?"

Mimi spoke clearly. "Who couldn't be in love with him? Certainly, if I were your age, which I'm not, and if I were single, which I'm not, I'd have no hesitation in falling for somebody like that."

It was the third such reaction. Florence Macreadie had said much the same thing, and then Grace. Now it was Mimi's turn. Nobody, it seemed, saw a problem. Or did the problem exist only in her imagination?

Isabel was about to speak. She suddenly felt she wanted to

tell Mimi about how she had agonised over her feelings for Jamie, and how it now seemed that it had all been unnecessary. But before she could say anything Mimi said, "A young man like that, of course, turns heads. He'll have people falling for him left, right and centre. Angie certainly did that evening. Did you see it?"

Isabel felt a sudden stab of anxiety. She had seen Angie talking to Jamie and it had been obvious that they were getting on well. And then there was the invitation for Jamie to join them at the house party. But she had not imagined that it was anything serious.

"They talked a lot, yes. But do you really think that there was more to it than that?"

Mimi laughed. "Oh yes, I do. She was devouring him with her eyes. Throughout the meal, she was hanging on his every word. Which made me think, I'm afraid."

Isabel smiled. "But I thought that you had already done that bit of thinking. I thought that you had your doubts about Angie's commitment to Tom."

Mimi made a gesture of agreement. "Yes. But this confirmed my suspicions in that respect. A recently engaged woman doesn't make eyes at a young man if she's happy with her new fiancé." She paused and looked at Isabel, as if for confirmation. "She doesn't, does she? And you don't need to be much of a psychologist to reach that conclusion."

At the far end of the lawn, under one of the oak trees, Susie clapped her hands together. Dinner, brought out on several large serving plates by a pair of young helpers, was now being served on the trestle tables. There would be a seat for almost everybody, Susie called out, and there were extra seats in the kitchen for those who could not be accommodated at the tables.

Isabel walked with Mimi towards the tables. Susie, seeing Mimi, came to her side and led her to a place in the middle of the larger table. Isabel, detaching herself, was preoccupied with what Mimi had said about Angie. So Angie found Jamie attractive; well, that was hardly earth-shattering news—any woman would, as Mimi herself had said. And if it was true that Angie was after Tom's money, then that was hardly anybody else's business, other than Tom's relatives, who could have an interest in his assets. Fortune hunters were hardly rare, and in places like Highland Park and University Park, those plush suburbs on the edge of Dallas where there were numerous oil and other fortunes—the Hunts, the Perots and others in that league—people must know about the need to be careful. If Angie had penetrated the defences of those tight circles and found a middle-aged man who was prepared to share his millions with her, then she was not doing much more than playing a wealthy society by its own rules, and nobody should be unduly surprised or concerned. And certainly she, Isabel Dalhousie, should keep out of it; she who had recently decided that she would mind her own business and not get caught up in the affairs of others. Yet this was the same she who found this so very difficult and who could not ignore the needs of those with whom she came into what she called moral proximity.

She found a seat at one of the tables, not far from the end, and sat down. She was beside a thin-faced man with a shock of dark hair and that almost translucent skin which goes with a particular strain of Celtic genes. She shook hands with him and they exchanged names. He was Seamus. Of course you are, she thought; that name went with the genes. And on her other side sat a tall, attractive girl of about twenty, with a wide smile and an Australian accent. Her name was Miranda, and she had come with one of the other guests, she said, adding that she knew nobody else in Edinburgh apart from the people she was staying with. "And I have to find a job," she said, the smile spreading across her face. "Or I'm going to starve."

"I could try to help," said Isabel, almost automatically. She sneaked a glance at Miranda's plate. It was stacked high with food. Perhaps this was her first proper meal for days . . . But then she had said that she was staying with people, and that implied that she was being fed. Unless there was a category of guests whom one did not have to feed. Isabel smiled at the thought. *Please come and stay with me, but I won't be able to feed you. I hope you don't mind . . .*

"Could you?" said Miranda eagerly. "Could you really?"

Isabel had not thought before she spoke, and now realised that she had no idea how she might help. How could she find anybody a job? It was moral proximity again; if one sat next to somebody one had to at least try to help her find a job. Certainly one could not let that person starve.

"Well, I'm not sure," Isabel said. "I don't know . . ."

The disappointment showed in Miranda's face, and Isabel immediately relented.

"What can you do?" she asked.

"Anything," said Miranda. "Anything general. I'm happy to do anything. I'm not fussy, you see. No worries." She laughed. "And I can cook too. No worries there either."

Isabel thought for a moment. She imagined living in a world as uncomplicated as Miranda's seemed to be. A world in which there would be, as Miranda had said—twice—no worries. She looked at Miranda and saw that there were small freckles on her face, and she noted, too, that her nose was aquiline, markedly so; and then there was a bracelet on her sun-tanned forearm, one of those plaited elephant-hair bracelets that people picked up in Nairobi or Cape Town or somewhere like that. And she looked up at the sky, just for a moment, at the high blue, which seemed to dance—a trick of the light, and the emptiness—and she thought of Jamie suddenly, and thought, *Bless him, look after him;* but to what gods she muttered this she had no idea. Gods of that empty sky, perhaps, gods who reigned over those spaces, dispensing a storm here, clement weather there, who answered, or ignored, the prayers of sailors and imaginative women.

She turned again to Miranda, who smiled back at her expectantly. Cat had talked about needing somebody during the summer, particularly if Eddie took a holiday, as she thought he might. He had not taken a holiday last year, but now he was talking of going to France with a nameless friend about whom Cat knew nothing, not even the gender. If Eddie did this—and Cat was keen to encourage him to do anything that would boost his confidence—then she would certainly be short-handed, particularly during the Festival, when the number of delicatessen-oriented people staying in the area seemed almost to double. Miranda could be the solution to this staff problem, so Isabel gave Miranda her telephone number and suggested that she call her the following day. She talked to both Seamus and Miranda during the meal, and they chatted with each other across Isabel while she spoke to the woman opposite her. It was an easy, relaxed atmosphere and the weather held.

At the end of the meal, people were encouraged to get up from the table and help themselves to coffee in the kitchen. Isabel left Seamus and Miranda deep in conversation. Seamus had been in Perth and wanted to go back. Miranda had lived there for a time, and they had discovered mutual friends whose exploits, related by Seamus, were causing them both hilarity. Now you know somebody, Isabel thought with satisfaction, and tomorrow you may have a job. She looked around for Mimi and Joe; they were in conversation at the other end of the table with Malcolm and Nicky Wood, both singers. She did not need to worry about them: the talk, which was already animated, would be about choirs. Mimi sang in the choir of a high Episcopal church in Dallas, one that claimed to possess a holy relic, a fragment of the true cross. Unlikely, thought Isabel, but then people believe in all sorts of things, some even more unlikely than that. How many people in the United States believed that they had been abducted by aliens? It was a depressingly large number. And the aliens always gave them back! Perhaps they were abducting the wrong sort.

Isabel walked across the lawn towards the kitchen door at the back of the house. There was a chill in the air now, not enough to spoil the evening, but a sign of the advancing night. A white night, she thought, like the midsummer nights of St. Petersburg, when it never became dark; it was so still; there wasn't a hint of breeze.

She moved across the small courtyard and headed toward the kitchen. There were several guests ahead of her: a man in a mustard-coloured linen jacket; a woman in a rather-too-formal dress with a stole across her shoulders; a young man with a high complexion who was regaling them with a story. The man in the linen jacket half turned and caught Isabel's eye. She knew him but could not remember his name or what he did. He looked at her briefly, obviously in the same position of uncertainty, and smiled before returning his attention to his companions. Then, in the kitchen, there were more guests, coffee cups in hand.

Isabel helped herself to coffee and began to move back towards the lawn. Peter and Susie had planned music and she could hear, drifting from one of the rooms further inside the house, the first strains of a fiddle tune. She turned round and went back down a corridor that led to the hall and the staircase. The music was coming from a room to the right—it was one of those lilting Scottish fiddle tunes that celebrated somebody's return or departure from Islay or Skye or somewhere like that, or a battle that took place a long time ago; maybe it was even that curiously named "Neil Gow's Lament for His Second Wife." She paused and listened. There was something about this music that always affected her strongly; perhaps because it came from such a particular place. It could not be the music of anywhere else. It was the music of Scotland and it spoke of the country she loved. She closed her eyes. What was Scotland to her? Her place, yes. And it was right that one's place should make one's heart stop with longing, particularly when it was as beautiful as was Scotland. *The rose of all the world is not for me,* MacDiarmid had written. *I want for my part / Only the little white rose of Scotland / That smells sharp and sweet—and breaks the heart.*

She opened her eyes. She was aware that somebody, a woman, had come up behind her. "That tune," she said. She made the remark, or the beginning of a remark, before she took in who it was, and now she gave a slight start of surprise.

"Yes," said the woman. "We've met before, haven't we? Cynthia Vaughan."

Isabel inclined her head. "Of course. I'm sorry, but I wasn't putting two and two together. I saw you outside, at the other end of the table, but hadn't . . ."

Cynthia raised a hand. "I wasn't sure either," she said. "And then somebody said yes, it was you. I can't remember exactly when we met last time, but wasn't it on that committee—the one to do with the hospital?"

They established where it was, and when, and they talked briefly about what had happened to the committee. Isabel thought: So this is her, Patrick's mother. The possessive one. She certainly looked the part—the matron, the galleon in full sail; she was tall, and there was that look Isabel always associated with political women—a firmness, a determination to stick to the agenda.

They had been standing near the door that led into the large dining room, where the music was coming from. "We're in the way," said Cynthia, gently steering Isabel away. "Here's a sofa. We can sit down here."

Isabel slightly resented being drawn away and told to sit down. What if she preferred to stand? But it was quite in character, she thought, for a woman like this to tell people what to do, and she found some amusement in that. And it was obvious that Cynthia had something to say to her, which intrigued Isabel; something about Cat, perhaps—if she knew of the connection.

"I gather that we have something in common," said Cynthia.

Isabel thought: She wastes no time. "Yes," she said. "You're Patrick's . . ."

"I'm Patrick's mother," said Cynthia. "Yes. And you are Cat's aunt, I believe. I must say that you look rather young for that."

Isabel smiled. There had been no declaration of war yet, but she thought it would probably come soon; indirectly, she thought, but then she looked again at the haughty nose and the firmness of the lips and decided that it might not be all that indirect.

"Cat was born when my brother was quite young. That makes me a young aunt," Isabel said pleasantly. "And Patrick came to my place for dinner. I liked him." She uttered the lie without thinking, and immediately said to herself: *Social lies are so easy.*

She had not intended that the comment should impress Cynthia, nor ingratiate her with the older woman, and it did neither. Cynthia took a sip of her coffee and stared into her cup, as if the compliment was so obviously true that she was not required to acknowledge it.

"Patrick's doing very well in his firm," she said. "He was with Dickson Minto, you know. Bruce Minto—I don't know if you know him, but he's one of the most successful lawyers in the country—he trained him. Personally. Then Patrick was offered this new job and he took it. He left with Bruce's blessing."

"It's always better that way," said Isabel.

Again there was no response to her remark. Isabel felt awkward. So far in the conversation she had uttered platitudes, and she felt foolish and ill at ease, as one does in a conversation where the other party has the advantage. There was no reason for her to feel this way, she was at least the intellectual equal of this political woman; it was a question of what people called alpha behaviour. Isabel was never sure exactly what alpha qualities were, but they seemed to have something to do with the desire—and ability—to dominate others. People usually spoke of alpha males, but there was no reason, surely, that there should not be alpha women. And if such people existed, then Cynthia was certainly one.

Cynthia had not been looking at Isabel as she spoke, but now she did, and Isabel felt the other woman's rather large brown eyes on her. "It's difficult these days," she said. "It's so competitive. Even for people like Patrick, who are . . . well, who are on top of things. They have to work all hours of the day. All those transactions, those deals that they get involved in."

She paused and Isabel felt that her agreement was required and that it would be all right now to say something trite. "Of course," she said. "How they do it—"

"Patrick was talking to me the other day," interrupted Cynthia. "He was telling me that they were involved in something or other which required them to sleep in the office! They were working until three in the morning and then had to get back to work at seven. They have fold-out beds and the lawyers sleep on those."

How ridiculous, thought Isabel. Firemen might do that, and doctors perhaps. But why should lawyers? She knew, though, that it was true. The whole culture of work had become so intrusive and demanding that people had to do it. And the result was that they were left with little time for simply living their lives, for going for a walk, for sitting in a bar, for reading a book. It was all work.

"Why do people have to work so hard?" she asked. "Do you think it's natural to work ten hours a day, every day? Were we made to do that, do you think?"

Cynthia frowned. She looked rather displeased by this remark, as if Isabel had interrupted the flow of her thought with some specious question. "That's how it is," she said. "It's China and India, isn't it? They are prepared to work for next to nothing, which means that our people have to run to keep still. Nobody can compete with the sweatshops."

Isabel thought that was probably right. If we believed that

we could survive on our wits without actually making anything, then we were living in a fool's paradise. But she was not sure that this applied to lawyers. So she simply said, "No."

"No," echoed Cynthia. "Anyway, Patrick does all this very cheerfully, I must say. And he's doing very well, as I said." She paused. "His career is very important to him, you know."

"I don't doubt it," said Isabel.

Cynthia reached out and picked a piece of fluff off a cushion and twisted it between her fingers. "I'm not sure that it's a terribly good idea for him to get too emotionally involved with anybody at this stage," she said quietly. "These next few years will be pretty important for him, job-wise. I imagine that he might be offered a partnership before too long. If he applies himself, that is."

Isabel tried not to grin. The approach had come, and she marvelled at Cynthia's effrontery. It amazed her that anybody would think this way, but it was even more astonishing that Cynthia felt that she could raise the issue like this. She was about to invite her, Isabel thought, to interfere.

"Emotional involvement is what people do," said Isabel. "All of us."

Cynthia drew in her breath. "I don't think they're suited," she said. "Sorry to have to say it. But I don't."

"It's difficult to say," said Isabel evenly. "Very different people, or people who strike others as being very different from each other, can get on very well. It's chemistry, don't you think?"

Cynthia's eyes were upon her again. "I know my own son," she said. "I know what he's like."

"I'm sure you do. But when it comes to these things, to . . . well, sex, it's a very private matter, isn't it? And can we ever tell who's going to get on well sexually with whom? I can't. I've never been able to."

Cynthia stiffened. "I don't know about that," she said. "I don't imagine that sex lies behind it."

Isabel was silent. Patrick's mother obviously did not know Cat. Isabel remembered telling Cat that she thought she sexualised the world too much. And Cat had laughed and said, "But, Isabel, the world is sexual. It is."

Cynthia looked at her, but when Isabel said nothing, she continued, "I don't know you well. But I'm sure that we both have the interests of Patrick and Kate—"

"Cat," corrected Isabel.

"Cat. We both have their best interests at heart. A word from you, perhaps, to your niece might help her see that this is not necessarily the best thing for them. Do you think so?"

"No," said Isabel. "I'm afraid I don't."

Cynthia suddenly got to her feet. "I'm sorry that I raised this," she said. "I thought that we might see things in the same way. We obviously don't."

Isabel rose to stand beside her. "Don't you think that we should keep out of it?" she said. "It's their business, after all." She wanted to add, "And it's time to let go of your son," but she did not, because she felt that it would be cruel to say that, even if it was abundantly clear that that was what Cynthia needed to do.

Later that evening, as she walked back with Joe and Mimi and she described the conversation to them, Mimi said, "You were right not to say anything more. Poor woman. He's all she has, and that's rather sad, isn't it? People cling. It's not the best way, but you can understand why they cling."

Isabel felt chastened. The needs of others were not a matter to be treated lightly, even when they were unreasonable, as was the case with Cynthia. I should feel sympathy for her, she thought, not irritation. And yet one could not hold on to somebody beyond a natural point, and Patrick, surely, had reached that point where his mother should let him go to live his own life. This made her think of Jamie, of course.

CHAPTER FOURTEEN

MIRANDA, the Australian whom she had met at the Steven-son party, telephoned at nine o'clock the following morning, reminding Isabel that she had offered to speak to Cat about a job. Isabel, immured in her morning room with her coffee and the *Scotsman* crossword, with Mimi seated opposite her reading *The Times,* was surprised that she should call so early and so soon after the offer was made. But she was not irritated, as one sometimes may be when a promise is called in. It was under-standable that Miranda should call and remind her; finding a job was a major thing for her. Then there was her age—nineteen or twenty-one is impatient, or less patient, Isabel thought, than thirty or forty. Isabel agreed to speak to Cat that morning and to telephone her once she had found out whether Cat could offer her anything.

"I hope you don't think I'm being pushy," Miranda said. "Calling straight away and all. But you did say . . ."

"I did," said Isabel. "And I'll do what I said I would do."

Isabel thought that it would be easier to discuss this with Cat in person, so she went into Bruntsfield an hour or so later.

Eddie was standing at the door of the delicatessen when she arrived. He turned to her distractedly and then spat out, "Somebody's stolen coffee again." Then he swore—a simple expletive, crude, dirty.

Isabel looked at Eddie. He was staring down the street, his lip quivering in anger, his face flushed, as if he had just come running from somewhere. There were times when he seemed on the brink of tears, from sheer injustice, Isabel had always thought, and from that ancient, unspecified hurt; now it was more immediate.

"Stolen coffee?"

Eddie turned to face her. "It happens all the time," he said. "They just go for it. It's always packets of coffee. Nine times out of ten."

Isabel looked down the street. It was that time in the morning when things were at their quietest: those going to work had caught their lumbering buses, and it was too early for the morning shoppers to come out. A man walked past with his dog, a small cairn terrier with a collar on which DOG was written helpfully in studs; the man glanced at Isabel and then at Eddie and smiled. There was a woman with a heavy bag, and a couple of boys of fourteen or fifteen, loose-limbed, dressed in black jeans sinking to the ground and voluminous T-shirts, engaged in the tribal debate of teenagers. She saw no fleeing shoplifters.

She followed Eddie inside, and the air changed; the smell of coffee (a temptation perhaps to the thieves), of ripening cheeses; the dry, itchy notes of pulses and cereals. Isabel had always felt that this was the smell of real food—supermarkets smelled of chemicals and detergents and cellophane wrapping.

Eddie, normally laconic, was vocal. "I don't know why they

go for it," he said. "They stuff their pockets with that Kenyan blend with the nice picture on it. Then they run out of the shop."

Isabel thought. She had been in charge of the delicatessen for a week not all that long ago, when Cat had gone to a wedding in Italy, and she had seen no signs of shoplifting. Had she missed it? She cast her mind back. She remembered stacking the coffee section, and she remembered packets with a picture. She had assumed that everybody who came into the shop was honest, which was the general assumption that she made about others.

She looked at Eddie, who was busying himself with counting the packets of coffee on the shelf. He was still quivering with rage.

"I always assume that people are good," said Isabel. "I'm naïve, I suppose."

"They aren't," muttered Eddie.

"I suppose I shouldn't trust people," Isabel went on.

"Don't," said Eddie. "Never."

She moved to the newspaper rack. What had happened to Eddie before he came to work here—and Isabel had never found out what that was—must have destroyed his trust in people. He had confided in Cat, she believed, and Cat had kept the confidence, not revealing what Eddie had said to her. But Isabel knew that it was something dark, and she did not want to know the details. So although she did not want to arouse Eddie's private demons, she did not feel she could let this denial of trust go answered.

She picked up a paper and went to stand beside Eddie. "You can't say that about trust, Eddie. You have to trust somebody."

The young man stopped in the act of counting, his hand

resting on the edge of the shelf. Isabel was aware of his breathing, which seemed to come more quickly than usual, as if he
had been exerting himself. He did not look at her, but kept his
gaze upon the packets of coffee in front of him.

"I don't," he said, his voice barely a whisper. "I just don't."

"Because of something that happened to you?" She had not
meant to say that, but it had come out.

He did nothing, said nothing. Isabel quickly thought, I must
get away from this topic.

"Anyway," she said. "Let's not talk about it. But remember
that there are some people you can trust. Me. Cat. You can trust
us, Eddie. And not everyone who comes into this shop is going
to steal something. They really aren't."

She moved back to the newspaper rack and replaced the
paper, since Cat had arrived, a shopping bag in her hand. Isabel
greeted her, leaving Eddie to his thoughts. "We've had shoplifters," she whispered. "Eddie's very upset."

Cat glanced at Eddie and sighed. With a nod of her head
she signalled to Isabel to follow her into the office at the back.

"He gets really upset over that," said Cat once they were out
of Eddie's earshot. "It's one of the things that seems to trigger
memories for him. He gets over it, of course, but I really feel for
him when it happens."

"He said something about not trusting anybody," said Isabel.

Cat opened her shopping bag and took out a small container
of nail polish, which she held against her nails to assess the
colour match.

"He doesn't," said Cat. "Poor Eddie. He doesn't trust anybody. Even himself."

Isabel frowned. The idea of not trusting oneself was a
strange one. It was possible to imagine not trusting anybody

else—bleak though such a position would be—but not to trust oneself? Did that make sense?

Cat put down the bottle of nail polish and looked up at Isabel. "Yes," she said. "That's what happens, I gather. People to whom really bad things happen don't trust their own feelings. Did they ask for it? Did they deserve it? Those sort of questions. And that means they don't trust themselves."

Yes, thought Isabel, you're right. And she remembered that when John Liamor had left her she had asked herself whether she had brought about his departure. For a time she had blamed herself for his womanising, for his constant affairs, and had felt, in some vague, unspecified way, that it was her failure to make him happy that had driven him into the arms of others. Such nonsense, of course, but she had believed it then.

Cat shrugged. "Leave him," she said. "He's getting a bit better—generally. Don't talk to him about it."

Isabel agreed. "But I do want to talk to you," she said. "Are you still thinking of taking on somebody else?"

Cat said that she was. "There's an Australian girl I met," Isabel said. "She's looking for something. I get the impression that she'd be a very good worker. And she's available pretty much immediately."

Cat was interested. "Will she be all right with Eddie?" she asked. "You know how he's frightened of people."

Isabel did not know how to answer that question. She knew very little about Miranda, now that she came to think of it. All she knew was that she came from Australia and wanted to work. But could she be trusted? Of course she could be, provided, of course, that one could trust somebody of whose past one knew nothing and of whose present one could not say much more than freckles, an engaging smile and an apparent optimism. Perhaps that was a good enough basis for trust, even in a world in which people destroyed the fragile sense of self of young men like Eddie and thought, one assumed, nothing of it.

"She seems nice enough." That poor, overworked word, she thought, *nice*.

"I'll try her now," said Cat, taking the piece of paper on which Isabel had written Miranda's telephone number.

Isabel left, pausing at Eddie's side on the way out. The young man was standing disconsolately, staring out of the window, his gaze unfocused. She took his hand, which felt warm to her, and a bit damp. "We're very fond of you, you know," she whispered. "Cat. Me. We're very fond of you."

She gave his hand a squeeze and, after a moment, she felt him return the pressure, not very convincingly, but detectably nonetheless.

MIMI WAS IN THE GARDEN when Isabel returned to the house. Isabel went out to join her, having seen her from the kitchen window, standing beside a large clump of flowering azaleas near the small wooden summer house.

"Something been digging here," said Mimi, pointing to the ground at her feet. "Look. A mole?"

Isabel looked down at the scratchings in the lawn. A few lines of dark earth had been scattered across a small area of grass and a bulb, dug from the edge of the flowerbed, had been left against a crenellation of mud. She looked for the familiar signs: a feather, perhaps; a fragment of bone from a vole or shrew, or even a chicken leg salvaged from kitchen pickings, but there was nothing.

"Brother Fox," she said. "This is his territory."

Mimi looked enquiringly at Isabel, the edge of the summer house reflected in the lens of her glasses.

"Brother Fox?"

"Our urban fox," said Isabel. "We call him Brother Fox because . . . well, I suppose it's because he has to have a name and Grace and I feel that we know him quite well. So it's Brother Fox."

"St. Francis . . ."

"Yes," said Isabel. "There is a Franciscan ring to it. Brother Sun, wasn't it? And why not?"

"No reason at all," said Mimi. "One of my favourite saints. You know that picture, do you, the one in Florence, where the saint stands with his arms out and all the birds are at his feet—those strange, naïvely painted birds, like little feathered boxes." She paused. "I'd like to see him, this Brother Fox of yours. Will he make an appearance?"

Isabel looked about the garden. "There's something unpredictable about him. Sometimes, though, I feel as if he's watching me. I just get that feeling."

"And he is? He is really watching you?"

Isabel knew it sounded unlikely, but it was true. "Yes. It's happened time and time again. I might be in my study, working, and I feel that there are eyes on me—eyes outside. And if I look up I see Brother Fox out in the garden, or see a flash of gold, which is him. He's very beautiful, you see. Reddish-gold. A most beautiful creature."

Isabel reached out and touched one of the flowers on the azalea bush. Nature was so beguiling in many of its corners; it was the tiny details that were important: the colour of these azaleas, somewhere between pink and red; the red-gold of fox fur. Why should we alone find the world beautiful? Or did

Brother Fox appreciate what he saw about him, and love it, as we did? No, we should not make the mistake of anthropomorphism: the world for him was really not much more than a struggle for food, for life; a matter of genetic survival against all the competing genes; just struggle. And we were the enemy, with our dogs and our gas and our huntsmen with rifles; all terror and pain for foxes. But Brother Fox was not scared of her; he was wary, when he watched, but not scared.

The azalea was next to a mahonia bush, with its yellow flowers and those spiky leaves, so different from the azalea. Isabel's hand moved on to touch the mahonia; it reminded her of holly, but it was more beautiful.

"I occasionally dream of Brother Fox," she said to Mimi. "In my dreams he can speak. It's very strange, but not at all odd in the dream, you know. He speaks with a slightly high-pitched, rather refined Scottish voice, but once he spoke French, and that surprised me. He used subjunctives and I remembered thinking how remarkable it was that an animal should have the subjunctive." She used the construction "have the subjunctive" without thinking that it might have sounded strange to Mimi. Scots said "I have the Gaelic" when they could speak Gaelic.

Mimi laughed. "And what did he say in these dreams? Small talk?"

Isabel searched her memory. Dreams are lodged in a very short-term part of the memory, but she had committed these to more permanent storage because they had been so unusual. Her last conversation with Brother Fox had been something about how we control our lives and how contingency plays a part in what we are. She remembered saying to him that he was a fox—and he had agreed—and that the pattern of his life was determined by that brute fact of biology. But then he had said,

And so is yours, and she had felt indignant that a fox should call into question her free will. Their conversation had ended in an atmosphere of polite distance, which Isabel regretted, as she had had a sense of the preciousness of speaking with a fox.

She told Mimi this, and Mimi said, "But he was right, wasn't he? Or you were, rather. Conversations in our dreams are really conversations with ourselves, aren't they? Have you ever thought of it that way?"

"No, but you're right. Internal rhetoric—that's what philosophers would call it." A mahonia leaf pricked the tip of her finger, just slightly, but she said to herself: *I must be careful of sharp things.* Internal rhetoric. "But . . . but surely, we don't have to agree with what is said by the people to whom we are talking in our dreams? Of course we may put words into their mouths—we are after all the director of our dreams—"

"And producer," interjected Mimi.

"Yes, and producer. But what is said in the dream by other people may just be what we think those other people are likely to say. The fact that we write the lines for them doesn't mean that we agree with the sentiments behind the lines, does it?"

Mimi felt that she needed time to think about this. Philosophy, she had always thought, was often just a matter of common sense; a matter of finding the words to describe what *is,* or, in some cases, what *should be.* What Isabel had just said might have sounded complicated, but in reality it was not. The playwright, the novelist did not endorse what their characters said—that seemed clear enough. But where did it all come from? Every word of Shakespeare was, after all, Shakespeare; if something came from the mind of the writer, then it was there in that mind, even if only as a possibility. And surely the insights of psychology underlined the point that what we talked about was

what we were interested in, and, sometimes, what we believe—
even if we said we didn't! That was why we sometimes criticised
others for doing exactly what we would want to do ourselves but
did not dare—which meant that the writer might not be believed
in protesting that the words on the page were nothing to do to
with him. They could well be.

Mimi thought of somebody she knew who often spoke of a
mutual friend's tendency to consult the plastic surgeon. "Such a
conservationist," the critic said. "She deserves some sort of
award."

And Mimi had politely observed that perhaps she, the critic,
would like to do the same thing, which had not gone down
well, because, she thought, it was true. But it had stopped the
remarks.

"Sometimes we say things which are the—" Mimi began, but
Isabel, who had not heard her, had started to say something else.

"I know that the dreams of others are tedious," she said.
"And I know I shouldn't bore you with these things. But I had an
extremely odd dream last night."

"About Brother Fox?" asked Mimi.

"No," said Isabel. "About Tom and Angie. Your friends."

"You must have been thinking about them during the day,"
offered Mimi. "I find that what I dream about very much
reflects what has been on my mind that day. It happens all the
time."

Isabel turned away from the mahonia and faced Mimi. "It
was very odd," she said. "Quite disconcerting, in fact."

"One shouldn't let dreams worry you," said Mimi reassur-
ingly. "Everybody does disconcerting things in dreams."

"Oh, I behaved myself," said Isabel. "I don't think I had
much to do or say in the dream. I was there, I suppose, because

I saw what happened. But I didn't do anything. I was just standing there, a bit shocked, I think."

Mimi raised an eyebrow. She waited for Isabel to continue.

"We were somewhere over in the west of Scotland," Isabel went on. "I think that it was on the Mull of Kintyre, or somewhere like that. We were in a house near the sea, and there was a room with one of those extraordinary cases of little stuffed animals dressed up in outfits, riding tiny bicycles, playing croquet. You know those strange things? The Victorians loved them. They would gas kittens, send them off to the taxidermist, and then put them into a sort of *tableau vivant,* or *tableau mort,* I suppose. An orchestra of kittens, with minute instruments. A court scene with kitten jurors and kitten lawyers."

Mimi made a face. She liked cats, and indeed had been the owner of a dynasty of distinguished cats, including Arthur Brown, an immense and dignified furry ball, who had been much admired by all in that part of Dallas, and who had died, suddenly, on the kitchen floor, of a heart attack, much as overworked businessmen dropped on the golf course. "I don't approve . . ."

"Neither do I," Isabel supplied. "But there was one of those cases in the room, and then in came Tom and Angie. They looked at the case, and walked out of the room. Then Angie came back in alone and started to read the *Scotsman* on the sofa. She turned to me and said, 'I've killed Tom, you know.' And that was it."

Mimi laughed. "Imaginative stuff!"

"I woke up feeling quite sad," said Isabel.

"One would." Mimi paused. "Of course there's a motive, isn't there? She would be better off if she did that. And the university would be worse off."

Isabel did not see what this had to do with SMU, and she asked Mimi to explain.

"Tom said years ago that he was going to make a major benefaction to Southern Methodist," said Mimi. "To the law school, in particular, but also to the Meadows School of the Arts. But then when Angie came along he stopped talking about this. Joe was very disappointed. He thought that she had got round him in some way. Anyway, all the law school people decided to take the long view. They thought that Angie would not be around for ever and that once she had got whatever settlement she had in mind, Tom would come back to the idea of giving money to the university. Joe hopes that too, but he's not so sure that Angie is a temporary fixture. He thinks that Tom would be more likely to go first. So there you have it."

"Of course," Isabel said wryly, "that gives people a motive to dispose of her, rather than Tom."

"Perhaps," said Mimi. "But remember that the people who would benefit are all very respectable. They wouldn't dream of doing anything like that." Of course they might *dream* of it, she thought, but not consider it. But Isabel would know what she meant.

"No," said Isabel. "Of course not. But I'm afraid that I can see Angie doing what she did in my dream. She just could, couldn't she?"

"No," said Mimi. "I don't think that she has the imagination." She paused, looking at her watch. "But, anyway, Isabel, this sort of thing simply doesn't happen. Outside novels, of course."

"Novels have nothing to do with real life?"

"Very little," said Mimi. "And that's what makes them such fun."

CHAPTER FIFTEEN

THAT FRIDAY was the day on which they were due to go off to stay with Tom and Angie. Joe and Mimi left in the morning, as they planned to visit Traquair House beforehand. Traquair, the oldest inhabited house in Scotland, had a maze ("Joe will get lost, so we won't be doing that," said Mimi) and a library ("Joe will spend the whole visit there") and the cradle in which James VI slept as an infant, a carved rocking cradle in which the future king had been laid by his mother, Mary, Queen of Scots.

"I feel so sorry for her," said Mimi. "What a difficult country this must have been. All that plotting and intrigue."

Isabel was sympathetic—up to a point. It was unfortunate having one's head chopped off by a scheming, suspicious cousin, certainly, but Mary had been no stranger to intrigue. "She did a fair amount of scheming herself," she observed. "And then there were those men . . ."

It was a non sequitur, she knew, but it seemed to add to the picture of misfortune. Mimi, though, was not going to let that pass. "But she never really had much choice," she said. "How old was she when she married the Dauphin? Fifteen, wasn't it?

And she'd been betrothed to him at the age of six or something like that. Today we'd call that child abuse."

"The Dauphin wasn't the problem, of course. That was just sad. It was the subsequent husbands."

Mimi raised a finger. She used to be able to quote several lines of the poem that Mary wrote on the death of Francis but now it was gone. Poetry went; no matter how fervently one wished it would stay, it went. She closed her eyes. *By day, by night, I think of him*—that came into it. He had doted on her, that little boy, and she had loved him in return, but rather as a sister would love her little brother, the child groom with his child bride. Her elegy to him had the drum-beat of real grief in its lines.

"And Darnley," said Isabel.

Mimi sighed. "You know, it always surprises me. People say that they can't understand why she chose to get mixed up with Darnley. But surely it's obvious. Or at least I think it is. Darnley was handsome, and he was the only man around who was taller than she was. He was also fond of a party."

"I would have thought those provided good enough reason. Women like handsome men who are fun. And then, a little bit later, they realise their mistake."

"Exactly," said Mimi. "Getting involved with anyone for their looks alone is folly. Sheer folly."

"And yet people do it, don't they? It's another example of human frailty, I suppose." Isabel thought: If Jamie did not look like he did, would I feel the way I do about him? What if Jamie were short, or overweight, or had an unflattering profile? Would I love him? These thoughts unsettled her. John Liamor had been good-looking—and had made use of the fact. He had that dark hair that the Irish can carry off so well, and chiselled features and, of course, I loved him for that. Of course I did. She remembered the poem that Yeats had written to Anne Gregory about how only God would love somebody for herself and not her yellow hair.

She knew that she would not feel the way she did about Jamie if he were not good-looking. And that, she thought, was a dispiriting conclusion, for it meant that it was really a love of beauty that was at work; we love the beautiful, and we find it in a person. The affection one feels for a person—that familiar, solid loyalty that grows around those to whom we have become accustomed, or on whom we have come to depend—is different from love, or at least from romantic love. It was a compromise; the ersatz coffee that we drink when the real is unobtainable.

Mimi brought an end to these thoughts. "Whatever miscalculations she made," she said, "Mary was a brave woman. Have you read her last letter, the one that she sent to Henry III? I find it terribly moving, that letter."

Isabel had, and recalled the dignity of the sentences in which she describes the shabby behaviour of those who had secured her execution; of how they had kept from the Queen of Scots her chaplain, so that he could not come to hear her confession and give her the comfort of the last sacrament. And how she sent to Henry two precious stones as talismans against illness; and the awful finality of the sentence, *Wednesday, at two in the morning*. It was almost unbearable, just to read, but worse was to come in the letter which Robert Wynkfielde wrote about the execution: a testament to her bravery and dignity, as well as to the loyalty of dogs; for Mary's little dog was found to be hiding in her skirts, unwilling to leave the body of its mistress, and had had to be washed of the Queen's blood. And that, thought

Isabel, was how it all ended in Scotland. We had a stirring history, which people romanticised, but at the end of the day it
ended in blood.

She might take Mimi, she thought, to visit her friend Rosalind Marshall, who had written about Scottish queens. They had
spoken about Darnley together in the supermarket in Morningside, of all places, when Isabel, who had been reading his biography at the time, had asked Rosalind's opinion.

"We must remember how young he was," said Rosalind.
"That explains a lot, you know. These days a young man like that
would be going to clubs and bars."

"Instead of marrying Mary, Queen of Scots," mused Isabel.

"Precisely," said Rosalind, reaching for a packet of Arbo-
rio rice.

After Joe and Mimi had left for Traquair, Isabel spent several hours working in her study. Grace was in the house, but
they had not spoken much that morning, as Grace had been in
one of her moods. Sometimes Isabel would enquire as to the
reason for the mood, and would receive a diatribe on some
issue, but usually she tactfully waited for the indignation or out-
rage to subside. This morning she suspected that it was political, as it had been a few days ago when the morning paper had
revealed the appointment by the Scottish administration of
three new commissioners: one to deal with obesity, one to protect the rights of children, and another to deal with issues of
access to the arts. One such commissioner would have been
provocation enough to Grace; the appointment of three was
insupportable. "All they want to do is to work out ways of regu-
lating us," she said. "But our lives are just not their business. If
we want to be overweight, then that's our affair. And as for the
rights of children, what about their duties?" The conversation

had ended at that rhetorical point, and Isabel, having only just opened her mouth, had shut it again. There would be no victory in debate with Grace; even a commissioner would come off second best in that.

She finished her work, which was the writing of a short piece to introduce a supplement of the *Review* devoted to self-knowledge. It had not been easy; for some reason she had felt that the piece had become too subjective, as if she were describing her own search for self-knowledge. She printed out what she had written and read through it. She had relied on Alasdair McIntyre as a starting point. He had suggested that the unity of the self be based on the unity of a narrative that started with birth and ended with our death. In other words, we made for ourselves a coherent life story, and that life story—that narrative—enabled us to understand ourselves. But was coherence a goal in itself? One might pursue bad goals consistently; one might be consistently self-interested, but would that make for a form of self-knowledge that had any value at all? Isabel thought not. Self-knowledge required more than an understanding of how things work as a narrative; it required an understanding of the character traits that lead to the narrative being what it is. And for this, she concluded, we might attempt to mould our character in the future. I can be better, she thought, if I know what's wrong with me now.

She put the sheets of paper down and sighed. Was this really a satisfactory way of earning a living? She was not at all sure whether what she wrote would change anything for anybody; it was doubtful that somebody reading her introduction would say to himself, *So that's how it's done!* If she wanted to do that, she would be better doing anything but professional philosophy. If she wanted to change the world and the way people looked at it, then she would do far better being a journalist, who at least would be read, or a broadcaster, who might slip in little bits of advice, or a teacher, who could pour thoughts into the ears of receptive pupils. And yet if she asked any of these whether they would wish to trade their lives for hers, they would all be likely to say that they would.

She packed, her mind still half on self-knowledge, half on the choice of clothing for the weekend. There would be walks, no doubt, and she would need something waterproof. And they might be fairly formal for dinner—Dallas people dressed smartly, she remembered, and so she would need something suitable for the evening. Angie would not dress down; she would wear a cocktail dress and there would be jewellery. She looked at her wardrobe, and felt, for a brief moment, despair. There were word people—idea people—and then there were clothes people—fashion people. She knew which group she belonged to.

An hour later, her weekend case in the back of her green Swedish car, Isabel drove across town to Stockbridge to collect Jamie. It was a teaching afternoon for him, and the last of his pupils emerged from the front door of his shared stair just as Isabel drew up in her car. The boy, swinging his bassoon with the lightheartedness of one who had just finished a lesson, noticed Isabel's car and made eye contact with her. She had seen him before, when she had come to Jamie's flat at the end of a lesson, and they recognised each other, but he looked away again sharply. Isabel smiled; there was a certain point in the teen years, for boys, when the sheer embarrassment of being alive was too much. And this came out in the form of hostility, of grunts, of silent glowers. The world was just wrong to the teenage boy, quite wrong, and all because it failed to understand just how important that particular teenage boy was.

She extracted her telephone from her bag and dialled Jamie's number to let him know that she was waiting for him. He would be two minutes, he said, and he was.

"I recognised that boy you were teaching," Isabel said as they set off. "I met him once before."

"He was nicer then, I suppose," said Jamie. "Something's happened to him. And his bassoon-playing."

"Puberty," suggested Isabel.

Jamie laughed. "They come out of it. One of them was horrible last year and then suddenly he started to act like a human being again. The excuses for not practising went away. The scowls. It all went."

Isabel turned the car into Henderson Row. She felt a sudden surge of excitement. It was Friday afternoon and she and Jamie were going off together into the country. They would be together until Sunday evening, which was the longest time she had ever spent in his company. And they had never been away before; that lent an additional spice to the moment.

"I've been looking forward to this weekend," she said. "I was feeling stale. I haven't been out of town for ages."

Jamie half turned in his seat and grinned at her. *Sic a smile,* she thought in Scots, *would melt ilka heirt*—such a smile would melt any heart. "I was thinking about it all morning," he said. "I had a deadly dull rehearsal in the Queen's Hall. I just wanted to get out of town. To get far away from conductors and other musicians."

"They'll want you to perform," warned Isabel. "There's a piano, I'm afraid. And I've brought some music."

"Singing with you is different," said Jamie. "It's . . . well, it's casual. I enjoy it."

Isabel said nothing. She looked ahead at the traffic, which

was light for a Friday afternoon. Sometimes one could get caught round about George Street or going up the Mound, but cars were moving freely now and she thought that it would not take them much more than an hour to get to the house, if that. They were heading for Peebles, to the south of Edinburgh, in roughly the same direction that Joe and Mimi had gone that morning. Tom and Angie had rented a house in a glen further to the west, a house off the normal track of visitors, but which Isabel was aware of. She had a friend who knew the owners. They were poor, in a genteel sort of way, and her friend had said that everything about the house—the furnishings, the carpets—was threadbare and worn, growing old in shadow, faded with age. That, apparently, had changed, and a decorator from Edinburgh had splashed colour and renewed texture about the place. Isabel wondered whether the soul would have been taken out of the house by money and the search for comfort. She could not imagine Angie roughing it, and nor, when he was asked, could Jamie.

"I don't think so," he said. "She's high maintenance, I think."

"An expensive woman."

"Yes," he said. "You could say that. But he's pretty well off, isn't he? So that doesn't matter."

"And do you think she loves him?" asked Isabel.

Jamie looked out the window. They were now approaching the edge of town and the slopes of the Pentland Hills could be seen rising before them. Behind them, over the North Sea, there were clouds in the sky, and slanting squalls of rain; behind the Pentlands, though, the sky was light, glowing, as if with promise.

He fiddled with a button on his jacket. It was hanging on by a thread, and he had meant to sew it before he came, but ran out of time. "I haven't given it any thought," he said quietly. "And I don't think you should either."

Isabel was quick to deny her interest. "Don't worry," she said. "I wasn't going to interfere."

"Are you sure?" Jamie sounded dubious. He had witnessed Isabel's interventions on more than one occasion, and if they had turned out well—or at least if they had not resulted in disaster—that was, he thought, owing in part to chance.

"All right," she said. "I confess that I'm intrigued. And who wouldn't be? A conspicuously wealthy, sophisticated man has a young fiancée with not a great deal of grey matter—well, one thinks about that."

"It's his business if he wants to take up with somebody like her," said Jamie. "That's what some men want." He paused and looked at Isabel. "They'll probably be blissfully happy."

Isabel conceded that. They could be happy, with each getting from the relationship what each wanted. But what, she asked, if he were to find out that she was interested only in his money? Could he be happy in those circumstances?

"He might be," said Jamie. "Presumably men like that have a pretty clear idea of what's what. He might be able to see through her and still say to himself: Well, I don't care if she doesn't really love me, I've got an attractive young wife, and as long as she behaves herself . . ."

"Which she might not do," said Isabel quickly. "What if she has an eye for other men?"

Jamie shrugged. "She'd be a fool."

Isabel drummed her fingers on the steering wheel. She wondered whether Jamie was one of those people who just could not understand the tides of passion; who thought that people calculated advantage and disadvantage in matters of the heart—they did not; people behaved drunkenly, irrationally when it came to these things. Perhaps that was why Mary, Queen of Scots, married Darnley, against all her obvious interest? But she did not want to go into that. Already their discussion had developed an edge which was not right for a romantic trip into the country—if that was what this was going to be. Suddenly she was aware of Jamie beside her, of his legs at an angle, of his right arm resting in a position where it almost touched her side, of the wind from the half-open side window in his hair, ruffling it; and the phrase *your ordinary human beauty* came into her mind, and it seemed to her to be so apt. Beauty that was so ordinary because it required no ornament, no false enhancement; that was ordinary human beauty and it was superior to any other beauty.

He said, suddenly, "Look at those sheep."

She looked. They were heading now up the hill from Auchendinny, and on the right side of the road there were fields and woods falling away to a river. The sheep were clustered about a hopper into which a farmer was siphoning feed of some sort. Little drifts of powdered feed, dust from the sheep's table, were being blown away by the wind.

"Their lunch," she said. They both laughed; there was nothing funny about it, but it seemed to them that something significant had been shared. When you are with somebody you love the smallest, smallest things can be so important, so amusing, because love transforms the world, everything. And was that what had happened? she wondered.

She remembered something. "You know, I came out here quite a few years ago, when the Soviet Union was still in business. Just. It was shortly before its end. There was a woman who was a philosopher who had been sent over here by the Academy of Sciences of the USSR, and I was asked to entertain her for a few days. Mostly she wanted to go shopping, because they had so little in their own shops and she needed things. But I brought her out here to Peebles, to have lunch, and she saw sheep in the fields and cried out, 'Look at all those sheeps! Look at all those sheeps!' Sheeps. That's what she said, understandably enough. And then she said, 'Do you know, in my country, we have forgotten how to keep animals.' "

Jamie was quiet. "And she hadn't seen . . ."

"She hadn't seen anything like it," said Isabel. "Apparently the Soviet countryside was pretty empty. Nobody on the collective farms kept animals. The bond between people and the land, between people and animals, had been broken."

Isabel remembered something else. "And here's another thing she said. We had a meeting at the Royal Society of Edinburgh. It was an open seminar on political philosophy, and this woman and the two male colleagues who had come with her came to it. They spoke in Russian, and there was a translator." She paused as she remembered the translator, a sallow-faced man who had been a chain-smoker and who had slipped out of the room every fifteen minutes to have a cigarette. "Members of the public were invited, but hardly anybody came. There was one man who did, however, a rather thin, very elegant-looking man who must have been in his late seventies, I think. At the end, after our guests had finished, he asked a question. He spoke in Russian, and I saw them turn and stare at him in what seemed to be astonishment. And when I looked to her, this woman philosopher, I saw there were tears in her eyes. I asked her what he had said, and she just shook her head and replied, 'It's not what he said. That's nothing. It's just that I haven't heard my language being spoken so beautifully, ever. Ever.' It tran-

spired that he was speaking pre-revolutionary Russian, that he
was the son of an exile who had been brought up speaking old
Russian in France. Our visitors were used to the brutality of
Soviet Russian, which was full of crudity and ugliness and jar-
gon, and that is what made her cry. To hear real Russian spoken
again."

TOM HAD FOUND Tarwhinn House through a friend from
Austin who had leased it a few years previously. The house had
been in the same family for almost three hundred years, or so
the owners claimed. It had been built in the seventeenth century by a man of some account in that part of Scotland, and it
had remained with his successors until an unwise choice in
the 1745 uprising—support for Bonnie Prince Charlie—had
resulted in the then head of the family being outlawed, pursued
to the very jetty from which he set ignominious sail for France,
and his property taken away from him. That was the point at
which the new owners acquired it by bribery, insinuating themselves into the position of the disgraced owner and eventually
assuming his arms and his name. "An early example of identity
theft," remarked Isabel, when she heard the story.

The current generation felt no need to gloss over the facts of
the shameful acquisition and wholeheartedly adopted the romantic associations of the property. But they had other fish to
fry, and the house and estate had been neglected. Eventually
repairs could be put off no longer—the roof, in particular, was
suffering from something which roofers call *nail sickness,* in
which the nail holes through the slates grow larger, the nails
weaken, and the slates begin to slip. The owners called in build-
ers and decorators, and the air of damp and fustiness which had

pervaded the house gradually began to be replaced by warmth
and light. But this was all an expensive process, and the long
summer lets to visitors became all the more important. Somebody like Tom, who was prepared to take the house for two or
three months, was ideal.

"There it is," said Isabel. "Can you see it? Over there."

Jamie looked in the direction in which Isabel had pointed.
Just above a stand of trees, the roof could be made out, and a
few of the windows on the top storey. But then the trees blocked
the view, and all he saw were Scots pines and a hillside rising
sharp behind.

"One of those tall, thin houses?" he asked.

"I've seen it only once," said Isabel. "And I don't remember
it very well. They had a Scotland's Gardens open day a few years
back and I saw it then. But I didn't go into the house."

They turned off the public road at a lane end marked with a
modest sign, a piece of painted board that announced TAR-
WHINN HOUSE. They were now on the drive up to the house, a
dirt track with only a little bit of gravel here and there. There
were potholes, filled with water from the last rain, and Isabel
slowed down to negotiate her way past them.

They rounded a large cluster of rhododendrons and the
house revealed itself. It was four storeys high and had the
small windows which marked the fortified houses which people
needed to build in those days. It looked rectangular—like a
cardboard box standing on its end—but there was a simplicity
about it which made it beautiful. The walls were pebble-dash
harling and painted with a soft terracotta-coloured wash with
just a touch of pink in it. This imparted to the house a soft
quality, a sort of luminescence, which the gentle sun of late
afternoon now caught, made glow.

"I love this place," said Jamie impulsively. "I just love it."

There were two cars parked on the edge of the large grav-elled circle at the front of the house; one was Joe and Mimi's hire car, a small red vehicle which somebody had dented at the back, and the other was the large car which Isabel remembered seeing in Edinburgh when she had first spotted Tom and Angie. She nosed her green Swedish car into position behind Joe and Mimi's car and stopped the engine.

Jamie, still in the car, looked round. "Yes," he said. "This is it."

"What?" asked Isabel. "What's it?"

"It's the place I wanted to be this weekend," said Jamie. "It's exactly what I wanted."

Isabel was not sure what to say. "Good," she said at last.

"You see," Jamie continued, struggling to release his seat belt, "I've never been invited to a house party. Not once. I almost went a few years ago when some friends rented a cottage up near Aviemore for a weekend, but they miscalculated the num-bers and two of us had to drop out. There were strict limits on the number of people who were allowed to stay, and so I didn't go. That was my house party."

Isabel laughed at this. She thought for a moment: This is where it shows, those years between us. He's *excited*. And was she? She had been to house parties before—there was nothing new in that from her point of view. But was there something else? Yes, she did feel it. She felt an anticipation, especially when she thought of what Jamie had said. This was something special for him; not just being here, but being here with her. Could she dare to think that?

They got out of the car. Jamie took both cases out of the back of the car—he had only a small weekend bag—and they walked over the gravel towards the door. Isabel looked up at the house, which seemed much taller when one was right up against it like this. These Scottish houses were really towers, small castles, and they must have seemed impregnable to their attackers. Of course there was always the possibility of a siege; it was all very well being behind three feet of solid stone, but food had to be brought in from somewhere. And then there was fire, and disease, and all the other hazards of having something to defend in lawless times.

Tom appeared as they reached the front door. "I was watching you from one of those little slots in the wall," he said. "Very useful, those. I can look all the way down the drive and see who's coming up to lay siege to me."

Isabel smiled at the joke, but then the thought came to her: *What if the threat is already inside?* Tom noticed how her expression changed suddenly, and he said, "Everything all right?"

"Yes," said Isabel quickly. "Yes. It is."

"Good," said Tom. He glanced over his shoulder—they were standing in the hall, and he looked towards a back door. "There's somebody who looks after us here. She comes with the house. Mrs. Paterson. She's made up your rooms and will show you to them."

Mrs. Paterson appeared, emerging from the doorway behind Tom. She was a middle-aged woman with a broad, weather-beaten face—the sort of face, thought Isabel, that one doesn't see in towns any more, where pallor reigns. She greeted Isabel and Jamie courteously in a Border accent and indicated for them to come upstairs.

They followed her into a corridor. "You've not been in this house before?" she asked.

"I visited the garden once," said Isabel. "Some years ago. But not the house itself."

"Oh, aye," said Mrs. Paterson. "I remember that. An awful lot of folk came out from Peebles to see the gardens. They should open them again some time. But I think that people who rent the house don't always like it. They want privacy—and who can blame them?"

"That's reasonable enough," said Isabel. "I'm not sure if I would want people traipsing through my garden, such as it is."

Mrs. Paterson made a sound that seemed like agreement. The corridor ran the length of the house, but because of the square shape of the house, it was not particularly long. Now they were at the end of it, outside a door of light, stripped pine, which Mrs. Paterson pushed open. "Your room," she said to Isabel.

She went in. Jamie stayed outside.

"You can come in too," said Mrs. Paterson, turning to Jamie. "Your room is next door. Through here." She pointed to an interconnecting door.

Jamie came in, looking embarrassed, thought Isabel. She turned away. It was a large room, with painted wood wainscoting around the walls and two windows. The floor was wooden, with wide, old boards, and there were faded Oriental rugs here and there. An ancient wardrobe, oak and irregular, stood against a far wall and there was some sort of chest of drawers opposite it. On the walls there were small, dark oil paintings of indeterminate country subjects: a hare at the edge of a field; stooks of wheat in a field; a winter landscape. There was a large double bed.

"I hope everything is all right," said Mrs. Paterson. "If you need to make tea or coffee or anything, the kitchen's off the hall you came in. You'll find everything you need there, even if I'm not around. And there's a bathroom two doors down the hall—we passed it. The hot-water pipes make a noise, but there's lots of hot water, all the time." She turned, smiled briefly at Isabel, and then left.

Isabel put her case down on the floor. Jamie had taken his case through to his room and had reappeared at the doorway between the two rooms. Now he moved over to her window and looked out.

"There's a rooks' nest in that tree," he said. "Look at them."

Isabel glanced at the tree. "It looks as if we're sharing a bathroom," she said.

Jamie looked round. "Fine," he said. He returned to the window. "We could be a hundred miles from Edinburgh out here. We could be in Argyll. It's amazing. Forty-five minutes from town."

She joined him at the window. She looked out. Behind the trees, the hill rose up sharply, green on the lower slopes and then, as the heather took over, purple and purple-red. *Sub specie aeternitatis,* she thought: In the context of eternity, this is nothing, as are all our human affairs. In the context of eternity, our anxieties, our doubts, are little things, of no significance. Or, as Herrick put it, rosebuds were there to be gathered, because really, she thought, there was no proof of life beyond this one; and all that mattered, therefore, was that happiness and love should have their chance, their brief chance, in this life, before annihilation and the nothingness to which we were all undoubtedly heading, even our sun, which was itself destined for collapse and extinction, signifying the end of the party for whosoever was left.

But she knew, even as she thought this, that we cannot lead our lives as if nothing really mattered. Our concerns might be small things, but they loomed large to us. The crushing under-foot of an ants' nest was nothing to us, but to the ants it was a cataclysmic disaster: the ruination of a city, the laying waste of a continent. There were worlds within worlds, and each will have within its confines values and meaning. It may not really matter to the world at large, thought Isabel, that I should feel happy rather than sad, but it matters to me, and the fact that it matters matters.

She decided to stop dwelling on that, because that was a question of meaning and philosophy, and philosophy and its concerns seemed so far away here.

CHAPTER SIXTEEN

THEY DID NOT SEE Joe and Mimi until they all met before dinner in the drawing room on the ground floor. This room had been sited without thought to the sun, and was north-facing, but there was a log fire in the grate—even in summer—which took the chill out of the thick stone walls. It was perfectly square, with a moulded ceiling displaying a cornucopia at each corner and four angelic heads about the central light. The furniture was right for the house—falling short of grandeur, but amounting to more than that which one might expect in a farmhouse, even a prosperous one. There was a cabinet of china, a revolving bookcase, a thin-legged walnut bureau, commodious sofas, silk cushions with chinoiserie motifs, pictures of dogs and children; the accoutrements, Isabel noted, of the Scottish country gentry. On the outer wall was what must have been the largest window in the house, under which there was an enticing window seat and a low table of glossy magazines of a rural nature, *Country Life, Scottish Field, Horse & Hound.*

Isabel imagined how quickly one might slip into such a life, content with the small rhythms, impervious to the strife and anxiety of the outside world. And could one be happy in such a

life if one came from outside? She suspected that one could—
and many were. One might be like Horace, perhaps, leaving
Rome for the consolations of his Sabine farm: the making of
wine; the writing of poetry; the anticipation of the harvest. But,
of course, it meant that one was entirely isolated from the life of
the majority of one's fellow citizens: a life of worry over all the
things that people had to worry about—crime, money, noisy
neighbours. It was better, she thought, to be of this world than
to be detached from it.

She glanced at Tom, who was standing near the drinks trolley with Joe, engaged in conversation, forgetting for a moment
Angie's request that he serve the Martinis that she and Mimi
had asked for. She wondered why they had chosen to come
here, into this world so far from Dallas. It was summer in Texas,
and Dallas was impossibly hot, but they came from an air-
conditioned world, did they not? They might not wish to remain
inside, of course, and then there was the sheer romance of Scotland, this soft, enchanting landscape with its pastel greens and
blues and its cool air. That was what they wanted; or what *he*
wanted; she was not so sure about Angie, about whether she fitted in. She's more *London,* Isabel thought: Bond Street, Mayfair, the highly refined and expensive pleasures.

Tom gestured to the drinks trolley and detached himself
from Joe. He had seen across the room, as Isabel had, the sign
from Angie, a mime of a glass tilted to the lips; not as discreet,
she thought, as the signs she had heard the Queen gave to her
staff: a slight twisting of a hand which would swiftly bring a gin
and tonic, part of an elaborate and tactful system of communi-
cation that enabled life to proceed. She had heard, too, that the
Queen liked to eat banana sandwiches, and that staff were
trained to make such sandwiches in just the right way; an

endearing touch to a public life, she thought, human simplicity in the midst of state fuss.

Tom brought Isabel's drink over to her and stayed to talk. She had worked out, now, how to look at him without having her eyes drawn to the painfully lop-sided face and to the grimace which Bell's palsy produced. By looking at the eyes, or just above them, the rest of the face became less important.

"I'm sorry about this face of mine," he said suddenly. "I know that it's hard for people." Isabel opened her mouth to protest, but he continued. "It looks very uncomfortable, you know, but it isn't. I'm aware of it, there's a certain muscular strain, but after a while it's nothing much. And I count myself lucky it's not worse."

"Of course," she said quickly. "And, really, it's nothing . . ."

He laughed. "It's not nothing. It certainly isn't. I can't bring myself to look at my photograph, you know. I say to myself, 'Oh no, that's not me, is it? I don't look quite that bad.' But then I gather that there are lots of people who can't stand looking at their own photograph, who prefer not to be seen. Probably most people, if it comes down to it."

"I'm one," said Isabel.

Tom looked surprised. "But you . . . Well, I would have thought that you would be proud of how you looked. Surely you don't have to worry."

"You're very kind, but I do. I've always thought that I'm too tall, for a start."

"Nonsense. Tall women are really attractive. I much prefer tall women."

Isabel glanced at Angie. She did not think about it, but her eyes flicked over, and then she looked back at Tom again, quickly, realising what she had done. Angie was not tall.

If Tom had noticed, he was too polite to let it show. "Tell me," he said, "do you like living in Edinburgh?"

Isabel felt a momentary irritation with him over this question. It was something one should not ask another, because it was either mundane to the extent of pointlessness, or tactless. If somebody did not like living where they lived, then that meant that they were trapped, either by marriage or some other domestic circumstance, or by a job, or by sheer inertia. Whatever the reason, if the answer to this was no, the background to that answer would be one of regret.

And there was another side to it. She had noticed that there was a tendency on the part of some Americans to believe that everybody, deep inside, wanted to live in America, and that it was inexplicable that people who could do so did not. And here was Isabel, half-American, and therefore in a position, one might assume, to live in America, living, instead, in Scotland. Was Tom one of those Americans? she asked herself.

"Of course I like it," she said. She hoped that her answer had not revealed her irritation, but she decided that it probably had, as he drew back slightly. She reached out to touch him. "Sorry. That sounds rather defensive. I do like it. But I'd be happy living in other places, I suspect. New York. Charlottesville, Virginia. To name just two. I'm sure I'd be happy there."

Her reply had the desired effect. "You might have thought that I was implying it was an odd decision to live in Edinburgh," he said. "Anything but. I'd love to live somewhere like that."

"Well, let me ask you, then, are you happy living in Dallas? Or even, why do you live in Dallas?"

His reply came quickly. "Because I'm from there, which is the reason most people live where they live, isn't it? Isn't that so all over the world?"

"It probably is. Most people don't choose to be where they are. They're just there." She paused. "But what about my other question? Are you happy there?"

This time his answer was slower in coming. He stared down into his glass, and Isabel knew that she should not have asked him.

"I'm sure you are," she said, before he could answer. "And I can understand why. It's comfortable. It's safe. There are things to keep you busy. Your friends are there." She knew, though, that true as those factors might have been, they were outranked by something else. And that, she thought, is not the usual thing—an unhappy marriage; it was that less common phenomenon—an unhappy engagement.

They talked about other things. He asked her about Scotland, and she realised that he had read widely on Scottish history, more widely, perhaps, than she had. One could not do everything, she thought defensively; it was difficult enough keeping up with what was being written in her branch of philosophy, let alone in other areas.

She looked over to the other side of the room, where Joe and Mimi were standing with Angie and Jamie. Mimi was saying something to Angie, and Joe, she saw, was staring at the picture above the fireplace. He did not look bored—he was too polite for that—but Isabel could not help smiling at Joe's expression. He looked as he did when he wanted to be elsewhere: slightly bemused. And he would have stood through many pre-dinner conversations with Dallas women, thought Isabel, and he would have been scrupulously courteous through all of them.

Angie, she saw, was studying her glass as Mimi spoke and

then, just briefly, she looked at Jamie, sideways—away from Mimi, but Isabel noticed.

"So," said Tom. "What do you think about that? I'd be interested to hear your views, since you live here."

Isabel had not heard the question. "I'm sorry," she said. "I was away with the fairies."

"Excuse me?"

"I'm sorry. That's a Scottish expression. It means that my thoughts were elsewhere. People used to talk a lot about the fairies in Scotland, especially in the Highlands. You probably wondered what I was going on about."

She saw his mouth shift, almost painfully, but she realised, from his eyes that he was smiling. "One would be careful about that expression back home," he said. "It might be misunderstood."

"Of course," said Isabel. "Two countries separated by the same language."

They lapsed into silence. Isabel was aware that he was staring at her, as if studying her, and she looked away in her embarrassment. Mimi had turned to Joe and he was saying something to her; Angie was now facing Jamie and was looking up at him. There was no mistaking her interest, Isabel decided; the body language was too obvious. She felt a pang of jealousy, primitive and acute, but then she thought: That is how any woman would be in the presence of Jamie. It could be expected from anybody, but certainly from somebody like Angie, who was obviously interested in men. She was a woman who would appreciate male beauty—of course she would—and she would not have met anybody like Jamie before, with his gentleness, that special Scottish gentleness. Texan men were not usually like that. But,

but . . . she imagined herself facing Angie and saying, *Sorry, he's mine, you know; he's not available. Sorry.*

Angie suddenly looked at her watch and announced, so that all might hear, that dinner would spoil if they did not go through.

Tom put down his glass. He nodded to Isabel and crossed the room to whisper something to Angie. Isabel watched Angie's expression. It changed, and then changed again as she listened to Tom. And what human emotions, she wondered, were written there? Boredom. Duty. Frustration. She paused. And resentment? Yes. Resentment that the wrong man was at her side.

For a moment Isabel felt sympathy for Angie. There were so many women—and, one might assume, men—for whom that could be said. So many of us had the wrong person at our side, and lived a life of regret at the fact. Loyalty kept people together—loyalty, and money, and sheer emotional inertia. But then, these were relationships which started with optimism and love and conviction that they were right. This, by contrast, was one which was starting, Isabel thought, through calculated greed and social ambition. And that, she felt, was undeserving of a great deal of sympathy. Angie should get out of it now. She should be honest with herself, admit her motives, and then say goodbye to Tom and to her ill-placed ambitions. But she has no intention of doing that, thought Isabel. She has something very different in mind.

AFTER DINNER they returned to the drawing room. Somebody had put more wood on the fire—the housekeeper, perhaps—and the flames were high, throwing dancing light on the dark Belouchi rug in front of the hearth. Coffee cups, small bone-china cans, were set out on a tray, with bitter chocolate mints to one side.

There was brief, inconsequential conversation, and then Isabel and Jamie went to the piano.

"Something Scottish," said Tom. "Please. Something Scottish."

Isabel nodded in his direction, then turned to Jamie as she sat on the piano stool. "Sing for your supper?"

"No alternative," muttered Jamie. But he was incapable of being churlish, and he smiled encouragingly as she opened the book of Scottish songs and put it on the piano.

Isabel pointed at the music and Jamie nodded. "Very suitable," he said.

" 'The Bonnie Earl of Moray,' " Isabel announced. "This is not exactly a cheerful song—sorry about that—but it's rather haunting, in its way. In fact, it's a lament, and a lot of Scottish music is about how things have gone wrong, about what might have been if things had turned out a bit better."

Mimi laughed at this. "Isn't that the same as country and western?" she asked. "All those songs about unfaithful women and faithful dogs."

"Perhaps," said Isabel. She played a few chords and turned to Jamie, who nodded. He stood by the piano, ready to sing.

When they reached the end of the song, and the last notes of the piano accompaniment, Mimi clasped her hands together, as if to clap, but did not, because everybody else was silent. Angie was staring at Jamie, and Tom, who had been watching Isabel's hands on the keyboard, was now looking at Angie. Joe had his hands folded on his lap and was looking at the ceiling, at one of the plaster cornucopias.

Isabel broke the silence. "The bonnie earl of Moray was murdered, alas," she said. "The earl of Huntly slayed him, and then laid him on the green, as the words have it."

"It's very sad," muttered Angie. "Very sad . . . very sad for his family."

Jamie caught Isabel's eye. He was daring her to laugh, but she looked down at the keys of the piano, and depressed one, a B-flat, gently, not enough for it to sound.

"Yes," said Isabel. "He was a much-loved man, I believe. And there's a line there, you know, which is very intriguing. *He was a braw gallant, and he played at the glove.* Apparently that means that he played real tennis—not lawn tennis, but real tennis. That's the game with those strange racquets and the ball that you hit off the roof. At first they played it by hitting the ball with their hands. Then they started to use a glove. Racquets came much later. There's still a real tennis court at Falkland Palace."

"We went there," said Tom, "didn't we, Angie? Over on the way to St. Andrews. Falkland Palace. There was an orchard—remember?—and that peculiar tennis court was there. That's where James V died, just after Mary, Queen of Scots, was born. Remember? He just turned his face to the wall and died because he thought that everything was lost. They told us about it—that woman who showed us around."

Angie frowned. She looked confused. "Which woman?"

Jamie came to her rescue. "I'd like to sing another song," he said. "This is by Robert Burns, and is one which you all will know. 'My love is like a red, red rose.' "

While Isabel paged through the book, Tom said, "That's a beautiful song. Really beautiful." He was sitting next to Angie on the sofa near the fire and now, as Isabel played the first bars of the introduction, he took Angie's hand in his. Isabel, half watching, half attending to the printed music, thought it was possible that Tom knew exactly what Angie had in mind when she accepted his offer of marriage, but had decided that she might grow to love him because love can come if you believe in it and behave as if it exists. That was the case, too, with free will; with, perhaps, faith of any sort; and love was a sort of faith, was it not?

But then she glanced at Angie, and she changed her mind again. *She would prefer him not to be around,* she thought. *That is when she would love him. She would love him much more then.*

CHAPTER SEVENTEEN

SHE AWOKE in the small hours of the morning, barely three, and heard him breathing beside her, that quiet, vulnerable sound, so human. Her pillow had slipped off the side of the bed and her head was against a ruffled undersheet. She was turned away from him; away, too, from the window through which the dim light of a sky that was never truly dark in the summer made its way through the gaps in the curtains. She was immediately wide awake, her mind clear, but she closed her eyes and drew the sheet up. It was warm; there was no need of blankets in that still air.

She went over what had happened. After the music the evening had come to an end. Mimi had been tired and said that she and Joe would go upstairs; Angie had looked at her watch and said that she, too, wanted to go to bed. Jamie had said, "I'm going to have a walk outside. Isabel? What about you?"

It was not an invitation that included Tom, and Isabel felt embarrassed, but then she thought that Tom would imagine he had been spoken for by Angie, who had declared that she was heading for bed. She said goodnight to Angie and saw that the other woman was looking at Jamie, and then at her, and was smiling. For a moment she wondered whether she knew what Isabel felt for him. Mimi had divined it; perhaps it was glaringly obvious.

She and Jamie had gone out together. It was half past ten and there was still enough light to see the details of the trees that clung to the side of the hills. And they could see, too, the sheep still grazing beside the dry-stane dyke that intersected the field at the bottom of the slope. There was a path that ran off the driveway beside the rhododendrons, which they had followed, Jamie leading, gravel underfoot, and twigs, too, pine needles, cones.

She had shivered, not because it was cold—it was not, and she did not feel the need of a coat—but because she was with Jamie and she felt that she would have to speak to him now, before they went any further. He could hardly have forgotten about their room; had he thought about what might happen?

"Jamie."

He was a few paces ahead of her on the path. Somewhere, not far away, there was a small burn descending from the hill above; there was the sound of water.

He turned round and smiled at her. "What an odd evening," he said.

She looked up at him. It was not all that odd; different, perhaps, from evenings they had spent together in Edinburgh, but not odd.

"Don't you think that we should talk?" she said. Her voice had a catch in it, out of nervousness, and she thought: I sound petulant. A philosopher in the countryside, where talking was not always necessary.

He looked surprised. "We've been talking all night, haven't we?" He paused, and his smile now was conspiratorial, as if he was about to confess a suppressed thought. "Or, should I say, Angie was. Did you hear her at your end of the table? That woman can talk. I hardly had to say anything."

No, thought Isabel, not that. "I didn't mean that. I meant that we should talk about what seems to be happening between us."

He was standing very close to a branch of a pine tree that had grown across the path, almost obstructing it. Somebody else had snapped off part of it and the pieces lay at the side of the path. He suddenly reached up and broke off a twig. It was something for his hands to do, something to mask the awkwardness of the moment.

He hesitated for a while before replying. "I'm not sure that anything's happening between us," he said eventually. "Or nothing that wasn't happening before."

He seemed to be searching her face for a clue, and, watching him, Isabel felt a momentary impatience. He was not a sixteen-year-old boy. He was twenty-something. He had had affairs. He knew.

"Look," she said. "Do you mind if I put it simply? Do you want to sleep with me? Do you?"

His eyes were downcast, looking at the path, at the litter of pine cones. Her words were hanging in the air, with the sharp scent of the pine cones and the sound of the burn somewhere near. I've shocked him, she thought; and she was secretly appalled.

He shrugged. "I . . ."

"You don't have to."

"No. I want to."

"Yes?"

"Yes. I said yes. Yes."

They went back.

SHE THOUGHT: How beautiful he is lying there. I have never seen anything as beautiful, never, than this young man, with his smooth skin and there, just visible, the shape of his ribs. I can place my hand there, against his chest, and feel the human heart beating.

He opened his eyes.

"You're awake too." She moved her hand upwards to rest against the side of his face. You are mine entirely, she thought; now, at this moment, you are mine entirely, but you will not be for long, Jamie, because I do not possess you. Oh my darling, darling Jamie, I wish I could possess you, but now, more than ever, I do not.

"Oh," he said. That was all: "Oh." And then, turning his head so that he looked into her eyes, he said, "I'm very sorry, Isabel."

"Sorry?" She touched his cheek again. "Why say that? You don't have to be sorry for anything."

"I rather . . . rather rushed things. Maybe you didn't want . . ."

She was surprised, and drew in her breath. Rushed?

He lifted his head and rested it against his hand, elbow-propped. "Have I upset you?" he asked.

"Of course not. Of course you haven't upset me, Jamie. Dear Jamie. No. Not at all."

"Then . . ."

She could not help but feast upon the sight of him: such perfection, clean—like a boy—with no spare flesh.

Then she whispered, "Of course you didn't. Don't be so silly. I was hoping . . . Yes, I was, I suppose. I hoped that this might happen."

She watched him as he thought about this.

"I'm very fond of you," he said.

"I know that."

He lay back again and looked up at the ceiling. "I'll never forget this. This."

"And neither shall I. Never. *Not a kiss nor look be lost.*"

"That poem?"

She nodded. "That most gravely beautiful of poems. I told you about it before." She would remember, too, with each memory folded and put away, like much-loved clothing in a drawer.

CHAPTER EIGHTEEN

Tom did not surprise isabel. She had not imagined that he would be one to sit inside and read, and he was not. Etiquette required that guests should not be forced to participate in activities that might not be to their taste. The possibility of a walk after breakfast was raised, "but people might want to do something completely different," Tom said quickly; what that was would be left to them. What, Isabel wondered, was completely different from a walk; only an activity that involved immobility would be completely different, and could immobility be an activity? It was a state, surely. She caught Jamie's eye over the breakfast table; he was sitting opposite her. The breakfast table, she reflected, was the test: regret, shame, the desire to forget—such were the emotions which might emerge in circumstances like these, but they hadn't. Things had changed between her and Jamie—of course they had—but there were none of those feelings as they sat at breakfast, only a warm fondness, something close to euphoria, or that is what Isabel felt.

"I'm going to go up the hill," said Tom, looking out the window at the cloudless sky. "It's about two hours there and back."

"And there are great views up at the top," said Angie. "You look out and you can see all the way down to . . ." She trailed off.

"You might be able to see the Eildons in the distance," said Jamie, adding, "maybe."

"You can," said Tom. "Walter Scott country. And Edinburgh too—a sort of smudge in the distance."

"Edinburgh is not a smudge," said Isabel.

Tom smiled, and bowed his head. "Of course not. How rude of me."

Angie looked at her watch. "I'll walk tomorrow," she said. "I want to go into Peebles."

Tom looked at her. Isabel noticed that he did not seem disappointed, but then a walk was a small thing.

"Isabel?" Tom said. "Are you coming for a walk? Jamie?"

Jamie looked across the table at Isabel. He was answering Tom, but looking at her. "Do you mind if I don't?" He gave no reason.

"Why not come to Peebles with me?" said Angie quickly. "I need somebody to help me carry heavy things. That is, if you don't mind . . ."

Jamie smiled. "I don't. Not at all."

Tom turned sharply. It seemed that he was going to say something to Angie, but he apparently thought better of it. Isabel wondered whether he was feeling annoyed about Angie's shopping sprees; heavy purchases sounded ominous and expensive. Another racehorse? Or a large bronze bust from an antique shop? She imagined Jamie staggering under the weight of a bust of Sir Walter Scott, trailing behind Angie through the streets of Peebles. But then she wondered if it was not resentment of Angie's shopping, but jealousy of her time and company. She

had declined to go on a walk with him and had invited Jamie to
go to town with her instead, rather quickly, Isabel thought. Any
man who saw his fiancée taking such obvious delight in the
company of an attractive young man must feel something, she
decided; unless, of course, that man was so secure in the loyalty
of the fiancée that it would not occur to him that there might be
anything but innocent pleasure for her in the company of the
younger man.

Joe and Mimi had their own plans. Joe, with unfailing
instinct, had located an antiquarian book dealer who lived
nearby and had arranged for them to visit him and have lunch
at the Peebles Hydro, a vast Edwardian hotel overlooking the
mouth of the Tweed Valley. The walk, then, would be done only
by Isabel and Tom.

"It's not compulsory," said Tom. "You really don't have to
traipse up there with me if you'd prefer to stay down here."

"I want to," she said. And she did. Angie might be unre-
warding company, but Tom was not; Isabel found him intriguing. And not the least of the interest was this: Why had he
become involved with Angie? Not that she could imagine that
being a subject of conversation, but light might be shed on his
character during the walk, and Isabel had a distinct sense that
Tom wanted to talk to her. There was something in the way in
which he looked at her which suggested that there were things
waiting to be said. And what, she wondered, would these be?
Nothing, she decided. You're imagining things—again.

Jamie agreed to meet Angie in the hall in fifteen minutes
and went upstairs. Isabel went too, a little later, and found Jamie
struggling with the zip of a light windcheater.

"It could rain," he said, looking out of a window towards the hill. "Make sure that you have something to put on up there. You know how things can change on the hills. One moment it's summer, then it's semi-arctic. Our delightful Scottish climate."

She moved forward and took over the struggle with the zip, which she eased past its obstruction. Her hand remained against the front of the garment, gentle against his chest. She looked up and into his eyes. There was light in them, and she wanted only to embrace him. She did not want him to go away; she wanted him to stay. She did not want to be anywhere but with him, because now, at last, she felt a happiness so complete that it was a mystery in its own right. Simple love, she thought, not a mystery, but the vision of *Eros*.

He leaned forward.

"My beautiful one," she whispered.

"Isabel."

"My beautiful one," she said. "Be careful of the rain."

"You too."

"NOT EVERYBODY UNDERSTANDS," remarked Tom during a pause halfway up the hill. "Not everybody understands why I should feel as I do about this country. I have a brother who has no interest—none at all—in Scotland. Even when I show him the papers that spell it out—how our people came from here, their names, the places they lived. He shrugs and says, 'A long time ago—we're Americans now.' How can anybody be so indifferent to the past?"

"It depends on the past," said Isabel. "Some people find the past just too painful. What if you come from a past that is full of unhappiness and indignity? A place in Russia or Poland where there have been pogroms and oppression? Would you want to be reminded of that? I'm not sure I would."

Tom used the end of his stick to prise an encrustation of mud off his boots. "Maybe. But don't you think that it's breaking faith with the people who had to put up with all that—to ignore, to forget about them now? And anyway, there's nothing like that in being from here. Our Scottish ancestors weren't miserable."

Isabel looked at him with incredulity. Texans, she thought, were at least realistic; did Tom not know what it was actually like? Having read as much as he seemed to have done about Scottish history, he surely could not believe that. She watched him scrape the rest of the mud off his boots and then wipe the stick clean on a clump of heather beside the path.

"I don't know how to put this," she said, "but those distinguished Scottish ancestors you've unearthed—they weren't exactly angels, you know. They can't have been; not if they were at all prominent. All the leading Scottish families were just a bunch of rogues. They plotted and raided and disposed of one another with utter abandon—utter abandon. The Sicilians could teach them nothing. Nothing."

Tom stared at her, and for a moment Isabel regretted what she had said. We have to believe in something, and a belief in the goodness of the place from which one had sprung, or one's ancestors had sprung, was one of the ways of arming oneself against the cold knowledge that it would all be over in a moment and was nothing anyway. Meaning—that's what we need, and if it helps to be Irish or Scottish or Jewish, or anything, for that matter, then we should let people believe in these scraps of identity.

"Of course one shouldn't make too much of it," said Isabel.

"Not everybody was ruthless. There were saints too—lots of
them. It's just that it's difficult to find many figures in Scottish
history who didn't have blood on their hands. You mentioned
Mary, Queen of Scots, Mary Stuart."

"She was wronged," said Tom quickly. "And she didn't kill
her husband."

"Darnley? No, there's no evidence that she blew him up.
But since you mention him, let's not forget that he was himself
a murderer. He was in on the plot to kill Mary's Italian secretary,
wasn't he? And when his friends came into the room he grabbed
Mary and pinioned her while they dragged Rizzio away from her.
He did. That's on the record. Which makes him a murderer."

It was not one of Edinburgh's most successful dinner parties, she thought. Mary Stuart had invited her guests to a room
off her bedroom in the Palace of Holyrood. The guest list was
small: her illegitimate brother, Lord Robert Stewart, and his
wife; the Laird of Creich; Sir Arthur Erskine; and, at the other
end of the table, David Rizzio. Rizzio was dressed in a gown
of fur-trimmed damask, a doublet of satin, and velvet hose.
He wore a cap, too, by permission of the Queen, which was
resented by those who had to remove their headgear in the presence of the monarch (everybody else, except Darnley, who was
married to Mary). The loutish Scottish lords came into the room
and seized Rizzio, who burst into Italian, and then French, in
his desperation. *Giustizia! Giustizia! Madame, sauve ma vie!* She
could not; she was just the half-French queen of a nation of
boisterous men. They stabbed him again and again, again and
again.

Tom pointed to the top of the hill, which still looked far
away. Now they would have to leave the path, a glorified sheep
track, as it followed the contour of the hill and they needed to

climb. They set out, making their way slowly over low heather. A female grouse broke cover suddenly, cackling in alarm, running along the ground, head lowered, to avoid what she thought would be her murderers. Isabel looked at her in pity, and felt a sudden tenderness, brought on by love. Love paints the world, she thought, enables us to see its beauty, its vulnerability, its preciousness. If we are filled with love, we cannot hate, or destroy; there is no room for such things. She closed her eyes for a moment, a dizzying moment, and she was back in that room, with Jamie beside her and the half-light of the summer sky outside, and her heart full of that very love she felt now.

"Are you all right?" Tom had stopped and was looking at her with concern. "Tell me if this is too steep."

She reassured him that she was fine, that she had only been thinking of something and had closed her eyes because of that. "I'm perfectly all right with this. I walk a lot in town, you know. I'm fit enough."

"Not everyone can climb a hill," said Tom. "We're so used to our cars. Our legs . . . well, we're forgetting how to use them. Or that's the way it is in Dallas. I try to walk as much as I can. I have a place out near Tyler. A nice bit of land. I've never managed to get the house as I want it. It's in the wrong place, but my hands are tied. I'd like to knock it down and build again, but it was left to me and my sister jointly. Her husband won't let her agree."

"And Angie? Does she do much walking?" asked Isabel. Angie had not been mentioned, and this was a chance to bring her into the conversation.

"She mostly drives," said Tom. "But she plays tennis from time to time. She'd like to do more of that when we're married."

"I see," said Isabel. She looked up at the sky; the rain was holding off, but was there in the distance, in the heavy purple clouds over East Lothian and the sea beyond. "Have you known her for long?" The question was innocent, even banal; casual conversation on a walk between two friends who wanted to get to know each other better.

"A year," said Tom, appearing to think. Sometimes we inflate times to make things seem better for us. "Or not quite."

"You must have a lot in common," said Isabel.

Tom did not answer immediately. Then he said, "Some things."

Isabel made light of this. "Well, that's a start. You'll develop fresh interests together, no doubt. That's so important in marriage. Without interests in common, well, I'm not sure what the point is." That was as far as she could go, too far perhaps. Tom just nodded. He did not say anything.

When they reached the top of the hill, the view was as Tom had said it would be. There were blue Border hills in the distance and there, in the other direction, were the Pentland Hills, with Edinburgh just beyond, Arthur's Seat a tiny, crouching lion. They sat down to get their breath back and Isabel laid back, looking up into the empty sky. The world is in constant flux, said the Buddhists, and she thought of this as she looked into the blue void; she imagined she could see the particles in the air, the rushing, swimming movement, the passage of the winds. Nothing was empty; it only appeared to be so. And then she thought: I am in a state of bliss. I am in love. Again. Finally.

JAMIE BOUGHT Isabel a jar of honey. It had been his only purchase in Peebles; a jar of honey which he placed in her hands with a smile. "Made by bees," he said.

Angie was watching as he did this. Her face was impassive. She had found an antique dealer and bought a small, marble-topped French table, which Jamie had uncomplainingly carried to the car—it had been heavy—and one of those Victorian bottles filled with coloured sand to make a striped effect.

"What's the point of that?" Jamie had asked.

"None," replied Angie. "It's a bottle with sand in it."

Tom showed a polite interest in Angie's purchases, but Isabel could see that they meant nothing to him.

"We're going to ship a lot of things back at the end of the summer," he said. "Angie's going to redecorate the house."

Angie stared at Isabel, as if expecting her to contradict this.

"I'm sure it will be very attractive," said Isabel. "And you're choosing the things yourself. Some people . . ." She almost said *some rich people* but stopped herself in time. "Some people get decorators to choose everything for them. Furniture, paintings—the lot."

"I couldn't live with that sort of thing," said Angie. "Another person's taste."

Isabel wondered if she was going to get rid of all of Tom's possessions when she moved in. And she thought that he might be thinking this, too, as he began to say something but was interrupted by Mimi, who started to talk about somebody in Dallas whom they both knew who had spent a year, and a fortune, searching for old possessions that had been mistakenly thrown out. He had tracked them down eventually and taken them back to the house. "Such loyalty," she said. "It was like old friends being reunited."

The conversation drifted off in other directions. They were all in the drawing room, drinking tea, which Mrs. Paterson had brought in from the kitchen and placed on a sideboard. As she did so, she turned to Isabel and whispered, "May I have a quick word with you, please?" She nodded briefly in the direction of the door and then left. Isabel, standing near the sideboard, took a few sips of her tea and then put down the cup and saucer and followed Mrs. Paterson.

The hall was empty, but the door that led off down the kitchen corridor was ajar. Isabel went through it and walked down the corridor. A child's rocking horse and a small, old-fashioned pedal car had been stored in the passageway. The rocking horse, with tangled mane, was painted off-white and was scratched with use; the pedal car was British racing green, with red leather seats. Both looked dusty, as if abandoned a long time ago by the children who had once loved them. Children, like cats, made a house into a home, and the echoes of their presence lingered.

Mrs. Paterson was standing near the large kitchen window, wiping her hands on a dish towel. She turned round when Isabel came into the room.

"Thank you, Miss Dalhousie," she said. "I couldn't speak to you through there. And when I looked for you this morning, you had already gone."

"Tom and I went for a walk," she explained. "There's a wonderful view from the top of that hill. We saw for miles and miles."

Mrs. Paterson nodded. "Willy liked that," she said. "My late husband. He was the factor here when this place was run as a proper estate. Though calling him the factor sounds a bit grand. There was only one other man working here, who looked after the sheep. Willy did the forester's job, too, because everything was so run down. Then when he died they stopped doing anything and just let out the land to the sheep farmer down the road, and I look after the house for the owners."

"You do a very good job," said Isabel, looking about the well-ordered kitchen, with its rows of gleaming copper saucepans and well-blacked skillets.

"I try my best. But it's tough work when we have the short lets. The Bruces are no trouble, because they're here for so long. And they're easy people to get on with."

Isabel nodded. "But you wanted to talk to me about something . . ."

Mrs. Paterson put down the dish towel. "I'm so embarrassed about this," she said. "You see, Angie asked me this morning to put some bottled water in your rooms. She said that there should be a bottle in your room and one in that young man's room too. Jamie, isn't it? Well, I said that you were sharing now. I didn't think, I just said it. And she was very surprised. I thought I shouldn't have mentioned anything. You see, when I made up the room . . ."

Isabel shook her head. "Don't worry about that," she said. "It's not important. It really isn't." She paused. "Being in adjoining rooms proved very convenient."

Mrs. Paterson looked up sharply. "Oh?"

Isabel shrugged. It was too late now to sidestep the issue. "Well, I suppose I'm just telling you the truth. We have to do that, you know. I could lie to you and pretend that I was embarrassed but I wasn't. It provoked a conversation between us, you see. And he stayed. Last night was the first time we were together."

Mrs. Paterson made a gesture with her hand which Isabel could not interpret. Was this shock? she wondered. A gesture of disapproval? People in Edinburgh might tolerate things which people in the more conservative Scottish countryside would not. Taking a younger lover might be just the sort of thing of which Mrs. Paterson might have a low opinion.

The older woman turned away for a moment and stared out of the window. Then she turned round again. "I'm sorry," she said. "Your private affairs are none of my concern."

"But I mentioned them to you," said Isabel.

Mrs. Paterson nodded. "That's true, I suppose that you did." She paused. "May I ask you something, Miss Dalhousie? Would you mind?"

Isabel wondered what the question might be. It was probably Jamie's age that she was interested in finding out. "Of course you can ask me."

"I know I'm older than you," began Mrs. Paterson. "But . . . but do you think that if I went to Edinburgh I might be able to find a young man like that? Do you think I'd have a chance?"

"Would you like me to help you?" asked Isabel. She burst out laughing, as did the other woman. They both knew that neither was serious, but Isabel thought, What if she said yes? How would I do it? And that question prompted another in her mind. How on earth had she found Jamie? How had that marvellous, improbable event happened? It was luck, surely, on the same scale as winning the lottery, or any of those things that were against wild, impossible odds, but which happened from time to time and made one believe in the operation of providence.

She returned to the drawing room. Joe and Mimi had gone for a rest before dinner; the country air, Mimi said, made one feel sleepy. Isabel agreed. She could have gone to sleep, she thought, on top of the hill when she had been lying there looking at the sky. She had done that once in Ireland one summer, with John Liamor, at the end of a long walk; they had lain down exhausted in a field one evening and woken up when it was dark and the sky was filled with stars. They had both been so struck by the beauty of the experience that they had said nothing about it, and now, strangely, when she thought about it she thought of John without that bitterness that had accompanied her memories of him.

Jamie was paging through a magazine. Tom and Angie were seated on a sofa.

"Well," said Jamie, putting down the magazine. "I'm going upstairs."

Isabel stayed where she was. Angie, she noticed, was watching her. She could not leave the room behind him—not now.

"Dinner is at seven-thirty," said Angie, transferring her gaze to Jamie. "Drinks at seven."

As Jamie acknowledged the information, Isabel, who had poured herself a fresh cup of tea, fiddled with her teaspoon. Then Angie said, "Is everything all right up there? Are you comfortable enough?"

Jamie was on the point of leaving the room. He stopped. "Yes," he said quickly. "Yes, it's fine."

"I'll come up and check on everything," said Angie. "I've left the arrangements to Mrs. Paterson, but I should see that everything's all right."

Jamie threw a glance at Isabel, and she looked at him helplessly.

"Don't worry," he said. "Everything's fine. Mrs. Paterson has looked after us very well."

"Yes," said Isabel. "Very well. You're lucky to have her."

Angie looked at Isabel, but only for a moment before she turned away, as if Isabel's intervention was hardly worth noticing. She put down her cup and rose to her feet. "I'll come with you."

Tom appeared uninterested in this conversation. He said to Isabel, "Do you know the Falls of Clyde?"

"The Falls of Clyde?" She was thinking of what Angie might do when she went upstairs. Did it matter at all that she had been told that her guests, whom she thought were merely acquainted, were occupying the same room? What business was it of hers? None, Isabel decided. In fact, it would probably do her good to be reminded of this, as it might lessen the eyeing up of Jamie which was going on. Was Tom completely unaware of that? Had he not noticed?

Jamie left the room, with Angie just behind him. Poor Jamie, thought Isabel. He's embarrassed about this. I have no need to feel awkward, but it must be different for him. She thought of the reason for this. It was the way that people looked at these things—from the outside. The younger man was seen as being used. Always. That's the way people thought.

She was not using him. And she would not hold on to him; she knew that there would come a time when one of them would need to let go—and it would be him. When that time came she would not stop him. But it was not yet. And it did not matter what the world thought of her. If people wanted to talk of cradle-snatching, they were welcome to do so.

CHAPTER NINETEEN

ON MONDAY, back in Edinburgh, she spent three hours at her desk and made a good dent in the submissions pile. There was an awkward letter to deal with, too, which took almost an hour: a letter from a member of the editorial board expressing concern about the direction the *Review* was taking. Since they had appointed this new member, a young professor from the University of British Columbia, he had written to Isabel four times. Normally she did not hear from the members of the editorial board, some of whom she suspected were only dimly aware that they were members and who never raised any issues. But this professor took his membership seriously and had a keen eye for what he saw as deviations from the main purpose of the journal. *We are a journal of applied ethics,* he wrote to Isabel. *There are plenty of journals that cover moral theory—our job is to look at the application of ethics to concrete situations: the real problems of real people doing real jobs.*

At his suggestion they had devoted an entire issue to lifeboat ethics. The discussion had been concerned with the decisions that one had to make in a lifeboat about who was allowed in and who should remain on the sinking ship if there were not enough seats. And then, once the lifeboat was launched and began to ride too low in the water, who would be thrown out. Should the oldest go first? How would one choose between the loafer and the hard-working doctor? And what if the people in the boat became really hungry and had no alternative but to eat one of their number?

Highly unlikely, another member of the editorial board had written to Isabel. Should we not concentrate on the problems of the real world?

And Isabel had replied:

I'm sorry to have to take issue with you on this, but I assure you that these questions have arisen in the real world. The case of the Mignonette *was very well documented, and it is just one example. A small group of sailors was ship-wrecked and found themselves in a lifeboat with the cabin boy. They drifted around for some time, becoming hungrier and hungrier, and eventually, in sheer desperation, two of them decided to kill and eat the cabin boy. This they did, and then, as luck would have it, help steamed over the horizon. The sailors were taken back to England and charged with murder. They argued that they were driven to do what they did through sheer necessity, but the criminal courts took a different view and they were convicted of murder and sentenced to death. Fortunately they were not hanged, and had to serve only short prison sentences. That happened.*

This had drawn a swift response. You said "fortunately" they were not hanged, wrote her correspondent. Aren't you justifying murder? By what principle can I kill an innocent person to save my own life?

I am *not* saying that, Isabel replied. I said that it was fortunate that they were not hanged because I have a very strong objection to the death penalty. Killing another as a punishment is an act of barbarism. It's as simple as that. And it also shows a terrible lack of forgiveness. That is why I said that it was fortunate that those two men were not hanged.

The reply came. I see. I stand corrected. But the point remains: Can you kill another to save your life even if your victim is not responsible for creating the threat to your life in the first place? That's the question.

The lifeboat issue had grown, and had eventually become two issues of the *Review*. And the focus moved from real lifeboats, which were, fortunately, manned by sailors rather than by philosophers, to the earth as lifeboat, which it was, in a way. And here the issues became very much ones of the real world, Isabel thought, because real people did die every day, in very large numbers, because the resources of the lifeboat were not fairly distributed. And if we might feel squeamish about throwing a real and immediate person out of a real lifeboat, then we had fewer compunctions about doing those things which had exactly that effect, somewhere far off, on people whom we did not know and could not name. It was relentless and harrowing—if one ever came round to thinking about it—but most of our luxuries were purchased at the expense of somebody's suffering and deprivation elsewhere.

She stopped work at twelve. The house was quiet, as Grace had the day off and Joe and Mimi were not due back from Tarwhinn House until that evening, having spent an extra night there. Isabel had returned with Jamie late on Sunday afternoon, driving back to Edinburgh in her green Swedish car in silence. It was not an awkward silence, though; neither, it seemed, felt the need to talk. Jamie had reached across and touched her lightly on the arm, and smiled, and she had smiled back at him; everything that they wished to say had been said earlier that weekend and it was as if they were replete.

But now Isabel felt restless. She could stay and have lunch in the house, but she did not relish the thought of sitting there by herself. What she wanted to do was to phone Jamie, just to hear his voice, but she could not do that as he was in rehearsals all day. And she thought, too, that it would be the wrong thing to do. She should not appear too keen . . . She stopped, and smiled. When had she last thought like this? Fifteen, sixteen— the age at which one spent hours pondering the reactions of boys to one's tactics. No, of course it was different; this was mature reflection, this was realism. Jamie would not want to feel crowded, and she would not crowd him.

She decided that she would have lunch at Cat's delicatessen. It was often quiet during Monday lunchtime for some reason, and she was sure to find at least one of the tables free. And she could offer to lend a hand in the early afternoon if Cat wanted a break; when she had run the delicatessen while Cat had been in Italy she had developed a taste for it and was happy now to help out when she had the time. Of course, Cat's new employee, Miranda, might be there, so there might be no need.

Miranda *was* there, standing behind the counter serving a customer while Eddie sliced ham with the electric slicer. He looked up and Isabel's blood ran cold; she hated that slicer, with its whirring circular blade, and she cringed each time she saw it. It had the same effect on her as the sound of chalk on a blackboard will have on others, or pumice stone on the surface of a bath: a chilling, nerve-wrangling effect. Eddie should not take his eyes off the ham, he should not; although the slicer had a protective device which meant that it would be difficult to remove a whole finger, it could still remove a top if one were not careful. She winced. When she was young there had been a butcher in Morningside Road who, as was common with butchers in those days, had cut off two fingers. He used to amuse children by placing the stub of one of them into his ear, or occasionally at the entrance to a nostril, and this caused boys to laugh with delight and girls to squeal with horror and disgust. There were no butchers like that any more; a lesson, somewhere, had been learned; the state had intervened.

Isabel pointed to the slicer and grimaced. "Careful," she mouthed.

Eddie smiled and returned to his work, sending shavings of Parma ham down onto a square of greaseproof paper below. The customer whom he was serving watched the process intently.

When she had finished serving the customer, Miranda came over to the table where Isabel had sat down and greeted her warmly.

"I've worked here two days already," she said. "And it's great. Cat's a great boss, and Eddie's a sweetie, he really is." She lowered her voice. "At first I thought that there was something wrong with him, I really did. Then I think he realised that I wasn't going to bite his head off and he was really nice to me. He showed me where everything is and he . . . Well, he was just very helpful."

"He's a bit shy," said Isabel. "But we like him very much."

"Has he got a girlfriend?" asked Miranda.

Isabel was slightly taken aback by this question. Was Miranda interested in Eddie? That seemed a bit unlikely; she could hardly imagine Eddie with this outgoing Australian, but then perhaps that was what Eddie needed—a girl who would make the first move. She could not imagine his making the first move, or indeed any move. Or was there another reason for the question: a veiled enquiry as to whether Eddie was interested in girls at all?

Isabel glanced across the room. Eddie had finished with the ham and was busy measuring out stoned black olives into a small white tub. She had felt that she had got to know Eddie better when they had worked together, but when she asked herself what she knew about him—about what he did in his spare time, about who his friends were—she came to the realisation that it was very little. He sometimes went to the cinema on Lothian Road—he had mentioned that once or twice—and there was a band that he liked to follow—Isabel could not remember its name and had called it the Something Somethings when she had asked him about it. But that was all she knew about him; that, and the fact that there had been some traumatic incident some time ago. She would not tell Miranda about that, though, as it had nothing to do with her.

"I don't know about girlfriends," she said quietly. "He doesn't talk about his private life. And I don't think that he likes us to ask."

Miranda looked thoughtful. "That's what he needs," she said. "He needs a girlfriend to give him confidence."

"It may not be so simple," Isabel objected.

Miranda looked over her shoulder to check that nobody was waiting at the till. "Every boy needs a girlfriend—or a boyfriend, depending, you know."

Isabel nodded. "Having somebody else is important." She looked at Miranda, at the fresh, open face, at the optimistic expression. That was what she liked about Australia and Australians; there was no angst, no complaining, just a positive pleasure in living. And there was such friendliness, too, embodied in that rough-edged doctrine of mateship that they liked to talk about. That had even found its way into the *Australian Philosophical Review,* where Isabel had found a curious paper called "What Is Mateship?" And mateship, it appeared, was a philosophy of looking after one's fellow man, and sharing in adversity. She had been doubtful that Australians had any monopoly on that idea, but then she had gone on to read about how mateship had saved lives in the Second World War when captured Australian servicemen coped much better with the privations of the camps because their officers had shared with the men and taken a greater interest in their welfare than had the British officers, with their insistence on separation and privilege. British officers might have something to say about that, she thought, but it was interesting. Of course, mateship had its negative side: one had to take one's mates' side in any argument with the authorities, which was immature, thought Isabel—she had never understood why people found such difficulty in accepting that their friends might be wrong. I am often wrong, she thought, often, and I assume my friends are too.

Miranda was staring at her. "You're a philosopher, aren't you? Eddie was telling me."

"Yes," said Isabel. "That's what I do."

"I might have guessed that," said Miranda. "Even if I didn't know. You seem to think so hard about things. Just then you were sitting there and thinking about something, weren't you?"

Isabel laughed. "Yes, I suppose I was. I find myself thinking at a bit of a tangent. I think of one thing and then I go on to think about something connected with it. And so it goes on."

"And you get paid to do that?"

"Very little, I'm afraid. Philosophy doesn't pay very well."

Miranda was looking at her quizzically. "And yet Eddie
says that you're rich. He told me that you live in a large house
and that you have somebody who works for you there."

There was no malice in the observation, and Isabel found
that she did not resent it. "I'm very fortunate," she said. "I'm
well-off. I was left money. That's where it comes from. But I try
not to splash it around, I assure you. I don't live in great splen-
dour or anything like that."

"Pity," said Miranda. "I would, if I had money."

"You don't know that. You might find that it made no difference. And it doesn't, you know. Once one has the minimum
required for reasonable comfort, any more makes no difference
to how you feel. It really doesn't."

It was clear that Miranda did not believe this, but the conversation came to an end as Cat came in the front door. "The
boss," said Miranda. "When the Cat's away the mice will play. I
must get back to work. Nice to talk to you, Isabel. And thanks
again for getting me this job."

Cat moved over to the counter and said something to Eddie
before she came over to Isabel's table and sat down opposite her
aunt. Isabel could tell immediately that there was something
wrong. Cat was tense, and her greeting of Isabel verged on the
cold. Patrick trouble, she thought. This was how Cat behaved
when her emotional life became complicated; it had happened
with Toby and with the others, and although it tended not to last
long, it was uncomfortable for everybody.

"Had a good weekend?" asked Cat.

Isabel hesitated. "Yes. I did. I—"

"I've just seen Mimi," said Cat. "I bumped into her in the
post office."

Isabel suddenly thought: Jamie, and she experienced a

moment of panic. She had not considered this, but of course she should have. "I thought that they weren't going to come back until later this afternoon," said Isabel. "We spent the weekend in the Borders. A house near Peebles."

"So she told me," said Cat. "And you had a good time?"

There was no doubt in Isabel's mind now that Cat knew—her tone of voice was unmistakably sarcastic.

"Cat," she said. "I was going to talk to you. I was going to . . ."

Cat leant forward slightly and lowered her voice. "How could you? How could you do it?" she half whispered, half hissed.

Isabel drew back. "What did Mimi tell you?"

"That Jamie was there."

Isabel wondered whether she should deny Cat's inference. Mimi would certainly not have told her about what had happened—and she had not discussed anything with Mimi. As far as Mimi was concerned, Isabel and Jamie were still just friends. But a denial on her part would be, quite simply, a lie, and one could not lie.

"Yes, he was. Jamie was there." She left it at that. She was not obliged to account to Cat, even if Jamie had once been her boyfriend. Cat had rejected him and made it very clear that she had no intention of taking him back. In the circumstances, then, she could hardly complain if Jamie became involved with somebody else. But then, that somebody else was Cat's aunt.

"Isabel," whispered Cat, "I can't believe that you would do it. That you would go off with Jamie. He was my boyfriend, for God's sake. Mine. I knew that you saw him, but I fondly imagined that it was just a nice little friendship—not this."

Isabel sighed. "I'm sorry, Cat. I really am. It was just a

friendship to begin with—I promise you that. I had no idea that you would be jealous of him. You knew that Jamie was head over heels in love with you. You knew that. But you're the one who got rid of him and you shouldn't really be jealous of him. That's hardly fair, is it? To him or anybody else for that matter."

Cat gave Isabel a look which disturbed her greatly. If it was not quite hate, it was close to it. "Jealous? Jealous?" She spat out the words. "I am not in the slightest bit jealous."

Isabel spoke calmly. "You must be. Otherwise you wouldn't behave like this."

"It is not jealousy," said Cat. "It's disgust."

Isabel was silent. Miranda and Eddie, from the other side of the room, had picked up that an argument was in progress and were looking in their direction with curiosity. She averted her gaze. Suddenly she felt ashamed. Disgust. That was what Cat felt about her conduct. Her own niece felt that.

"Think about it," Cat went on. "He's twenty-eight and you're forty-two. You could be his mother."

Isabel looked up. "Hardly," she said. "I was fourteen when he was born."

"So what?" Cat said abruptly. "He's much younger than you are. Much. And anyway, don't you think that there's something a bit disgusting in an aunt taking her niece's boyfriend into her bed? Or did you climb into his bed? Did you? Is that what happened?"

"You have no right to talk to me like that. You don't know what you're saying, Cat."

Cat sat back in her chair. The anger now seemed to drain out of her expression and Isabel noticed that there were tears welling in her eyes.

"Cat," she said, reaching out to her. "Please don't be upset. Please."

"Go away," said Cat. "Just go away."

Isabel reached for the shopping bag that she had placed on the floor below the table. Cat kicked it, and the bag fell over, spilling the contents on the floor.

Eddie watched from the counter. Then, when Cat rose to her feet and went silently into her office, he walked over to Isabel's table and bent down to retrieve the items that had fallen out of the bag.

"She sometimes gets into a bad temper," he whispered to Isabel. "Usually it's when her boyfriend is being difficult. She gets over it."

Isabel tried to smile as she thanked Eddie, but it was difficult. What had she done? When she had entered the delicatessen that morning she had still been feeling elated over Jamie. Now that had changed. She simply had not thought about the impact her affair with Jamie might have on Cat. It was remiss of her; she spent so much time thinking about other things, about the moral ramifications of every act, that when it came to something so close to her, something as important as her relationship with Cat, how could she not even have thought about the implications?

But then she thought: Why should I feel guilty? I *should* feel elated, not guilty; elated that I have the affection of somebody like Jamie; elated that I have been the recipient of such an unexpected gift. That is how she should have felt, but did not. Guilt over Cat put a stop to it.

CHAPTER TWENTY

Isabel?"

She had answered the telephone in her study. In front of her, a particularly impenetrable—and dull—manuscript bore the markings of her blue pencil. "The Ethics of Tactical Voting" was not easy reading. Was it acceptable to vote for somebody you did not like in order to prevent somebody else from winning an election? Of course it was, thought Isabel, because in those particular circumstances you did like the person for whom you voted; you liked him more than you liked the opposition. So the fundamental premise that you were indicating approval where you really felt disapproval was false: *that was not what your vote meant.* Normally, this paper would have been rejected, but it had been written by a member of the editorial board and comity had to be borne in mind. The telephone call was a welcome diversion, and indeed Isabel had been on the point of getting up to make a cup of tea—her third that morning—in order to give herself an excuse to stop reading. She was also distracted, of course, by the row with Cat. That had been terrible, and she had tried to put it out of her mind, but it was there nonetheless, a background feeling of dread. And Jamie had not telephoned.

She had dared to hope that it would be Jamie, but she recognised Tom's voice. "I've been meaning to call you to say thank you," she said. "That was a wonderful weekend."

He said that the pleasure was entirely his—and Angie's of course—which Isabel doubted, as she was certain Angie would have been just as happy, or happier perhaps, had she not been there. There was a silence after this, but only a brief one. The Tom said, "We're coming into town today. I don't know how busy you are . . ."

She glanced at "The Ethics of Tactical Voting." "I'd welcome an interruption," she said. "If that's what you were going to suggest."

He sounded pleased. "I was. Could I drop by?"

Isabel hesitated, not through any unwillingness to see Tom, but through uncertainty about what he had in mind. Was Angie coming?

He answered the unspoken question. "Just me, I'm afraid. Angie has a hair appointment and I believe that she has some shopping to do. So it'll just be me."

They agreed on a time, and Isabel went through to the kitchen to switch on the kettle. She was sure that Tom was not just calling for a casual chat; he had sounded as if there was something that he wanted to talk about. She was not sure what it was, though. Over the weekend they had conversed a lot together, and they had got on well, but it could hardly be a case of something being left unfinished. One did not come into town to discuss a point in an interrupted conversation.

She made her tea and returned, reluctantly, to her study. It would be three hours before Tom arrived, and in that time she could finish her editing of "The Ethics of Tactical Voting." The other possibility was to let the paper go forward in its existing form. That would please the author, she was sure, but it would involve a lowering of her own standards—not that anybody would read this particular article, anyway, and so perhaps nobody would notice. Or would they? There were people who thought about nothing other than voting behaviour; they liked this sort of thing. Psephologists. She sighed. There were psephologists.

TOM ARRIVED at the house at three o'clock, exactly the time they had agreed upon. Isabel had just finished editing the article and was pleased with the result. What had been dull and unintelligible had now become dull and intelligible, which was little achievement, but enough for the day. It was a warm afternoon and the air was still. They could sit out in her summer house, drink their tea, and Tom could say whatever it was he wanted to say. For a few moments she fantasised. He would say, "I've gone off Angie in a big way. I feel a bit bad about it. But I realized that . . . well, you were the one I really wanted. What about it?" And she would say, "Oh, dear, Tom, I'm so sorry. Bad luck for Angie, of course, but there we are. As for me, I've got a boyfriend at the moment and can't take up your kind offer. Thanks anyway." She smiled at the ridiculous thought. Absurd fantasies were fun, provided one did not overindulge in them. People could begin to believe their fantasies—she had known several who did. Her poor neurotic friend, Mark, who had been adopted, believed that he was really the son of a wealthy Glasgow shipowner who would come to claim him and induct him into his inheritance; he believed that in spite of the lack of any evidence.

"You're dressed for tea in the garden," she said to Tom when he arrived. He was wearing a white linen jacket, open-necked white shirt, and loose beige trousers. She noticed the air of crumpled expensiveness about the jacket, and the belt through the loops of the trouser waist—a discreet, yachting-club stripe.

He laughed. "I have a Panama hat back home, but didn't think I'd need it in Scotland."

She led him into the garden, which seemed drowsy that afternoon. The summer house, which had been her father's retreat, was at the end of the lawn, backed by rhododendrons and a high stone wall that gave the entire garden privacy from the neighbours. This was Brother Fox's territory, of course, and one year he and his vixen, whom she never saw, had raised their cubs under the foundations of the summer house itself. She had heard them scratching there when she had been sitting in her chair, and she had thought of the warm, dark comfort of their den, and of the vixen, Sister Fox, she supposed, who might at that moment be licking the fur of her cubs with pride, and of their small eyes which even at that tender age were so full of fox knowledge and wisdom.

She poured the tea and passed him his cup. It had not occurred to her before that the Bell's palsy might make it difficult for him to drink, but now she saw that when he raised the cup to his lips he had to turn it carefully to the side. He saw her watching.

"I have to be a bit careful," he said. "When this first happened, I spilled coffee all over the place. I'm used to it now."

"I'm sorry," she said. "I didn't mean to stare."

He was quick to reassure her. "I really don't mind. I remind myself that it really makes very little difference to the things I can do. And as for the disfigurement . . . well, we've all seen far worse, haven't we? People who have had bad facial burns. And dwarves. Imagine what they have to put up with. People embarrassed to look at them and not knowing how to speak to them."

"But attitudes have changed, surely."

He lowered his cup. "Maybe. Until this happened to me, though, I had no idea what people with . . . with disabilities have to put up with. The looks. The pity. Yes, that's difficult to take. The pity. It's well meant, but we don't want it, you know. And it also made me realise something that I never thought about. Dallas is part of the South, in its own way, and I never thought very much about what it was to be black in a white world. Now I think I know a little bit about what that might have been like. A bit late to get that education. This thing—this illness, just a virally damaged facial nerve—gave me wisdom. How about that? The wisdom of the facial nerve."

She did not say anything, but she knew exactly what he meant. To be able to imagine the other, and the experience of the other, was what wisdom was all about; but nobody talked about wisdom very much any more, nor virtue, perhaps because wisdom was not appreciated in a world of glitz and effect. We chose younger and younger politicians to lead us because they looked good on television and were sharp. But really we should be looking for wisdom, and choosing people who had acquired it; and such people, in general, looked bad on television—grey, lined, thoughtful.

Tom picked up his cup again and looked into it. "Coming to Scotland has been important for me," he said. "We almost went to France, but decided that it would be Scotland this year."

"Tarwhinn is a lovely place. You must be happy there."

He took a careful sip of tea. "Oh, the house is fine. But it's not really that. It's just that I've been able to do some thinking."

She listened attentively. The sun had moved to fall through the open doors of the summer house, against the side of his trouser leg and on his left hand, which was resting on the arm of his chair. She noticed the signs of early sun damage on his skin, a dryness and freckles—Dallas, of course, and the harsh Texas summers.

"I don't know how to say this, Isabel."

She was about to pour more hot water into the teapot, but she stopped.

He took a deep breath. "Everything's wrong," he blurted out. "Everything."

She did not know what to say. It was the engagement, obviously. He had made a mistake. People found out about other people when they went on holiday with them, and perhaps that was what had happened; it was a simple falling of scales from the eyes. And sometimes it took different surroundings to reveal a person's inadequacies. Angie may have been fine in Dallas, where she made sense, but out there in Peeblesshire, amongst those hills, she could well seem strident, brittle.

Tom continued, "I can't help myself. When I met you, I realised what sort of person I should really be looking for. Somebody like you." He looked at her, gauging her reaction. She smiled, but her smile was weak and uncertain. He was sufficiently encouraged, though, to go on. "I suppose that I'm a little bit smitten with you. In fact, I'm downright smitten. There you are. I've said it. Sorry. It's very rude of me."

This was not welcome, but his manner was so formal, so polite, that it somehow seemed not in the least threatening. She reached across and placed her hand on his forearm. The linen of the sleeve was rough to the touch. "Tom, you don't have to apologise. You—"

He interrupted her. "I agonised over telling you, but then I decided I had to. I know that it's ridiculous—"

"It isn't."

"Yes, it is," he insisted. "You've got your friend, Jamie. I'm an engaged man, and I've got this . . . this face. I know that nothing can come of it. But I couldn't bear just sitting there with this knowledge about myself and not being able to talk to anybody about it. That's why I had to come and speak to you. I shouldn't have."

Her relief showed. He was not going to press her. "Of course you should."

He looked at her. There was anxiety in his face. "You don't mind?"

"Of course I don't. I'm flattered. I really am. But, as I'm sure you'll agree, it really doesn't have much of a future, does it?"

He appeared to think about this for a moment. And Isabel, for her part, controlled the urge to smile at the thought of how this meeting had followed the script of her fantasy, thus far at least, although there had been no direct mention of Angie.

"And what about Angie?" she asked.

For a while he said nothing. Then, speaking quietly, he said, "She doesn't really care for me. In fact, I think she'd be quite happy to get rid of me."

He looked at her to see her reaction. If he had expected her to be shocked, then she disappointed him, for she was not. It was as she had thought. She had known all along, in the way that one knows some things that cannot be explained, beliefs of unknown aetiology. She had just known that, and had felt embarrassed when she expressed the fear to Mimi. And Tom had known it too.

She spoke very carefully. "How do you know that?" She would not tell him about her dream; it would be too melodramatic. But she would make it clear that she did not think that what he said was outrageous.

He joined his hands together in a gesture that seemed close to hand-wringing. "I think she tried. We went to the Falls of Clyde. I was trying to get a photograph, right at the edge, from a place where I suppose one shouldn't go because there was a sheer drop just a foot or so away, and suddenly I felt that I had to turn round. And I did, and Angie was right behind me."

"And she tried to . . ."

He shook his head. "No. I lost my balance, and I started to go backwards. It was very strange. I was teetering, I suppose. It must have looked as if I were going to go over."

"And?"

He closed his eyes for a moment, as if reliving the scene. "She didn't do anything. She just looked. She didn't reach out."

Isabel had felt a knot of tension within her, which now dissipated. It was that old favourite of the moral philosophers, the act/omission distinction. Was it as bad to fail to act as to act, if the consequence in each case was the same?

"You think that she should have done something?"

"Of course she should." He paused. "I know that one might panic in such circumstances, one might freeze. But when that happens the eyes show it. I looked into her eyes and saw something quite different."

"Which was?"

"Pleasure," he said. "Or perhaps one might describe it as excitement."

She thought about this, and then asked Tom whether he

had said anything to her about it. He replied that he had not, and the reason for this was that he could not be sure. It was a terrible thing to accuse anybody of, and he found that he was not able to do it.

"But you can't stay with somebody if you think that she's capable of that," said Isabel. "You can't do that."

He spread his hands in a gesture of resignation. "I'm engaged to her. All Dallas knows. I can't turn round and . . . and end it just on the basis of a suspicion."

Isabel felt a growing anger within her. "You can't? Of course you can. People break off engagements all the time. That's why we have them. A trial period."

He looked at her helplessly. "I can't bring myself to do it. I can't tell her." He sighed. "And maybe I'm wrong anyway. Maybe the whole thing is my imagination."

"No," she said. "I don't think it's that. But the point is, surely, that you don't want to marry her. You've just told me that meeting me made you feel that. You did mean that, didn't you?"

He nodded vigorously. "I did. Yes, all that was true. This other thing—the thing at the falls—that's something on top of it. An extra difficulty. But—and I know this sounds weak—I just can't bring myself to break it off. She would be devastated." He met her gaze, as if pleading. "I just can't decide. I know I have to, but I can't."

"Why would she be devastated if she wants to get rid of you?"

Tom sighed. "I don't know. I just don't."

Isabel decided. "Do you want my advice?"

"No. I have to make my own decision."

"But you've just told me you can't do that."

Now he looked anguished. "I'd be a coward if I let somebody else do my dirty work, do my thinking for me."

"Yes," said Isabel. "It would be cowardly. But all of us are cowards from time to time. I certainly am, and just about everybody else is, if they're honest with themselves." She looked at him searchingly. "One thing occurs to me, though. I take it that if she wants to get rid of you, she would want to do so after your marriage, not before. For financial reasons."

He shifted in his chair, as if the question made him feel uncomfortable. "She stands to benefit from my death, even now. I have already made arrangements. My lawyers advised it when we got engaged."

"I see." She picked up a small silver teaspoon from the tea tray and began to play with it between her fingers. "Do you think she might accept a settlement?"

"You mean that I should pay her off?"

"Yes. Because if she doesn't really like you, then why is she engaged to you?"

"Money?"

"It looks that way," said Isabel. "Don't you think?"

Tom said something that Isabel did not catch. But then he repeated himself. "How horrible to have to put it that way," he said.

Isabel thought so too. Human affairs, though, were reduced to monetary calculation all the time, and marriage had traditionally been about money every bit as much as it had been about love.

He was staring at her. "Should I do that? Should I offer her money?"

"What do you think?"

"No," he said. "I'm asking you what you think."

"All right. Yes, I think that you might offer her something. You don't have to, but if it's important to you that she releases you, so to speak, then do it." I should not be interfering, she thought. I have resolved not to interfere in the affairs of others, and now I'm doing this. But he had asked her, had he not? He had pressed her to give her advice, and she had done so. Did that amount to interference? She was not sure.

CHAPTER TWENTY-ONE

JAMIE TELEPHONED. He did so shortly after Tom's departure, when Isabel had stacked the teacups in the dishwasher and returned to her study to work. He wanted to have dinner with her, he said, if she was free. Of course she was, although she tried not to say so too quickly. But she was quick enough.

At Jamie's suggestion, they met in a pub, the St. Vincent Bar, on his side of town. It was a small bar tucked away near the end of a wide Georgian thoroughfare that went down the hill from George Street. This road came to an architectural full stop at an imposing, high-pillared church on St. Vincent Street; beside it was a much more modest Episcopal church, also known as St. Vincent's, in which high rites were celebrated. This was the home, too, of a slightly eccentric order, the Order of St. Lazarus, the members of which paraded in ornate uniforms and claimed descent from Templar-like chivalrous organisations; harmless enough, thought Isabel, and evidently satisfying two deep-seated male desires—to have secrets and to belong.

The afternoon weather had held, and as Isabel made her way down the hill from George Street the high northern sky was still filled with evening light. It was shortly after eight, but it would not get dark until well after ten, and even then the darkness would be attenuated by a lingering glow, the *simmer dim* as they called it in the far north of Scotland. The air was warm, too, but with that touch of freshness that reminded one that this was Scotland after all.

The door of the bar was wide open and there were several people sitting on the stone steps outside, enjoying the warmth. Jamie was already there, sitting at a table just inside the doorway, a glass of beer on the table in front of him. When he saw Isabel his expression lightened. He rose to his feet and took her hands. Then he leant forward and kissed her lightly on the cheek. Isabel felt herself trembling, like a schoolgirl on her first date. He has obviously had no regrets, she thought; he feels now as he felt over the weekend.

She sat down at the table while Jamie went to buy her a drink. She looked around the bar, taking in the small groups of friends, the couples, the one or two solitary drinkers seated on stools at the bar itself. There was nobody she knew, which did not surprise her. This was not her territory. And the thought of territoriality made her think, inconsequentially, of Brother Fox. She imagined that she might come into this bar and find him seated on a stool, his neat furry legs crossed elegantly, sipping a glass of . . . What would Brother Fox drink? Sherry perhaps, or something even more sophisticated, one of those cocktails with elaborate names that one saw listed in grander bars. Brother Fox would drink something called a "St. Francis," she thought: two parts gin, one part lime and one part chicken. And Brother Fox would have a group of somewhat raffish friends—people like Charlie MacLean, perhaps, that man who wrote books on whisky and whose whisky-nosing she had once attended down in Leith; he and Brother Fox would get on well, telling each other stories. Absurd, but she smiled.

Jamie came back with her drink. When he sat down, his knee touched hers under the table, but he did not move it.

"I've got a present for you," Jamie said, fishing into the battered leather music case that he habitually carried. It was a case that served every purpose, from carrying musical scores to transporting cartons of milk and groceries from the supermarket.

He took out a compact disc in a small plastic bag and handed it to her. "It's a wonderful mixture of things," he said. "And some of them we're going to have to do ourselves. I'll try to do arrangements if we can't find the music. And I suspect that we won't be able to find some of these things."

"Thank you," she said. "You're . . . you're very sweet." She took his hand briefly and squeezed it. She examined the disc. *"Mood Scottish,"* she read.

"A play on *Mood Indigo,* I think," said Jamie. "But don't worry. It's all very good. Some lovely stuff. Look."

He took the disc and pointed to an item on the list of tracks. " 'Sinclair.' It's a Faroese song about a Scottish soldier in Sweden. They went there a long time ago. By invitation, unlike most British soldiers . . ."

"I know all about that," said Isabel. "That's why you come across Scottish names in Sweden. Macpherson and such like. But Swedish now."

Jamie tapped the CD case. Isabel noticed his finger, which was tanned light brown. It was gentle; so beautiful. "This Sinclair was on his way to battle," he said, "and was warned by a mermaid not to go. By a mermaid, mind you."

"One should always listen to mermaids," said Isabel. "They

address one so infrequently that anything they have to say must be important."

He looked at her in surprise and burst out laughing. Nobody else would say things like that; just Isabel. That was one of the reasons he found her irresistible.

"He didn't," Jamie went on. "And he was killed as a result. Poor Sinclair. But the song is wonderful—it goes on and on. Very odd stuff."

Isabel pointed to something else. "And some Peter Maxwell Davies," she said. " 'Lullaby for Lucy.' I met him up in Orkney once."

"Max," said Jamie. "We played his 'Orkney Wedding.' Complete with a piper. Very dramatic." He paused, took the disc and examined the cover carefully. Then he handed it back to Isabel. "We could listen to 'Sinclair' after dinner. Would you like that?"

"Yes. I would." Her heart was racing.

"Or we could go to the flat now and have dinner there. In Saxe-Coburg. How about that?"

That, she thought, was even better. "Do you want me to cook?"

"No," he said. "I'll manage something."

They finished their drinks in the bar and then walked down St. Stephen Street, back to Jamie's flat.

"That flat round the corner," Jamie said. "Have you decided?"

"I have," said Isabel. "I shall buy it. Grace looked at it the other day and liked it very much. She also met our friend Florence. They hit it off. She'll probably recruit her for her spiritualist meetings."

"Florence is too rational," said Jamie. "Still, it's a happy ending."

"I suppose so. And there's nothing wrong with happy endings, is there?"

"No," said Jamie. "Except, perhaps, for that fact that they are rather rare."

They passed a small antique shop on the way and Isabel paused in front of the window. "I knew the man who ran this shop," she said. "He used to sit in a chair, right there, dressed in a black suit with a waistcoat and a rose in his lapel, and everybody who went in received a great welcome and a story. He had Scottish literature on those shelves over there, and all other writers, including English, were shelved under foreign literature. But he didn't mean it unkindly. He was just making a point."

Jamie pressed his nose against the glass. The chair was empty, the shop dusty. "A point about what?"

"About cultural assumptions," said Isabel. Seeing the empty shop saddened her. There were pockets of character, of resistance, that held out against all the forces that would destroy local, small-scale things, even small-scale countries; little shops were on the front line, she thought.

"I don't like shopping in great big shops," she muttered.

Jamie looked at her in puzzlement. "Excuse me?"

She smiled, and drew him away from the window to continue down the street. "I don't like the idea of little shops like that disappearing. That's all. I like small things."

"Convenience," said Jamie. "Isn't there something in convenience?"

"I suppose there is. But then . . ." She trailed off. Perhaps it was too late, and the logic of the large scale was unstoppable, but it all led to sameness and flatness, and who wanted that? Francs had gone, marks had gone, the insanely inflated Italian lira had gone; cars looked the same wherever you went, clothes too. All the colour, all the difference, was being drained out of life. And species were dying too; every day insects disappeared for ever, strange little lives that had been led for millennia in the undergrowth came to an end with the destruction of a last toehold of habitat. It seemed like a relentless return to barrenness, to unrelieved rock. She looked at Jamie and wondered whether he cared about this. Or did one need another fourteen years to understand, or even to feel, these things?

"I'm hungry," said Jamie.

"Then let's go," said Isabel. She was about to slip her arm into his, but stopped herself. Could she do that, or would that embarrass him? The early days of any relationship raised questions of that sort, of course; the easy familiarities came later, and seemed natural then, but at this stage they could be awkward. And they were not officially a couple, in the sense that people did not necessarily know about it, and would he want them to know? They walked separately.

In his flat, Jamie took from Isabel the disc that he had given her and slipped it into the player. His kitchen, which ran off the living room, was small, and Isabel watched him as he prepared the meal: mozzarella and tomatoes, followed by pasta. He poured her wine and they raised their glasses to each other in a toast.

"To you," she said. And Jamie replied, "To me," and then laughed. "I mean, to you."

"To me, one imagines," said Isabel, "is the toast of the Egotists' Club. What do you think?"

Jamie agreed. "I'm sure it is," he said. "Their dinners, though, will be difficult occasions. Everybody will want to give an after-dinner speech."

"And they'll all think that there are too many members," she said.

There was silence for a moment. Jamie picked up the bottle of dressing that he had prepared for the mozzarella and tomatoes and shook it so that the black of the balsamic vinegar suffused the olive oil.

Isabel fingered the stem of her glass. "Jamie," she said. "Are you happy about this . . . about what has happened between us? Are you sure that you're all right with it?"

He looked at her intently and she thought, *I should not have said that. There are some things best left unsaid.*

"Of course I am," he said. "Of course."

"You would tell me if you weren't?"

"I would tell you."

"Promise?"

He moved his right hand in a quick crossing of the heart. "Promise." Going back into the kitchen, he said over his shoulder, "Have you spoken to Joe and Mimi about last weekend?"

"Briefly."

"And?"

"They both enjoyed themselves."

"And Tom and Angie?"

Isabel hesitated. She wanted to speak to Jamie about her talk with Tom, but she feared his reaction. He had always lectured her about interfering in others' affairs, and she had just engaged in a major intervention, having encouraged Tom to get rid of Angie. Of course Tom had asked for that advice—he had effectively insisted that she be involved—but she was not sure whether Jamie would appreciate that.

"Tom came to see me today. Just before you phoned. He wanted to talk."

Jamie, who had been stirring the pot of pasta, turned away from the cooker and looked at her quizzically. "Talk about what?"

She would not tell him of Tom's confession of feeling for her, but she decided that she would tell him the rest. "About him and Angie."

Jamie had put down the spoon and was standing in the kitchen doorway, wiping his hands on a tea towel. "What did he say?"

Isabel lifted her glass and took a sip of wine. "He thinks she isn't very fond of him. He's decided to end the engagement."

Jamie looked down at the floor. "I'm not surprised," he said.

"You think that they're unsuited too?"

He shrugged. "I don't know about that. Maybe. But . . ."

Isabel detected his uncertainty and encouraged him. "Go on. You can tell me."

He stared at her, embarrassed. "Well, I don't know. I'm not sure . . ."

"You have to tell me now."

He joined her at the table and sat down. "When we went into Peebles on Saturday morning, something happened."

Isabel caught her breath. "What happened?" Her voice was small.

Jamie shifted in his seat. "I don't really like to talk about this," he said.

Oh, she had eyes for you, that woman, thought Isabel. And her feelings, now, were ones of anger.

Jamie mumbled, "She made a pass at me. Or I think she did."

This should be no surprise—Isabel had seen her looking at him—but she had not imagined that it would be translated into action. Where, though, was the doubt? "But you must know. Either she did or she didn't. What did she say?"

Jamie's embarrassment seemed to be mounting. "It was while we were driving back. She put a hand on my knee. Suddenly. Just like that. But quite far up." He blushed, and Isabel lowered her eyes.

"Was that all?" she asked. It was, she thought, and she felt relieved.

"Maybe she didn't mean it like that," said Jamie. "I don't know."

"I should think that she meant it exactly like that," said Isabel. "Come on, Jamie. Women don't do that sort of thing by mistake." She mused for a moment. "What did you do?"

Jamie bit his lip. "I told her a lie."

"Oh? That you were married?"

"That I had a girlfriend."

Isabel smiled. "And that had the desired effect?"

"She looked at me and she just said, 'Pity.' And then she took her hand away."

They sat in silence for a while. Isabel reflected on what she had heard and thought: It is exactly as I imagined. Angie is not in love with Tom. And since that is true, then my encouraging him to bring it to an end is the right thing to have done.

"I told him to end the engagement," she said. "I told him that he should talk to her about it. And he's going to do it."

Jamie shrugged. "That's probably for the best," he said.

He turned to go back into the kitchen. Isabel was relieved that he had not criticised her for interfering, and she started to talk about something else. Jamie, too, seemed pleased to move off the subject of Tom and Angie. He moved the disc back a track and played Isabel something that he wanted her to hear. Then they sat at the table and began their meal.

He put down his knife and fork, although he had just begun

eating. He took her hand. "You can do no wrong, you know," he said. "Not in my eyes."

"What a funny thing to say. But very nice."

"I mean it."

She felt the pressure of his fingers on the palm of her hand. It was gentle, as everything about him was. Gentle. Love is not a virtue, she thought; not in itself. But it helps us to be virtuous, to do good for those whom we love, and in that sense it can never be wrong, wherever it alights, whatever direction it takes.

She looked at Jamie, in fondness. But she found herself thinking: He said that he had lied to Angie when he told her he had a girlfriend. Therefore I am not his girlfriend. So what does that make me?

He let go of her hand and returned to his meal.

"Can we go away together?" he asked. "Somewhere on the west coast? Or one of the islands?"

"Yes, of course."

"I'd like to go to Harris," he said. "Have you ever been to the Outer Hebrides?"

"Yes," she answered. "And there's a hotel I know there, just a small one, a converted manse. It looks down on a field that is full of wild flowers in the spring and summer, with the sea just beyond. Cold, green waves. The very edge of Scotland. It's very beautiful. We could go there. Would you like that?"

"Very much."

She smiled at him, and put her hand to his cheek, as she had done before, on that first discovery. But as she did so, she thought: I am going to break my heart over this, but not now, not just yet.

CHAPTER TWENTY-TWO

HAPPINESS. Over the next few days, Isabel felt herself to be in state of blessedness. She spoke to Jamie every day, and saw him briefly, for a snatched lunch in the small café opposite the gate of the Academy; he had an hour between pupils and they talked, low-voiced because a couple of the boys from the school were sitting at a nearby table, sniggering. Isabel eventually smiled at them and they blushed scarlet and turned away.

Isabel's happiness, though, was qualified by her anxiety over Cat. There had been rows with Cat before, and they always resolved themselves after a few days. The normal pattern would be for Isabel to apologise, whether or not she was in the wrong, and for Cat, grudgingly, to accept the apology. Isabel thought that she might wait a little longer before she went to speak to her niece; that would give Cat time to simmer down and also, she hoped, to begin to feel guilty about her own behaviour. This time it really was not her fault, she thought. Cat had no right to Jamie, having rejected him and turned a deaf ear to his attempts to persuade her to take him back, and even if Isabel had perhaps been insensitive to the need to talk to her about her feelings for Jamie, she considered this to be a light offence.

She made her way to the delicatessen in the late morning. She had written a note which she would leave for Cat—a note in which she confessed her lack of sensitivity and asked Cat to forgive her. *I've been thoughtless,* she wrote. But then, in self-defence, *It may be hard for you—I understand that—but please let me be happy. I had not imagined that this would happen. Please give me your blessing.* She had read and reread the note, agonising over the wording, but had eventually decided that the words were just right because they were true.

Cat was not there. Miranda and Eddie were behind the counter, Eddie cleaning the slicer—Isabel's blood ran cold even at that—and Miranda serving a customer. Both of them glanced at her; Miranda smiled and Eddie acknowledged her with a slight nod.

"Cat?" she asked Eddie.

"Out," he said. And then added, "Patrick."

Isabel sighed. Even if Patrick was as busy as his mother suggested, he still seemed to have a lot of time for lunch with Cat. She wondered whether his mother knew about these trysts, and whether, if she did, she would try to interfere.

She asked Eddie to pour her a cup of coffee. Then she picked up a newspaper and went to sit at one of the tables. The world was in chaos, the front page suggested: floods had destroyed a large part of somebody's coast, and there were pictures of a couple stranded up a tree, the woman wailing, her skirts torn and muddied; there were people building nuclear weapons; a large lake somewhere had been found to be poisoned, dead. So we frighten ourselves daily, thought Isabel, and with reason.

She folded the newspaper up and put it away. She would look out at the street, watching passers-by, and then, if Cat had not returned in twenty minutes, leave the note. She stared through the window, past the carefully arranged display of bot-tles of olive oil which Eddie had set up to lure customers inside. Eddie was in charge of the window displays, and looked forward to the beginning of each week, when he would rearrange them.

He brought Isabel her coffee and sat down opposite her, his cleaning cloth draped casually over his shoulder. "I heard your news," he said, grinning as he spoke. "Congratulations."

Isabel sipped at the scalding, milky coffee. She had not an-ticipated this; Cat must have told him. "She told you? Cat did?"

Eddie nodded. "She wasn't pleased. Or at least not at first. She said that I'd never believe what you'd got up to. Then she told me, expecting me to side with her."

Isabel watched Eddie as he spoke. He would never have been this forthcoming a few months ago. And when he had first come to work for Cat he would hardly have said more than a word of greeting, and mumbled at that. This was progress.

"And you didn't?" she asked.

"Of course not," said Eddie. "I laughed. She didn't like that."

"I'm not surprised," said Isabel. "She virtually accused me of stealing him."

"That's nonsense," said Eddie. "And I told her she had no right to be jealous."

Isabel told him that that was exactly what she had thought. But one was dealing with irrational feelings here, she pointed out. Jealousy was something which people found difficult to control; sometimes it was impossible.

"I know," said Eddie. "Anyway, I talked to her about it and she calmed down. Then, at the end, she said that maybe she should be proud. She said that . . ." He trailed off, and Isabel looked at him quizzically.

"Go on," she encouraged him. "She said what?"

Eddie looked sheepish. "She said that not everyone had an aunt who was capable of running off with a younger man. She said that it showed a certain style."

"And that was how you left it?"

He nodded. "Yes. Then we started talking about Miranda. We—"

Isabel glanced across the room and cut Eddie off. Miranda had finished dealing with the customer and was coming over to join them at the table. "Here she is. Here's Miranda."

Miranda came up to stand behind Eddie. She greeted Isabel, smiling warmly, and then she rested a hand on Eddie's shoulder. Eddie half turned, smiled and lifted a hand to place on hers, patting it fondly. Isabel watched in astonishment.

"Yes," said Eddie.

"Well," said Isabel. "Well . . ."

"You should have told me, Isabel," said Miranda in mock admonition. "You should have told me that the nicest boy in Scotland worked here. As it is, I had to discover that myself."

Eddie beamed with pleasure. "We must get back to work." He rose to his feet and touched Miranda gently on the shoulder. "Come on."

Isabel watched them return to the counter. For each of us, she thought, there is our completeness in another. Whether we find it, or it finds us, or it eludes all finding, is a matter of moral luck. She had a good idea of what it was that had happened to Eddie, but now she saw that shattered, timid life begin to be made confident and whole, and she felt a warm rush of satisfaction and pleasure. She reached into her pocket and took out the note she had written to Cat. It was in its rectangular white envelope, the flap tucked in. She took it out and reread it. It had taken time to choose and weigh each word; now she tore it up in seconds and tossed the pieces into the bin used for scraps of sugar wrappers and the like. The next move was Cat's rather than hers, and she would wait for it with impatience. She did not have to apologise for Jamie; she did not have to apologise to anybody for her happiness.

MIMI AND JOE were out when she returned to the house, but Grace told her that they had said that they would be back in the late afternoon. There had been a change in their plans, and they had decided to go off the following day to Skye for a week. Joe wanted to write up his article on adoption and there were distractions in Edinburgh. "If I go somewhere really remote, I shall get it done," he said. And Mimi had agreed. Skye, she said, was far enough away and, more important, there were few, if any, bookshops to distract him. For her part, she had reading to do, and could do it as well on a small island as on a big one.

Isabel would miss them, but would see them briefly on their return. And they had persuaded her to make a trip to Dallas to stay with them, which she had agreed to do before too long. "My *sainted American mother* would have liked me to . . . ," she had said, and faltered. No. There was no reason why her mother should not still be called *sainted*. A saint might still fall in love; indeed, would it not be most likely that those who loved their fellow man in general might feel all the more strongly inclined to love their fellow man in particular? I love Jamie, she thought, and has that not made me love the world all the more? Of course it had.

That evening Mimi sat in the kitchen while Isabel did the

cooking. They talked about Skye, and what Joe and Mimi might do there. They could stay in Claire Macdonald's hotel; they could walk; they could watch the slow movement of the sea; they could sniff at the peat smoke in the air.

"Come with us," urged Mimi. "There's room."

"I'd love to," said Isabel. "But I have my work."

"Be irresponsible for once," said Mimi.

Isabel smiled at the thought. I'm being very irresponsible as it is, she thought, and it's immense fun. "I can't, I'm afraid," she said. "The journal . . ."

Mimi conceded. "Of course. But if you change your mind, jump in the car and join us."

Isabel, standing at the cutting board, neatly sliced an onion into rings. She felt tears come into her eyes and wiped them away with the back of her hand. "Not real tears," she said to Mimi. "Nor even crocodile ones. Just onion tears."

"A nice name for tears that don't mean anything," said Mimi.

"Yes. We'll need to think about that."

She looked out the window. To the west, the sky had clouded over to the west and was heavy and dark. "Rain," said Isabel. "I hope that you're not washed out on Skye. It has a tendency to rain over there, as you know." She remembered a couple of lines which Michael Longley had written about such landscapes: *I think of Tra-na-Rossan, Inisheer / Of Harris drenched by horizontal rain.* It was such a powerful image of the rain that came in off the Atlantic, relentless, horizontal across the island.

"I'm not put off by rain," said Mimi. "Rain can be beautiful, don't you think? And there's no point becoming depressed by it. That never changes anything."

"That's fine if you're from Texas," said Isabel. "Rain doesn't outstay its welcome down there."

"Perhaps," said Mimi. "But still . . ." She played with a button on her sleeve. "We had lunch in town today," she said. "An interesting encounter."

"With?"

"Angie, no less. She's moved into town and is going back home tomorrow. Just her. The engagement with Tom is over, it seems. Very dramatic news. I've been itching to tell you. Joe, though, has been a bit embarrassed about it. He feels that it's indecent to crow too much, even in a case like this. I told him I wasn't crowing."

Isabel moved the chopped onion to the side of the board, neatly, making a small white pile. So Tom had acted. "I'm sorry to hear that," she said. And she was, in a sense; it was a tale of unhappiness from start to finish—an unhappy, false beginning and now an unhappy ending.

"Yes, it's a bit sad really," agreed Mimi. "I felt rather sorry for her at the end."

Isabel looked up in surprise. "For Angie?"

"Yes," said Mimi. "She said that she felt she had to do something about it. She didn't want to hurt Tom, she said, but she felt that it just wasn't working."

Isabel stared at Mimi wide-eyed. "She said that she was the one who ended it?"

"Yes. I must say that I was a bit taken aback. I'd thought of her, as you know, as a gold-digger. But a gold-digger doesn't end an arrangement like that. A real gold-digger would have hung on in. She didn't."

Of course she wouldn't, thought Isabel. She would have

received her pay-off. There would be no reason to hold on after that.

"Then she said something really surprising," Mimi went on. "She said that Tom had offered her money to end the engagement. She said that she had been quite shocked and had turned him down."

"Turned him down?"

"Yes."

No, thought Isabel, highly unlikely. "Did you believe her?"

"Yes, I did," said Mimi. "She seemed completely sincere."

Both were silent for a while. In Isabel's case, it was a silence of indecision. If Angie was telling the truth, then Isabel had completely misjudged her. But had she been telling the truth?

Mimi, though, seemed to be in no doubt. "I've learned a bit of a lesson," she said. "Or rather, I've been reminded of something that I suppose I knew all along—that you just can't be certain about people and their motives. You can't. You think you know, then . . ."

Mimi could be right, thought Isabel. And then reminded herself that she had encouraged Tom to end the engagement on the basis of her own, possibly misguided, feelings about Angie's venality. But did that make any difference to the outcome? If Angie had ended it of her own accord, then the fact that she had urged Tom to tackle her about it was quite irrelevant. It occurred to her, though, that if Angie was not telling the truth and the break-up had really been at Tom's insistence, then her own encouragement of Tom may have played a part in the end result.

She looked helplessly at Mimi, wondering whether she should tell her cousin about what she had done. Mimi, though, had guessed that there was something on Isabel's mind. "You're feeling bad too?" she asked gently. "You shouldn't worry about it, you know. Angie probably misjudged you too."

"Maybe. Maybe she did. But she wouldn't have thought of me in quite the terms I thought of her. I doubt if she thought I was up to committing murder."

Mimi looked at Isabel in astonishment. "And you thought that of her? That she was capable of murdering Tom?"

Isabel confessed that she had, and told Mimi of the conversation in which Tom had described Angie's reaction to the near-disaster at the Falls of Clyde. Mimi listened thoughtfully, and then, when Isabel had finished, looked up into the air, as if searching for the solution to a conundrum. "Very curious," she said at last. "Because, believe it or not, she said something rather similar to me. She said that she felt unsafe in Tom's presence, as if there was something in him, something not always apparent, something buried deep within him, and this thing, this hidden thing, was a propensity to violence. She said she feared that he might use it against her."

They looked at each other. "Well," said Isabel. "Who's to be believed?"

"Both?" asked Mimi.

Isabel considered this. It was true that people were inclined to rewrite their personal histories, like overly generous biographers, so that they appeared in the best light. But even if there was no such rewriting here, it was quite possible that two people might feel threatened by each other and harbour fears that the threat might materialise; that was quite believable. It was also perfectly possible that Angie had made the first move to end the engagement, and that Tom, feeling guilty, had still offered her a financial settlement, and that she, out of pride, had turned it down. If this were so, then everything had worked out for the best, for everybody. A loveless marriage was staved off, Angie's pride was intact; and Tom, on mature reflection, might conclude that he had no need to feel guilty about anything.

She turned to Mimi to answer her question. "Perhaps," she said. It was not much of an answer, but there were circumstances in which "perhaps" or "maybe" were the only answers one could honestly give.

She pondered, though. She pondered the question of whether she had done a wrong to Angie—a wrong which somehow needed redress. She had thought ill of her, and although Angie might never have been aware of what was thought of her, Isabel had gone further and actually spoken ill of her. That, in any system of reckoning, was a wrong against another. But she was not sure if she had the moral energy to pursue the matter and, besides, what could she do: write to her and apologise? Only the most conscientious person would take moral duty to those lengths, and Isabel decided to leave matters where they lay. She had learned her lesson about leaping to conclusions and judging people unfairly, and that perhaps was enough. Again it was a question of a "perhaps."

JOE AND MIMI went to Skye, where it rained, and came back to Edinburgh, where it rained too, but not so persistently. Then, after a few more days there, they left for Oxford, where they planned to spend the rest of the summer. "Joe's happy there," said Mimi. "He was a Rhodes Scholar, quite a few years ago now, and it's full of memories. I'm not sure whether we're happiest at that time of life, but we often think we were."

I'm happiest now, thought Isabel. She wanted to say that to Mimi, but hesitated, because it seemed to her that one might so easily slip into sentiment; and protestations of happiness could sound almost boasting to those whose happiness is incomplete. One did not boast of perfect skin to one affected by dermatitis; for the same reason, perhaps, one should take care in proclaiming one's happiness. Not that Mimi was unhappy in any way; she seemed equable, content and, indeed, Isabel need not have felt reticent, as Mimi, detecting Isabel's state of mind, commented on it. Mimi had enough experience of life to sense the presence of love in the life of another, and to understand its transforming power. And she knew, too, how strong may be our wish to show off the object of our love, to say, *Look, here he is, here!*

"I know what's happening to you," Mimi said, reaching for Isabel's hand. "Enjoy your good fortune."

To her own surprise, Isabel did not feel any embarrassment. "I have to pinch myself," she said. "I have to persuade myself that it's real."

"It seems real enough to me," said Mimi.

"And I know that it can't last for ever," said Isabel. "Auden said—"

Mimi smiled. "*I thought that love would last for ever: I was wrong.* Yes, we all think that. But don't be too realistic about it. Love can last an awfully long time. Even after the other person has gone away, one can still love him. People do that all the time." She paused, and looked enquiringly at Isabel. "Is he likely to go away?"

They were sitting in Isabel's study during this conversation, and Isabel glanced up at the shelves of books as she answered. Her life was filled with baggage: a house; all these books, all these philosophers; a garden, a fox . . . Jamie's life had none of that. He could go away at any time if a good job came up somewhere in an orchestra. He had almost joined an orchestra in London not all that long ago, and he had also talked of living in Berlin as if it were a real possibility. She had never thought of living in Berlin, and would have no idea how to go about it; that was the difference between them, that and those fourteen years.

"He might," Isabel said. "I think we're at different stages of our lives. We really are. He might want to go off and work somewhere else. He's just starting. He could do anything."

Mimi reached for a magazine on the sofa beside her. She flicked idly through the pages, and then turned again to Isabel. "There's an expression that people use these days—have you noticed it?—which is actually quite useful. They just say 'whatever.' It sounds very insouciant—and it is—but there are occasions . . ."

"And you feel that you want to say it now?"

"Yes," said Mimi. "Whatever. There you are. Whatever. It more or less sums things up. Things will sort themselves out. That's what it means. Things will sort themselves out and we don't really need to do anything."

"Whatever," said Isabel.

"Yes," said Mimi, tossing the magazine aside. "Whatever. And do take some advice from me on this, Isabel. You know that I don't like to play the older cousin, but maybe just this once. May I?"

Isabel nodded her assent. She could not imagine herself ever resenting advice from Mimi. "Yes. Of course."

"Just let this thing evolve naturally," said Mimi. "Stop thinking about it. Just for the moment remember that first you are a woman, then, second, you're a philosopher. Can you do that, do you think?"

It would be hard not to be a philosopher, because that is what she was, and, thought Isabel, you don't easily forget what you are. But she could try, and she told Mimi she would. This satisfied her cousin, who only wanted Isabel to be happy, that was all. And Isabel wished the same for Mimi, and knew, too, that she would miss her when she went back to Dallas. They would write to one another, and speak on the telephone, but it was never the same as being in the same room, without three thousand miles of sea and half a continent between you.

On impulse she rose to her feet and bent down to plant a kiss on Mimi's brow, which made Mimi smile, moist-eyed for a moment at this friendship between cousins, something one could never replicate afresh, even if one had the recipe, relying as it did on a long past, and so much that had been said and not said.

OVER THE NEXT TWO WEEKS Edinburgh basked in unusual warmth. Isabel found that she could sit out in her garden and work there, in a shady spot to avoid the heat in the sun. She had to water the lawn, which had started to dry out, and when she did so she caught the Mediterranean smell of settling dust, and the scent of thyme, too, wafting from her herb bed. It was a time of long afternoons and the humming sound of bees attracted by the low lavender hedge about her lawn. She and Jamie had several meals outside, lunches and dinners, sitting lazily on the grass itself or on the old canvas deck chairs which Isabel had taken from their dusty storage place in the garden shed. With his pupils away on holiday, Jamie had less to do than usual. He was working on a composition, he said, but it was going slowly: "It's about islands," he said, and that was all he told her.

Isabel would find him gazing at her sometimes, just gazing, and he would smile when he saw that she had noticed. She asked him on one such occasion what he was thinking, and he replied, "About you. I'm thinking about you." He said it with guilelessness, with a sort of innocence, and she felt something happen within her, some suffusion of warmth, that made her want to hold him, there and then, hold him to her.

He stayed for days at a stretch, going back to his flat in Saxe-Coburg Street only to pick up the mail and find things, a bassoon reed, a page of his composition which he had scribbled and left somewhere, a book he was reading. For much of the time they were alone, but once they invited friends round for a dinner at which they sat out until midnight, under a sky which was dark, but only just, dotted with faint stars. They talked, united in a common feeling of contentment and peace, and then sat silently, with neither saying anything for a long time, each looking up at the sky, alone in his or her private musing.

Isabel bumped into Cat in Bruntsfield, in the post office. It was an awkward meeting; Cat was polite but seemed embarrassed, and Isabel's efforts at a normal conversation were too studied to be anything but stiff. They parted after a few minutes, nothing resolved. Isabel asked herself whether she should try another apology, but decided again that there was nothing for her to apologise for. It was taking a long time, but Cat would come round eventually. She almost told Jamie about it, but stopped herself because it occurred to her that he might interpret Cat's jealousy as a sign that she wanted him back, which Isabel knew was not the case.

Then came the letter from Mimi. They were back in Dallas, and she complained about the heat. Joe had gone to a legal history conference in Denver. It was cooler there, he had told her, and she wondered whether she should have gone too. Then: *Something bad happened here a couple of days ago. Tom Bruce, who entertained us all, had a fire at his place near Tyler. He has a house there, and he goes there for weekends now and then. It went up pretty quickly, I'm afraid. He was in it at the time.*

Isabel strained to make out Mimi's handwriting. A word had been smudged, but the rest of the sentence was clear.

> *In spite of that . . . he managed to escape out a window. The front door had been locked by somebody who had a key. He said that he didn't bother to lock up at night. But the fire people thought that he had probably done so and had forgotten. I've done that myself, haven't you? Forgotten whether or not I've locked something. But I imagine that somebody else might have had a key.*
>
> *Tom was all right, apart from having breathed in smoke, which made them keep him in hospital for a night. Hank and Barb Lischer saw him. They said that he was pretty shocked, but otherwise none the worse for it all. It's not a very nice story, bearing in mind that the fire chief in Tyler says that the fire was deliberately started. He's adamant about it. Apparently they can tell if gas has been used, and they said it had. So who did it?*

Mimi then wrote, and underlined, *We know, of course.* She understood, and shared, Isabel's liking for crosswords, and wrote, *Take the saint from German anxiety, that is.*

Isabel smiled at the clue, which was hardly a revelation. She would be more direct, though, and called Mimi immediately. "I've had your letter," she said. "That fire: you know, I know—do you think Tom knows?"

"He's not stupid," said Mimi. "I imagine he does."

"But are you sure?"

"No," said Mimi. "I'm not."

"Sometimes when things concern us intimately, we don't see the obvious."

"We don't," said Mimi. "Often we don't."

There was silence as each waited for the other to say something. It was Isabel who spoke. "Go and ask him if he's done something about his will," she said. "He said that he had made arrangements after the engagement."

"He must have done something about that," said Mimi. "He has his advisers. I can't imagine that sort of thing would be left."

"But it can be," Isabel protested. "You're always hearing about people who don't bring these things up to date. Then they die and their first wife gets everything and the second nothing."

Mimi sounded doubtful. "But is it our business?"

"Yes," said Isabel firmly. "It is. But, if you like, I'll call him. Just give me his number."

"I'll speak to him," said Mimi.

"And tell him to tell Angie," added Isabel.

"To tell her what?"

"To tell her that the provision he made has been unmade. That's very important." She paused. "Of course it may have nothing to do with it. It may just be a settling of scores. She feels rejected. A fire might restore her *amour propre*."

"It's unlikely that they will be able to prove anything," said Mimi. "And anyway, even if he has an idea that it's her, would he want to take matters further? Probably not.

"You may be right, though," Mimi continued. "Anything else?"

"Just an observation," said Isabel. "A question for us. How wrong can you be?"

"Perhaps we should trust our intuitions," said Mimi.

"Of course, there are other reasons for arson," said Isabel, as an afterthought. "Especially in the country. Local issues. Local jealousies. Resentment over boundaries, trees, livestock. Anything." One just could not tell. And until there was proof, nothing was clear, which was the way that so much of life was—vague, ambiguous, by no means as simple as we imagine it to be.

"And people set fire to their own property," said Mimi. "That's very common, apparently. And not just for insurance purposes."

Isabel said nothing. She remembered a conversation she had had with Tom on their walk up the hill, about something to do with a house not being in the right place. They had talked about it. But she could not remember exactly what had been said, and after puzzling for a few moments, she stopped thinking about it.

She rang off. In her mind there was a counting rhyme, one of those rhymes one learns as a child, and which stays in the mind for ever. Eeny, meeny, miny, mo: he lies, she lies, he lies, she lies, he lies . . . And the finger ended up pointing at the child who was in the wrong place when one finished counting. Liar!

CHAPTER TWENTY-THREE

THE CONVERSATION with Mimi took place on a Monday; the next two days were days of activity and revelation. By Wednesday she knew that she had to talk to Jamie. He had gone to Glasgow to take part in a musical workshop organised by the chamber orchestra in which he occasionally played. That was due to finish on Friday afternoon and he would return, he said, on Saturday afternoon: there were friends he wanted to meet in Glasgow. Isabel said to him, "You don't think that you would be able to come back for Friday evening? We could have dinner."

"What about Saturday evening? Are you doing anything on Saturday evening?"

She was not, but she needed to talk to him. It could wait, of course—most things can wait—but she wanted to talk to him as soon as possible.

"There's something we need to discuss," she said, trying not to sound too insistent, but fearing that she did.

Jamie's hesitation was very brief, but enough to convey anxiety. "All right," he said. "I'll come round on Friday evening. We can discuss whatever it is. What is it, by the way?"

"Do you mind waiting?"

A note of irritation crept into his voice. "No, not really. But . . ."

"It would be better," she said.

After that their conversation came to an end. She knew what he was thinking: that she was proposing to end their affair and that she wanted to do it face-to-face. He must be thinking that, she told herself—if only he knew.

She decided to make a special meal for that evening and went into Bruntsfield to buy supplies. When Isabel went into the delicatessen Miranda was serving, standing behind the counter with Eddie. They had been laughing at a shared joke.

"Something amusing happen?" asked Isabel.

Eddie glanced at Miranda, and burst into giggles.

"Eddie said . . . ," began Miranda, but she, too, started to laugh.

Isabel smiled, not at the joke, whatever it was, but at the sight of the two of them so obviously enjoying themselves. She had so rarely seen Eddie smiling, let alone laughing, and the sight pleased her. "Don't bother," said Isabel. "Some jokes just don't translate."

"She said . . . ," Eddie began, but again burst into squeals of laughter.

Isabel shook her head in mock despair. She saw that the door of the office was open and that Cat was sitting at her desk. She approached the door, knocked and stuck her head in.

Cat looked up. When she saw Isabel, her expression changed. There was a flicker of a frown, but only a flicker. Then she gestured to a chair in front of the desk.

"I mustn't stay," said Isabel. "I thought that I might just . . ."

She had not thought of what she might say to Cat, but now she knew. The time for reconciliation had arrived. "I thought I might just say that I'm sorry."

Cat looked down at her desk. "I'm the one who should be saying that," she mumbled. "I got carried away."

"We all get carried away," said Isabel. "It's a risk of being human—being carried away."

The tension that had been in the room disappeared. "May I come round on Sunday? To tea?"

"Of course," said Isabel. In her relief, she decided to include Patrick. "And Patrick too. Please bring him."

Cat's frown returned. "Patrick and I . . ."

Isabel looked up quickly. Patrick's mother had won. "I'm sorry," she said. "I didn't know."

"Well, now you do," said Cat. "We're no longer seeing each other."

"His work?" asked Isabel. "Was that the trouble?"

Cat seemed surprised by the question. "How did you guess? He said that he just didn't have the time at the moment to continue to be involved."

Mother, thought Isabel. That interfering woman had got what she wanted. And Patrick joins the ranks of Cat's former suitors.

"Oh well," said Isabel. "You'll be all right."

"I am," said Cat. "I am all right."

"Good."

"And you?" asked Cat. It was not a prying question.

"I'm all right too," said Isabel. "You know how it is . . ." It was a vague, pointless thing to say, and for a moment she thought of adding *whatever,* but did not.

She left Cat's office and made her purchases. Miranda and Eddie were still laughing with each other, and Isabel's presence seemed to tickle them all the more. "Anyone would think that you were high on something," Isabel said good-naturedly.

There was a sudden, sober silence. *You are!* thought Isabel. And that, she thought, must be Miranda's doing. She would have to speak to Cat about it, discreetly. She did not like the idea of Eddie being led astray by an older woman. Young men are easily led astray, she thought, but then . . .

Eddie pointed to a large box filled with crumpled silver-paper wrappings. He smiled guiltily. "Liqueur chocolates," he said. "Cat found a time-expired box and gave them to Miranda. Rum. Cointreau. Even crème de menthe. We've eaten them. All of them. Thirty-two."

He turned to Miranda, as a conspirator turns to an accomplice; she put a hand to her mouth in an elaborate display of greed discovered, but then burst out laughing again. Isabel shook her head and smiled, then left the delicatessen. Once again I jumped to the wrong conclusion, she thought; I am often almost right, she told herself, or right but wrong.

She made her way back to the house, walking slowly along Merchiston Crescent in the warmth of the afternoon, deep in thought. There was no turning back; she would not do that, she would see things through. Once back at the house, she laid out the provisions she had bought. Grace was about to leave, but before she did she showed Isabel the rearrangement she had made of the spice cupboard. "The nutmeg was all mouldy," she said accusingly. "I had to throw it out."

Isabel would not be held responsible for mould and she ignored Grace's remark.

"And as for the pepper," Grace went on, "you had three opened jars. That makes pepper dry and dusty. I put everything into one jar and sealed it."

Isabel accepted the reproach. "I'll try to remember to finish each one before I open another," she said.

They finished with the spice cupboard, and Grace gathered her things in readiness to leave. Isabel asked her about her plans for the weekend and was told that there was a session at the spiritualist centre that night. "A *very* good medium," said Grace. "She's very direct, and she doesn't hesitate to warn us."

She looked challengingly at Isabel, as if expecting contradiction. But Isabel said only, "How useful." She was wondering when she should speak to Grace, when she should tell her; next week perhaps.

Then Grace said, "I've not said thank you properly. For the flat. I'm very grateful to you, you know."

Isabel looked away. She felt awkward about thanks; she knew that she should not, but she could not help it. She knew how to show gratitude; it was harder to accept it, and she would have to learn.

"I'm glad that you like it," she said. "I took to it straight away."

Grace nodded. "Shall I pay you the rent monthly?"

Isabel frowned. "There's no rent," she said.

"But I must," said Grace. "You can't . . ."

"I can."

"I won't accept it," said Grace. She could be stubborn, as Isabel knew well.

"In that case we'll agree on a peppercorn rent," said Isabel, pointing to the spice cupboard. "A jar of peppercorns."

The matter was left at that; they would discuss it later.

Grace left Isabel in the house shortly before five. Jamie would be coming at seven, and she had things to make ready. But although she had things to do, she could not do them. She sat down at the kitchen table, feeling suddenly weepy; she rested her head in her hands, staring at the stripped pine surface. The table—a long one—had been bought by her father when it was no longer required by a psychiatric hospital on whose board of trustees he had served. It had seen sorrow, she thought, confusion, unhappiness. And she remembered, as she sat there, a short film she had seen about the life of a man, a quiet, gentle man, who had been taken from his small farm on one of the Hebridean islands and had been detained in that hospital for seventeen years. He had been a weaver, and had made figures out of reeds and rushes; she realised, as she watched the film, that her father had known this man and had brought back for her one of these small figures, a corn dolly, and she had kept it on her window sill amongst her other dolls. When he had been allowed to go back to his croft, after all those years, he had been looked after by a sister, who had waited for him to return and was ready to care for him again, as she had done before. That was all that the film was about: exile and return, and the small needs of quiet people. She had wept then, as she watched the film, as she wept now, for very different reasons.

SHE MET JAMIE in the front hall and led him through to the kitchen, where she had been preparing their supper. He yawned, stretched and said, "I'm really tired, you know. We had a party last night—the people from the workshop. I didn't get to bed until two."

"We can eat early tonight," she said.

"I didn't mean to be rude."

"No, I know that." Her heart was beating hard within her; her stomach felt light, topsy-turvy. She walked over to the fridge and took out the opened bottle of New Zealand white wine which she had put in to chill. She poured Jamie a glass of wine and a glass of ginger ale for herself.

He took the wineglass from her, looking at her glass as he did so. "Ginger ale?"

"Yes," she said, trying to steady the glass in her hand, which was shaking.

He raised an eyebrow. He knew that Isabel enjoyed a glass of wine in the evening, particularly at the end of the week. "Why?"

She closed her eyes. Her glass was chilly on her fingers, moist. Now was as good a time as any, perhaps the best.

"Because I'm pregnant," she said.

He dropped his wineglass. It fell to the floor, to the Victorian stone flags; it shattered, although the stem remained intact, a little glass tower catching the light from the window. There was the sharp smell of wine, released in a sudden rush of bouquet.

She looked at him. "Oh, Jamie."

He fell to his knees and began to pick up the glass. He cut a finger, just a small cut, but there was blood, and she bent down beside him and took the cut finger and pressed it against her blouse. It was his blood; his blood. Their faces were close together, and she kissed him. He kissed her back, and placed a hand on her shoulder, steadying himself.

"How clumsy of me," he said. "I'm sorry."

"You couldn't be clumsy if you tried," she said.

He looked at her in amusement, and then laughed. They stood up. He held her hand in his. There was a small patch of blood on her palm now; his blood. He squeezed her hand.

"What are we going to call him?" he asked.

THEY ATE TOGETHER in the garden room at the back of the house, because it was so warm. The French doors were left open, and there was the scent of lavender on the air; there was only one topic of conversation, of course. She allowed herself a half-glass of wine, and they raised their glasses to each other. She had been uncertain as to how he might react, but she had not expected this enthusiasm. "I'm glad for you, and for me," he said. "I love children. I love them. I really do. And you'll let me help, won't you?"

"Of course," she said. "After all, you will be the father."

He repeated the word, and dwelt on it. "All of a sudden I feel very responsible," he said.

She said nothing. He might not feel this way later on, she thought; she would have to see. But for the moment, her happiness was profound, and that was sufficient.

They sat together. Later, without ringing the bell and announcing her presence, Cat left a peace offering for Isabel at the front door: a package of French cheeses and a spiced Italian sausage from the delicatessen. She had taped a note onto the package which simply said, *We must never have another argument. Never!* And then, in a spirit of what might have been realism, or humour, or both, she added, *Until the next one!*

Shortly after Cat had left this present outside the door, Brother Fox, skulking through the front garden, hungrily sniffing at the evening air, detected its presence and padded cautiously up to the small package. He made short work of the wrapping paper—no challenge for a fox—and ate the sausage within a few minutes, spitting out the open elastic stocking in which it had been encased. After that he moved on to the cheeses, which he also ate, although not in their entirety, leaving small bits of rind littered about the path, evidence of the gift that he had so fortuitously intercepted. Then, replete and content, he moved away, back into the welcoming shadows, the undergrowth.

THE ISABEL DALHOUSIE SERIES

THE SUNDAY PHILOSOPHY CLUB

Isabel Dalhousie is fond of problems, and sometimes she becomes interested in problems that are, quite frankly, none of her business—including some that are best left to the police. Filled with endearingly thorny characters and a Scottish atmosphere as thick as a highland mist, *The Sunday Philosophy Club* is an irresistible pleasure.

Volume 1
978-1-4000-7709-0 (pbk)
978-0-375-42298-0 (hc)

FRIENDS, LOVERS, CHOCOLATE

While taking care of her niece Cat's delicatessen, Isabel meets a heart transplant patient who has had some strange experiences in the wake of surgery. Against the advice of her housekeeper, Isabel is intent on investigating. Matters are further complicated when Cat returns from vacation with a new boyfriend, and Isabel's fondness for him lands her in another muddle.

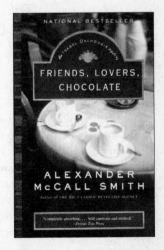

Volume 2
978-1-4000-7710-6 (pbk)
978-0-375-42299-7 (hc)

THE RIGHT ATTITUDE TO RAIN

When Isabel's cousin from Dallas arrives in Edinburgh, she introduces Isabel to a bigwig Texan whose young fiancée may just be after his money. Then there's her niece, Cat, who's busy falling for a man whom Isabel suspects of being an incorrigible mama's boy. Isabel is advised to stay out of it all, but the philosophical issues of these matters of the heart prove too tempting for her to resist.

Volume 3
978-1-4000-7711-3 (pbk)
978-0-375-42300-0 (hc)

THE LATEST IN THE ISABEL DALHOUSIE SERIES

THE CAREFUL USE OF COMPLIMENTS

There's a new little Dalhousie on the scene, and while the arrival of Isabel's son presents her with the myriad wonders of life, it doesn't in any way diminish her curiosity about other things. While attending an art auction, she discovers a mystery revealed in one of the paintings, launching her into yet another intriguing investigation.

Volume 4
Coming in Hardcover August 2007
978-0-375-42301-7

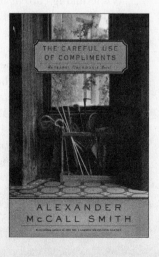

ANCHOR BOOKS
ORIGINAL TRADE PAPERBACKS
THE 44 SCOTLAND STREET SERIES

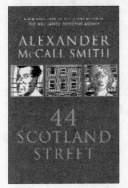

44 SCOTLAND STREET
All of Alexander McCall Smith's trademark warmth and wit come into play in this novel chronicling the lives of the residents of an Edinburgh boardinghouse. Complete with colorful characters, love triangles, and even a mysterious art caper, this is an unforgettable portrait of Edinburgh society.

Volume 1
978-1-4000-7944-5 (pbk)

ESPRESSO TALES
The eccentric residents of a converted Georgian townhouse in Edinburgh are back. From the talented six-year-old Bertie, who is forced to arrive in pink overalls for his first day of class, to the self-absorbed Bruce, who contemplates a change of career in between admiring glances in the mirror, there is much in store as fall settles on 44 Scotland Street.

Volume 2
978-0-307-27597-4 (pbk)

THE LATEST IN THE 44 SCOTLAND STREET SERIES

LOVE OVER SCOTLAND
Complications continue in the lives of the denizens of 44 Scotland Street. From conducting perilous anthropological studies of pirate households to being inadvertently left behind on a school trip to Paris, the wonderful misadventures of these residents will charm and delight.

Volume 3
Coming in Paperback November 2007
978-0-307-27598-1

THE NO. 1 LADIES' DETECTIVE AGENCY SERIES

THE NO. 1 LADIES' DETECTIVE AGENCY

Millions of readers have fallen in love with the witty, wise Mma Ramotswe and her Botswana adventures. Share the magic of Alexander McCall Smith's No. 1 Ladies' Detective Agency series in three alternate editions:

978-1-4000-3477-2 (pbk)
978-1-4000-9688-6 (mm)
978-0-375-42387-1 (hc)

TEARS OF THE GIRAFFE

The No. 1 Ladies' Detective Agency is growing, and in the midst of solving her usual cases—from an unscrupulous maid to a missing American—eminently sensible and cunning detective Mma Ramotswe ponders her impending marriage, promotes her talented secretary, and finds her family suddenly and unexpectedly increased by two.

Volume 2
978-1-4000-3135-1 (pbk)

MORALITY FOR BEAUTIFUL GIRLS

While trying to resolve some financial problems for her business, Mma Ramotswe finds herself investigating the alleged poisoning of a government official as well as the moral character of the four finalists of the Miss Beauty and Integrity contest. Other difficulties arise at her fiancé's Tlokweng Road Speedy Motors, as Mma Ramotswe discovers he is more complicated than he seems.

Volume 3
978-1-4000-3136-8 (pbk)

The mysteries are "smart and sassy . . . [with] the power to amuse or shock or touch the heart, sometimes all at once."
—*Los Angeles Times*

THE KALAHARI TYPING SCHOOL FOR MEN

Mma Precious Ramotswe is content. But, as always, there are troubles. Mr J.L.B. Matekoni has not set the date for their wedding, her assistant Mma Makutsi wants a husband, and worst of all, a rival detective agency has opened up in town. Of course, Precious will manage these things, as she always does, with her uncanny insight and good heart.

Volume 4
978-1-4000-3180-1 (pbk)
978-0-375-42217-1 (hc)

THE FULL CUPBOARD OF LIFE

Mma Ramotswe has weighty matters on her mind. She has been approached by a wealthy lady to check up on several suitors. Are these men interested in her or just her money? This may be difficult to find out, but it's just the kind of case Mma Ramotswe likes.

Volume 5
978-1-4000-3181-8 (pbk)
978-0-375-42218-8 (hc)

IN THE COMPANY OF CHEERFUL LADIES

Precious Ramotswe is busier than usual at the No. 1 Ladies' Detective Agency when the appearance of a strange intruder in her house and a mysterious pumpkin in her yard add to her concerns. But what finally rattles Mma Ramotswe's normally unshakable composure is the visitor who forces her to confront a painful secret from her past.

Volume 6
978-1-4000-7570-6 (pbk)
978-0-375-42271-3 (hc)

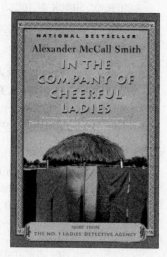

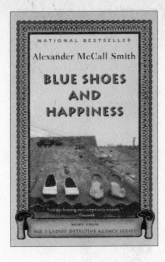

BLUE SHOES AND HAPPINESS

Mma Ramotswe and her invaluable assistant, Grace Makutsi, have their hands full with finding a cobra in their office and investigating the medical clinic and the local advice columnist. But the most troubling situation is in Mma Makutsi's personal life. When her wealthy fiancé misses their customary dinner date, and Mma Makutsi wonders if he's having second thoughts about the engagement, Mma Ramotswe once again steps in with calming, sage advice.

Volume 7
978-1-4000-7571-3 (pbk)
978-0-375-42272-0 (hc)

THE LATEST IN THE
NO. 1 LADIES' DETECTIVE AGENCY SERIES

THE GOOD HUSBAND
OF ZEBRA DRIVE

In the life of Mma Ramotswe there is rarely a dull moment, and lately her estimable husband, Mr J.L.B. Matekoni, has been keeping her occupied above all else. He has been hinting for some time now that he intends to do something special for their adopted daughter, Motholeli, but when his plan hits some snags he finds himself doubly lucky to be married to the ever-resourceful, ever-understanding Precious Ramotswe.

Volume 8
978-0-375-42273-7 (hc)
Coming in Paperback Spring 2008
978-1-4000-7572-0

THE NO. 1 LADIES' DETECTIVE AGENCY
3-VOLUME BOXED SET

The first three books in Alexander McCall Smith's beloved bestselling series, featuring the traditionally built, eminently sensible, and cunning proprietor of the only ladies' detective agency in Botswana, are available in a beautifully designed boxed set.

Includes: *The No. 1 Ladies' Detective Agency, Tears of the Giraffe,* and *Morality for Beautiful Girls*

978-0-679-78975-8 (pbk)

ANCHOR BOOKS
ORIGINAL TRADE PAPERBACKS

THREE NOVELLAS
INTRODUCING THE ECCENTRIC AND EVER-LIKABLE
PROFESSOR DR VON IGELFELD

Welcome to the insane and rarified world of Professor Dr
Moritz-Maria von Igelfeld of the Institute of Romance Philology.
Von Igelfeld is engaged in a never-ending quest to win the
respect he feels certain he is due—a quest which has a way
of going hilariously astray.

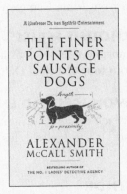

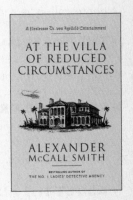

978-1-4000-7708-3
(pbk)

978-1-4000-9508-7
(pbk)

978-1-4000-9509-4
(pbk)

The Official Home of Alexander McCall Smith on the Web

WWW.ALEXANDERMCCALLSMITH.COM

A comprehensive Web site for new readers and longtime fans alike, with five exclusive content areas:

- ## THE NO. 1 LADIES' DETECTIVE AGENCY SERIES
  The original site for McCall Smith's bestselling series. Explore Precious Ramotswe's Botswana through book descriptions, a photo gallery, advice from Mma Ramotswe, and more.

- ## THE ISABEL DALHOUSIE SERIES
  Enter a Scottish atmosphere as thick as a highland mist, complete with a photo tour of Isabel Dalhousie's Edinburgh.

- ## PROFESSOR DR VON IGELFELD ENTERTAINMENTS
  Three original paperback novellas introducing the eccentric and ever-likable Professor Dr von Igelfeld, his colleagues, and their comic adventures.

- ## ABOUT THE AUTHOR
  Read about Alexander McCall Smith and get updates on tour events and other author activities.

- ## JOIN THE COMMUNITY
  Share the world of Alexander McCall Smith with friends, family, and fellow book club members. Print our free Reading Group Guides and sign up for the Alexander McCall Smith Fan Club and e-Newsletter.